THE LEFT-HANDED
HUMMINGBIRD

DOCTOR WHO – THE NEW ADVENTURES

Also available:

THE NEW

ADVENTURES

THE LEFT-HANDED
HUMMINGBIRD

Kate Orman

First published in Great Britain in 1993 by
Doctor Who Books
an imprint of Virgin Publishing Ltd
332 Ladbroke Grove
London W10 5AH

ISBN 0 426 20404 2

Cover illustration by Pete Wallbank

Phototypeset by Intype, London

Printed and bound in Great Britain by
Cox & Wyman Ltd, Reading, Berks

For David, for Kyla, for Glenn,
for Sarah, for Stephen, for Antony,
for listening

The author wishes to thank the University of Oklahoma Press for kind permission to reprint Aztec poetry from *Pre-Columbian Literatures of Mexico*, by Miguel León-Portilla. Copyright © 1969 by the University of Oklahoma Press.

Oh no, I think I'm turning into a god.
                    Suetonius, *Divus Vespasianus*

Prologue

He had come such a long way.

Such a long way from the teenager who loved the Beatles and who had grown his hair long, Beatle-long, to the despair of his parents.

Such a long way from the young man who had tried every psychedelic drug he could get his hands on, unable to find the big trip, the best trip.

Such a long way from the religious fanatic who hated the Beatles because John Lennon had said they were more popular than Jesus.

Such a long way from the irascible, ordinary little man with the interest in lithographs and firearms.

Such a long way from Hawaii.

There were cassettes of the Beatles' songs in his pockets. There was a copy of *The Catcher in the Rye*. Tomorrow everyone in the world would know what had been in Mark's pockets.

And deep inside him, something Blue was itching, something Blue was wrapping itself around him like a shroud. It was possible, even probable, that he was not aware of it. But the Blue was there, an unnatural colour, a spreading stain in the soft greyness of his brain.

It was a warm evening, a warm evening in New York. He looked at his watch. Nearly eleven o'clock. Surely they

1

would be back soon? In their limousine, their sell-out stretch. They'd be back.

They were back.

She came first, walking past Mark, not even seeing him in the New York darkness. But she was not the object of his interest.

The air was warm. He took up a firing stance, holding the .38 revolver out in front of him. It was a line between them, a connection. Matthew, Mark, Luke, and John. Mark and John.

'Mr Lennon?' he said.

First Slice

He who fights with monsters might take care lest he thereby become a monster. And if you gaze for long into an abyss, the abyss gazes also into you.
Friedrich Nietzsche, *Jenseits von Gut und Böse*

Chapter 1

Mexico (Not Tenochtitlan)

Dear Doctor, please come to the above address ASAP. Bring Bernice and Ace if they are with you. Urgent!!! – CXA, 4 December 1993

Mexico City, 1994

The Doctor stood alone in the darkness, listening to the city breathe.

Had you been watching from above – say, from a high-rise over Guatemala Street – you would have seen Mexico City stretching away to every horizon, buildings crammed together under an umbrella of industrial filth. The stars were blotted out. There were more houses and cars and flats and dogs and shops and garbage and streets and cockroaches and people than you could possibly have imagined.

The Doctor heard Mexico breathing. Something industrial, far away, pounding like a giant heart. The background chatter of the *chilangos*, the city dwellers, awake in the steamy midnight. A car skidding its tyres. A bell tolling. A shout. A CD playing. Snores. The sounds swelled together to become the city's pulse, its music.

If you had been watching from the high-rise, and your eyes were sharp enough, you might have seen him there – a shadow amongst the shadows, ignored by the passers-by. His eyes were closed, his lips slightly parted, his face taut and yet relaxed with concentration. He leaned on his umbrella, a small, almost comical figure in his battered fedora and his crumpled white suit. You might even have mistaken him for human.

You might have wondered what he was doing there, standing alone and unnoticed.

But if you happened to be Huitzilin, standing at the window of the hotel room with one ghost hand pushing back the curtains, you would have known. And you might have smiled. There you were, a mere eight floors above him, winning the game of hide and seek.

But the story does not begin at midnight on Guatemala Street. It begins the morning before, in room 104 of the Hospital of Our Lady.

The sunlight oozed through a gap in the venetian blinds. It crept across the face of a man in his forties, alone in the pale green bed in the pale green room. There were no flowers.

His skin was Indian dark, his hair Indian black, shot through with early grey. He was thin, and even in sleep his face was tense. The skin around his eyes was deeply lined with worry. One hand held onto the bedclothes, clutching them to his chest, rising and falling in the quiet rhythm of sleep.

A door slammed. Cristián jerked awake with a cry.

He lay there for a few seconds, taking deep breaths, his heart thumping irregularly somewhere in the vicinity of his mouth. Telling himself it was right, all right, everything was going to be all right.

He had been in hospital for three weeks.

The Doctor still had not answered his message.

But it would be all right. *Give him time*, he thought.

He climbed out of bed with difficulty. His right arm was in a sling, the hand curled in the cloth like a dead spider. He wriggled his feet into his slippers and went to the window, tugging the blinds open.

Mexico looked in on him. The sky was full of grey, a haze of filth that clung to the windows. The sun was hot and

6

bright somewhere behind that shroud; he could feel its warmth when he pressed his fingers to the glass.

Distantly, the sun was glinting off El Angel, the golden statue blowing its trumpet over the Paseo de la Reforma. He wondered how many steps there were in the statue's base now. Long ago his father had told him that as Mexico City sank into the swamp, new steps had to be added to keep the statue at the same level. It had occurred to the four-year-old Cristián Xochitl Alvarez that Mexico City was sinking away from the angel, sinking away from heaven.

Down in the street, a boy who couldn't be older than nine was eating petrol fire from a wooden loop. The drivers tossed him small change as they stopped at the lights. Cristián pressed his forehead to the glass and wondered if the four-year-old had been right.

There was a small noise behind him, and he turned, too fast, leaning against the window-sill for support.

'Cristián Alvarez?' said the silhouette in the doorway.

'You're here,' said Cristián, very nearly smiling. 'I knew you'd come.'

The Doctor came into the room, followed by Professor Summerfield and Ace. Cristián closed his eyes for a moment, comparing them to his mental photograph. The Doctor with his squashed hat, his penetrating blue eyes. The Professor in white slacks and blouse, her short dark hair hanging in a fringe. Ace in some sort of green military jacket and pants, wearing a black T-shirt that said *Hard Rock Café Svartos*.

The clothes were different, but the faces were the same. They hadn't changed at all.

Cristián opened his eyes. They hadn't changed at all.

For a terrible moment he thought he was imagining them. That he would wake up, and the room would be pale green and empty.

Then the Doctor said, 'UNIT passed your letter on to us.'

Cristián sat down on the bed, feeling vulnerable in his

tatty blue pyjamas. Three pairs of eyes looked at him. Ace's were invisible behind her sunglasses.

'May I call you Cristián?' continued the Doctor.

'What else?' said Cristián tremulously. He felt his heart start to kick irregularly. 'Don't you remember me?'

'We were having a holiday in Switzerland in 2030 – '

'Holiday?' said Bernice. 'I wouldn't call that a holiday – '

' – when we dropped into UNIT HQ in Geneva. They passed your note on to us.'

'Just like in *Back to the Future*,' concluded Benny.

Cristián just blinked at them. 'Why don't you remember me?' he said. 'How can you not be any older?'

'When was the last time you saw us?' asked Bernice, sitting down on the bed next to him.

Cristián found himself pulling back from her, uncertainly. 'December the eighth, 1980, in New York. And before that, January the thirtieth, 1969. In St John's Wood.'

'London,' said Ace from behind her shades.

'Let me try to explain,' said the Doctor.

Cristián Alvarez lived by himself in an apartment building squashed between two other apartment buildings. The front was white, but dirty rainwater had eaten great streaks of grey into the paint. Flowers, blue and red, exploded in earthenware pots on the balconies.

Bernice found herself helping the Mexican up the stairs. He moved slowly, like someone who had been ill for a long time, and he still smelt of hospital. '*Muy amable*,' he mumbled, fumbling with the door keys.

A tabby came bounding out of the kitchen and tangled itself in Cristián's ankles as Benny manoeuvred him to the sofa. '*Hola*, Ocelot,' he said, tickling the cat under its chin. 'Did Señora Caraveo look after you properly?'

The tabby purred its assent. Then it jumped into the Doctor's lap, curled up, and went to sleep.

Ace sat on the floor, looking around the flat. There was a PC on a white card-table next to the phone, a couple of sofas, a wall-hanging with an Indian design. No sign of a television. A photo sitting on a coffee table caught her eye. Then it caught her mind.

It showed the Doctor and Bernice at what had to be a party – there was a streamer caught in his hair, and part of a sign read *MAS* in the background. Ace realized she was sitting behind him, on a sofa, looking up from a bowl of noodles. Caught in mid-lunch. Her shades were white with the flash.

'My memento,' said Cristián. Once again he almost smiled.

'Weird,' Ace said. 'This photo is part of your past, but part of our future.'

Cristián said, 'It should have occurred to me that you might receive the note even before you had met me.'

'Occupational hazard of time travel,' shrugged the Doctor.

'How much should I tell you?' said Cristián. 'About your future, I mean.'

'As much as you think we need to know,' said the Doctor seriously. 'Obviously nothing catastrophic happened to us, or you wouldn't have expected us to come.'

Cristián opened his mouth and shut it again. 'Where should I begin?'

'Why not start with why you wrote the note?'

It was October 31, 1993, when Cristián went shopping in the tiangui.

He should have gone to the cine. *He should have gone to Chapultepec Park. He should have visited his sister. He should have stayed home.*

But he went shopping in the market on Guatemala Street, and bought three courgettes and a bag of tomatoes. He carried them in a string bag that bumped against his leg. He put down the bag as he stopped at a refreshment stall to buy himself a slice of watermelon. He never did pick it up again.

It was 4:33 in the afternoon when the Hallowe'en Man came to life. Witnesses would later remember that he had been standing there all afternoon, his face blank, his

9

*arms slack by his sides. No one really took any notice of him
and his pale North American face.*

*At 4:33, the Hallowe'en Man pushed aside his coat to
reveal a Chinese SKK semi-automatic rifle. He pulled it out,
snapped off the safety, and shot six stall owners, thirteen
passers-by, eight children, four police and a dog.*

'Why?' said Bernice. 'What *for*?'

'What do these people do anything for?' said Cristián
quietly. 'It is as though the gun needs a reason for existence, so it attaches itself to someone. Someone weak or
afraid. It makes them insane.' He looked at Bernice, and
his face was as blank as it had been throughout his story.
'The insane do not need a reason to do anything.'

The Doctor said, 'But you think you know the reason.
Don't you, Cristián?'

For the first time, the *chilango*'s face took on an
expression. It was fear.

*If you had asked Cristián X. Alvarez what he would do if a
man pulled out a gun in the marketplace, he would have
laughed. Such things do not happen in* la Republica. *If you
had insisted, he would have said something sensible. Run
away. Dive to the ground. Get behind cover.*

*For thirty-seven seconds, Cristián X. Alvarez stood with
his mouth slightly open, a slice of watermelon held tightly
in his hands. The juice ran down into his sleeve as he
watched. As bullets thudded into the walls around him. As
people screamed and fell down for no reason his brain
could get a grip on.*

And the Blue was there.

*It ran out of the Hallowe'en Man like a stain, like paint
pouring from an overturned bucket. It coloured everything,
the walls, the scattered vegetables, the blood. It filled up
Cristián's eyes, forced its way into his lungs, expanded inside
his mind. For the first time in decades, Mexico City had a
Blue sky.*

*He wanted to faint, but he couldn't. Something was hold-
ing him up.*

The Hallowe'en Man's eyes were Blue. They looked into Cristián's.
He shot him.
And then he shot himself.

'They were blue?' said the Doctor.

'No. They were Blue. Like – a bit like yours.'

'Tell me about the time we first met,' said the Doctor.

Cristián nodded. 'I was living in London.' He spoke slowly, as though choosing his words with care. 'London was full of Blue in those days. I thought I was going mad. You found me. And you told me that I wasn't.'

'And what did I tell you?'

'You said – you said I'd had a profound psychic experience.'

'You're telepathic?' said Bernice.

Cristián shook his head. 'No. I can't read anybody's mind. But the Doctor said I was sensitive. To things. To events and places. *Zeitgeist*, you said.' He smiled fleetingly. 'I had to look that up.'

The Doctor sat back, looking thoughtful. 'Normally, when a human has psychic abilities, it's very obvious. Psychokinetics can juggle without using their hands. Telepaths can tell you what you had for breakfast, and the word you are thinking of right now.'

'You said my powers were dormant. That just the tip of the iceberg was showing.'

Ace said, 'This colour Blue – what do you think you were sensing?'

The Indian's eyes dropped to the floor. 'Something frightening. Something so frightening that I spent over a month in a mental hospital.'

'Was that where we met you?' said the Doctor gently.

'No, that was after – ' He stopped short.

'After what?' asked Ace.

'After the Happening,' said Cristián. 'I don't think I'd better tell you about that.'

And so, at midnight, the Doctor stood on Guatemala

11

Street, straining his senses for any trace of what Cristián had described.

He had left his companions at the apartment. Cristián, with Mexican hospitality, had offered to put them up for a bit. The Indian ought not to be left alone: he was too obvious a target.

The whole situation was intriguing. These little temporal paradoxes were simple enough to create, especially when your path through space and time was so tangled. But they could be very complex to handle. Causality operated backwards, the future affected the past, affected people's actions. His actions.

What was it Cristián didn't want to tell him about the Happening?

For that matter, could he be sure the Mexican's story was genuine? Cristián struck him as truthful, but he had the advantage of them, in more ways than one. There was the photograph, of course, but there was no way to know the circumstances under which it had been taken. No way to know if they had left him as friends or enemies.

The Doctor opened his eyes. Nothing. He couldn't sense anything.

He had the knack of sensing spirit of place, but he couldn't feel anything unusual here. As far as he could tell, the Hallowe'en Man had been acting with the true spontaneity of the random mass murderer.

Whatever the Happening had been, it had badly damaged Cristián Alvarez. And, whatever had happened, it was the result of the Doctor's actions. Normally he was in and out of people's lives so quickly that he didn't get to see the long-term effects of his handiwork. Life was a series of hellos and goodbyes.

Ah well, he had all that to look forward to.

He stood back to admire the ruins.

The Aztecs' greatest temple had been at the centre of their magnificent city: Tenochtitlan, mighty Tenochtitlan, whose armies and glory swelled to fill all of Mexico.

Of course, when the Spanish had arrived, they had levelled the place. The Great Temple had been burned to the ground. Tradition had it that the rubble was used to build the first Christian church in Mexico.

But tradition was often wrong. They had found the remains of the Great Temple under the streets of Mexico City, purely by chance. The link with the past was unbroken – one city built on another, intertwined with the ancient stones.

He looked down into the pit of excavations. The stones loomed out of the night, dimly lit by the street-lights, angular, meaningless shapes. The odour of wet earth mixed with the smell of petrol fumes and garbage. Like all of Mexico City, the Great Temple was sinking into the swamp. This unexpected reminder of the past would eventually be swallowed.

He sighed, remembering the temple in its full glory, remembering Barbara's futile attempt to change the *Mexica*. They were a proud people, ferocious, their entire way of life based on war and sacrifice. It had been their constant quest for sacrificial victims that had driven them from one shore of the land to the other. His companion had not known what she was up against when she tried to convert them, tried to do away with the killing. And that had been in their early period, before thousands upon thousands had died under the stone knives. He had tried to explain to her that you don't just get up in the morning, eat your cornflakes, and go out and change history – change an entire way of life.

But it had hardly mattered. The Aztecs had had only a few more decades of glory left. It had not helped that Cortés and his conquistadors had shown up in the year One Reed, when the *Mexica* expected their white-skinned god Quetzalcoatl to return. Barbara's English complexion was part of the reason they had mistaken her for a goddess.

The Doctor shrugged, shaking himself loose of his memories. There was more to do tonight. Human beings spent half their lives asleep – rather more than half, in most cases. But it was all office hours to the Doctor.

From his hotel room, Huitzilin watched the Time Lord leave. He grinned, an invisible slash of white in the

13

darkness. '*Otiquihiyohuih*,' he said, and his voice rang in the air like a bell.

Ace had heard about Mexican water. She found a six-pack of *agua mineral* in the fridge, cracked one open, sat on Cristián's faded sofa and watched the gunk in the lava lamp ooze up and down.

Cristián had long since gone to bed, and Bernice was dozing on a mattress in the kitchen. Ace was wide awake. She was jet-lagged, or TARDIS-lagged, or something. The space-time vessel had failed to synchronize their arrival time properly. Obviously. But she also had the nagging feeling that someone ought to keep watch.

She held the photo in her lap, trying to pull more details out of it. St John's Wood, Christmas, 1968. Bernice was wearing a caftan over a pair of battered jeans. Ace was wearing a leather jacket. They looked relaxed, enjoying themselves.

There was a small turntable in one corner of Cristián's living room, with a single rack of LPs underneath. She thumbed through them. Most of the groups she hadn't heard of: Cream; Yes; the Byrds; Dave Dee, Dozy, Beaky, Mick and Tich. Ah – *Sergeant Pepper*. Her mother had a prized copy of that, with the little bit of gibberish in the pick-up track.

Cristián lived in a world of his own, behind his wooden door and his black curtains. He rarely went out. In the day a newspaper sent him stories through the modem and he sub-edited them on the PC-compatible. At night he stayed home and – did what? Read, or listened to his old LPs, or watched Mexico City out of the window.

She had been watching him in the taxi. His hands had been shaking. Between whatever had happened in 1968 and the Hallowe'en Massacre, Cristián Alvarez had become one of the walking wounded.

She suddenly realized that the coffee table was a TV hidden under a tablecloth. She lifted its skirts and watched *Star Trek: The Next Generation* in Spanish until she fell asleep.

* * *

14

The attendant nearly spat coffee all over his newspaper. 'Señor!' he said in a strangled voice. 'You frightened me almost to death.'

'My apologies,' said the visitor. His Spanish had a continental lisp. 'I would have thought that, working in a place such as this, you would need very strong nerves indeed.'

'I've grown used to the presence of the dead,' said the attendant. 'I just wasn't expecting to meet the living.' He glanced at his watch; it was almost one in the morning. 'What can I do for you, Señor?'

'Doctor,' said the visitor. 'I want to look at your records.'

'Do you have a permit?' said the attendant, sitting up in his seat.

El Médico leaned across the table and looked him in the eyes. 'That isn't important,' he said.

'No, I suppose not,' said the attendant. His mouth hung very slightly open as he waited for *el Médico* to ask him something.

'Just tell me one thing. No, two things. Were you on duty when they brought the Hallowe'en Man in?'

'*Sí.*'

'And you took a good look.'

'I . . . *sí.*'

'What colour were his eyes?'

Cristián awoke in his own bed. He sighed and stretched, his toes poking against the tabby curled on the blanket. It was good to be home.

Ocelot bounded into the kitchen, preceding him. He felt alive again; no longer amongst the sick, once more amongst the living. Well, almost: according to the kitchen clock it was three in the afternoon.

He discovered the Doctor doing creative things with maple syrup. Bernice sat at the kitchen table. Ace was curled up on the sofa, snoring gently.

The Doctor smiled and passed Cristián a stack of pancakes. '*Otiquihiyohuih*,' he said.

'What?'

15

'*Buenas tardes*,' he translated. 'Just curious. How much do you know about your ancestors?'

'The *Mexica*? Mostly what my grandmother told me. The Aztecs ruled this country for over a century. Then the Spanish came.' He sat at the table, eyeing the fat tortillas curiously.

The Doctor said nothing, watching Cristián's face as he continued. 'Grandmother told me a lot, when I was a child. But I haven't kept the old stories, the old ways of life.'

'Difficult, in a big city like this.'

'Yes. It's ironic, isn't it? I've even forgotten most of the *Nahuatl* language she taught me. She made me go to school, learn good Spanish so that I could work in the city. And she made me learn English, in case I had the chance to emigrate to the United States.'

The Doctor started pouring milk into a saucer. Ocelot nuzzled his ankles. 'Cristián,' he said, 'I need to know more.'

Cristián put down his fork and clasped his hands. 'What can I tell you?'

'What colour were the Hallowe'en Man's eyes?'

'Blue.'

'And have you had that spirit here since 1969?'

Cristián rubbed his eyes with his good hand. 'Twice.'

The Doctor sat down at the table with him. Despite Cristián's grey hair, the Time Lord seemed far older. 'Bernice, Ace,' he said, clapping his hands together. 'Why don't you two go shopping?'

'I don't *believe* you just said that,' said Ace, around a pancake. Bernice just arched an eyebrow.

'I'm serious. There's nothing to eat in this flat. Besides, I'm sure Ace has a few things she'd like to buy for herself.'

Bernice raised her other eyebrow.

'What do they use for money?' said Ace, swallowing her mouthful.

Perhaps the TARDIS was alone.

It stood unnoticed in a narrow canyon between two buildings. The air was thick with the yellow shimmer of

16

exhaust fumes. Brightly coloured washing hung between the two buildings, flapping slowly in the warm morning air. The alley was dusty with November drought.

Perhaps no one noticed the TARDIS at all, just another bit of junk like the cardboard boxes, the smashed refrigerator lamenting its fate amongst the trash. Perhaps the *chilangos* passed it on their way to the subway or the market without a second glance.

Perhaps alien fingers raked across its surface in a paroxysm of recognition, feeling every atom of the illusion of blue paint. Ghost fingers, hidden from the city.

Or perhaps the TARDIS was alone.

Cristián wasn't eating.

'You have to tell me everything,' said the Doctor. 'I can't help you unless I have facts. Information. Something to chew on.'

Cristián said nothing, tracing elaborate patterns in the maple syrup with the tines of his fork.

'Why are you afraid?' said the Doctor.

'Afraid,' said Cristián. 'I'm always afraid. When I wake up in the morning, I get scared before I get out of bed. The sunset triggers it, and flowers, and moving vehicles. I'm frightened when I eat and I'm frightened in crowds. Any time you see me, you can assume I'm afraid.'

The Doctor did not take his gaze away. 'You suffer from chronic panic attacks.'

'Yes!'

'Are you on any medication?'

'I don't – ' Cristián stopped short. He pushed his plate aside.

'You don't trust doctors.'

'Not any more,' Cristián said at last.

'Then why did you ask me to come here?'

'Because I thought – because you're the only person to have any understanding of this situation. But you don't. It hasn't even happened to you yet.'

'Cristián,' said the Doctor carefully, 'there's a chance that things will come out differently the second time.'

17

Cristián looked at him slowly, letting the import of those words sink in. 'Do you want to know your future?' he said.

'At the moment, I'm not as interested in my future as I am in your past. I need to know more.'

'But I can't remember. It's . . .' The Indian cast around for words. 'When I try to think about it, my mind just slides off. Like a drop of water on an orange peel. As though someone does not want me to think about it. Only . . . I think that person is myself.'

'I can help you remember.'

'How?'

Preston had been sitting in the complimentary lounge for twenty minutes, trying to work out if the girl was looking at him or not. She wore the kind of mirrored sunglasses that Californian cops wore; she ran that reflective gaze over the souvenir shop junk, taking in *piñatas*, pet cacti, leather goods. And occasionally turning in his direction, the shades showing a distorted view of the hotel foyer. She was wearing a leather jacket, black skirt, fingerless gloves.

If Preston hadn't been so bored, he probably wouldn't have had the courage to get up and walk across the foyer, his shoes shuff-shuffing on the red carpet. The girl turned as he came towards her. 'Hi,' he said. 'Er. You a tourist?'

Brilliant opening, Casanova. But the girl was smiling, good teeth between glossy lips. 'Yeah. Looking for something to take home to my mother.' Her voice was English, with traces of other accents.

'Can I get you a coffee?'

'Thanks.'

Good sign. He went back into the complimentary lounge, trying to guess her age. She followed, hands in the pockets of her jacket. The black-stockinged legs that emerged from her miniskirt were thicker than Preston liked, muscled. He wondered if she was an athlete.

The machine disgorged two plastic cups of watery coffee. The girl's shades steamed up as she sipped. 'Been here long?' she asked.

18

Preston shrugged. 'I'm from Texas. On vacation.' With Mom and Dad, he didn't add.

'And you run out of tourist attractions eventually.'

Dammit, how old was she? The English accent made it even harder to tell. 'Yeah, I know what you mean. How about you?'

'Well . . . I'm just curious.'

'Curious?'

'Call it a morbid curiosity.'

It took Preston a few moments to work out what she was talking about. 'Oh,' he said. Brilliantly.

She took another sip of the coffee.

Bernice pushed open the door of the flat with her toe and dumped her bags of shopping on the floor. Cristián lay on the sofa, still in his pyjamas, his feet propped up on the arm. The Doctor sat beside him in one of the kitchen chairs. He looked up sharply when she came in. *What are you doing back so soon?* 'Where's Ace?'

'You were right,' Bernice said shortly. 'She had some shopping of her own to do.' She dragged the groceries into the kitchen.

'Doctor, Doctor,' said Cristián, a smile flickering across his face. 'My wife thinks she's invisible.'

'Tell her I can't see her,' said the Time Lord, returning the smile.

Cristián's half-grin faded into anxiety. 'They tried counselling me. Hypnosis also. We didn't get anywhere.'

'All right,' said the Doctor. 'Close the curtains, would you, Bernice?'

She obliged, and sat cross-legged on the floor to watch. Distantly, the sounds of traffic reached them.

The Doctor folded his hands in his lap. 'Cristián, you are now in a state of deep hypnosis. Can you hear me?'

The answer was a few seconds in coming. '*Sí . . .*' said Cristián dreamily.

'That's it?' whispered Bernice, but the Doctor waved her silent.

19

'Cristián,' he said, 'how many times have you experienced the Blue?'

'Four,' he said. 'Christmas '68. And Hallowe'en.'

'Tell me about the other two times.'

'One was Christmas again.'

'And that was in Mexico? Or London?'

'Not Mexico. Not London. New York, December the eighth. 1980.'

The Doctor's eyes narrowed, as though he were searching his inner calendar and did not like what he saw. 'And the other time?'

'That was Mexico.' Ocelot jumped up onto Cristián and curled on his chest, purring. Absently, he stroked the cat's head. 'Mexico City. 1978.'

'Can you remember the date, Cristián?'

'*Veintiuno de febrero.*'

'All right. You're doing very well. Now, I want you to tell me about the time in New York City.' Cristián frowned, tightening his grip on Ocelot. The tabby squirmed. 'Let's start with simple things. Where were you?'

'In a hotel room. There were orange flowers on the walls.' He laughed. 'Hotels always buy the most revolting lampshades and pictures. So no one will bother stealing them.'

'I want you to think yourself back to that hotel room. Look at your mental map. You are here.' Pause. 'What are you doing?'

'I'm getting myself a glass of water.' He laughed again. 'And they say Mexican water is *no potable.*'

'And now what's happening to you?'

The sky explodes inside Cristián's head. The glass of water hits the floor of the bathroom. It shatters, like a grenade, like a rose dipped in nitrogen. Pieces of glass spray in all directions, making screeching music as they skid across the tiles.

He follows the glass to the floor, his cheek slapping the cold tiles. Bits of glass embed themselves in the side of his face. His mouth is open, but no sound is coming out. The scream is too big to fit through it.

Ocelot squeals and jumps out of his hands. Cristián says nothing, his eyes and mouth dark circles in his face.

'Cristián?' says the Doctor urgently. He kneels beside the Indian. 'Can you hear me? Cristián!'

'Oh, God, Doctor, do you think he's – ' Bernice is on her feet, not knowing what to do.

Cristián's hand lashes out and grabs the Time Lord's wrist. His fingernails pierce the skin. The Doctor tries to pull away and cannot break his grip.

'*Otiquihiyohuih,*' Cristián snarls, with a smile.

Preston, thought Ace as she sliced into her steak, rated about a six. Two for looks, two for brains, two for having a good memory. He had bleach-blond hair, and was wearing one of those red jackets with a big 'P' sewn onto the shoulder. He was from Houston, where he was busy failing college and chasing girls. But his family was rich, and he could afford to take English tourists to dinner in the hotel restaurant.

'I used to see the guy every day – at breakfast, or going back into his room,' he was saying. 'He had these little dark eyes. A real psycho.'

'What colour eyes?'

'Brown,' said Preston, hesitantly. He was obviously finding her curiosity very morbid indeed.

'Were you here when the massacre happened?'

'Yeah, I was stuck in the room with Montezuma's revenge!'

'Tell me about the massacre.'

'It's weird,' said Preston. 'Dallas is famous for being where JFK got shot. And we had that Waco thing last year. Everybody in the States has a gun. Everybody. In the glove box of their car, or on their bedside table. My dad has three – he keeps one of them with his golf clubs.'

'Go on,' she prompted.

'We get a lot of psychos with guns,' Preston said. 'A lot.

21

But it's not supposed to happen in Mexico. One reason we came here was that there's not much crime, well, not much violent crime, anyway. I have to watch the news for my media studies course. Do you know how depressing watching the news is? All the news?'

He looked older than he actually was, Ace thought. 'I can imagine,' she said.

'In the twentieth century, the world has been at peace for eight per cent of the time. I read that somewhere. Can you believe that? There's always a war on. Anyway. I was in my hotel room, watching TV. I could have been in the street market,' he said. 'But I was lucky. Damn lucky.'

'Did you hear the first shot?'

'There wasn't really a first shot,' said Preston. 'It was a semi-automatic. It went *tick-tick-tick*. Then the voices started.'

'Voices,' said Ace.

'Screaming and shouting,' said Preston. He was trying to sound cool, but his high cheekbones had gone quite white. 'I was at the window by that stage. I saw them running, everybody running in different directions. I couldn't see the Hallowe'en Man – he was somewhere in the crowd. People were running over the roofs of cars. I saw one old woman on her knees praying. Her groceries were spread out around her on the pavement.'

'All right,' said Ace. 'Stop.'

Preston stopped. 'You can't imagine it,' he said at length.

'I don't have to imagine it,' said Ace.

She wanted to take his hand. But this was business.

'He doesn't remember any of it.'

Bernice gently closed the bedroom door. She squatted down next to the Doctor, who was sitting on the rug, scowling and nursing his wrist. Four deep scratches stood out against the pale flesh.

'This whole situation,' said Benny, 'is extremely suspicious. It smacks of being some kind of trap.'

'Trap? Trap? A cryptic message? A mysterious man

22

from our past? Of course it's a trap! But the question is, did Cristián set the trap, or is he the bait?'

The Doctor extracted a small plastic box from his pocket, with a red cross on it formed from two bits of electrical tape. He opened it and started bandaging his wrist with surprising ease.

Benny watched him. 'Do you think it's got anything to do with what happened to us in Oxford?'

'Maybe. Too early to tell. It's certainly not the Garvond.'

'You know I didn't mean that.'

'Yes, I do. You mean whatever caused our brush with our skull-faced friend, and the jaunt with the Silurians too. I'm not sure. So far nothing tastes of temporal interference, but all the same . . .'

Benny said, 'You must have uncovered something pretty powerful in Cristián's memory.'

'Possibly,' said the Doctor. 'So much for New York. We still need to know what happened in Mexico on February 21, 1978.' He held the bandage in his teeth and tied it off with a deft motion.

Bernice silently jerked her thumb at Cristián's computer.

The Doctor beamed, his bad mood forgotten. 'I should have thought of that,' he said, jumping up.

He started up the computer, found Cristián's password taped to the keyboard, drummed his fingers on the table while the PC connected with the newspaper's mainframe. Within a minute he was in their archives.

The screen went white, changing to a scan of the newspaper's front page. The Doctor glanced at the headlines, paged down, and again. 'Here,' he said. 'February 21, 1978. The sacrificial stone at the base of the Great Temple was uncovered by electrical workers laying cables under Guatemala Street. Depicting the goddess Coyolxauhqui, it – '

'What's this?' said Bernice, poking a finger at the screen.

' "Our Lady deluged",' the Doctor translated from the Spanish. ' "At least three dozen *chilangos* were admitted to the Hospital of Our Lady last night, suffering from an unidentified illness. Each victim collapsed suddenly for no

23

apparent reason. Staff have not released the names of the victims, nor have they given any indication of what the illness might be. All the victims were Indians".' He typed rapidly, calling up an index, and the screen emptied and filled in rapid succession. 'This one's a week later. It says that the illness is still being hushed up. "One of those struck down was the famous clairvoyant Señor Feliciano Nahualli, whose readings have been sought by celebrities".'

'What happened to him?'

The Doctor called up the index again, and scanned a page, absently rubbing his wrist. 'Nahualli is still at Our Lady. He never regained his sanity.'

Preston had retreated after dessert. Ace had been surprised – no coffee, no come-back-to-my-room? But then she'd thought about his memories, and the old woman's groceries lying scattered on the street like green tears. He wouldn't want to talk to her again.

Her sunglasses reflected the mirrored wall of the lift back at her. She watched the foyer disappear behind the doors. The floor lurched gently as the lift started to move.

Whatever it was, it hit her all at once.

She made a tearing breathing sort of noise and hit the wall of the lift, spinning around, her own reflection looking back at her. The reflection was clawing at its left side. Her sunglasses came off as she spun around again.

When Ace had been four years old, she had been stuck in a lift when the doors closed unexpectedly behind her. She had been too little to reach any of the buttons.

Ever since then, she had had a recurring dream about a lift that went sideways, that became unreasonably small, that went impossibly fast.

Now she was in a lift that did all of these things. The mirror cracked clear across as she smacked into it, her mouth open in an O of surprise. She clawed open the zipper of the jacket, tore loose the Browning 9mm pistol that was taped to the skin under her T-shirt, clutched it

24

uselessly as she spun and fell. The carpet was rough under her cheek. The gaffer tape tangled in her fingers.

Someone put their hand in through her face. They hadn't bothered to cut their fingernails.

Pieces of mirror showered onto her. If she screamed, the carpet ate the sound.

It was a quiet evening.

Bernice and Cristián played draughts on the card-table. The television lit the walls in alternating dark and light blue. *Capitan* Picard was arguing soundlessly with an alien. Cristián had had to explain to Bernice that it was not a documentary.

'How are you feeling?' asked Bernice.

Cristián kept his eyes on the board. 'Do you resent being left here as my nurse?' he said.

Bernice laughed, surprising him. 'I hadn't thought of it in that way. Look, you did have a pretty serious experience this afternoon.'

'I'm fine,' said Cristián. He moved a quarter that was substituting for a missing piece.

'I just want to know if I can help,' said Bernice gently.

'Help,' said Cristián. 'Just keep playing draughts with me. And don't talk about it.'

Benny shrugged on the inside. Cristián seemed like a resentful teenager caught in the body of an old man – like someone who hadn't had a chance to grow up in their own time. Like someone who'd been pushed and pulled until they had no direction of their own. At least Benny was prepared for the strange twists her path took. At the age of eighteen, Cristián hadn't been ready for . . .

Whatever.

Bernice knew that whatever was going to happen – whenever it was going to happen – she would live through it. Or at least, if what Cristián was telling them were true, and the time-line didn't change or do whatever it did, and . . .

'You must want to ask me a million questions,' said Cristián.

25

Bernice pushed a counter forward. 'To be honest, I'm not sure I want to know the answers.'

'The Doctor says maybe the same thing won't happen again. Maybe none of this will have happened to me. Just think. Who might I really be?'

'I don't understand how this time-line business works,' Benny admitted. 'Not properly. I do know that the Doctor will do whatever he can to help you.' She hoped. If someone was using Cristián as bait, what might the Doctor use him for?

'I'm sorry about the nurse joke,' said Cristián hesitantly. 'I appreciate your staying with me.'

'It hardly seems fair to answer your communiqué and then galumph off without you, does it?' She smiled. ' "They also serve who only stand and wait".'

'Is it a quotation?'

'Milton. He was talking about being blind. His idea was that he could serve God by just bearing the burden he had been given.'

Cristián looked up for the first time. His eyes were watery.

Bernice, feeling awkward, said, 'Do you want something to drink?'

Cristián shook his head.

He heard her rattling about in the kitchen, the old fridge humming as its thermostat kicked in. He heard the distant sounds of traffic, the wind blowing through the ravines of the city.

He heard the sizzling of a moth caught in an electric trap in the fast-food shop downstairs. He heard his own blood pushing through his capillaries.

He gripped the edges of the table as the badness kicked in, starting just under his ribs, just to the right of his stomach. The badness crawled to the back of his neck, to his scalp, pushed an angry finger up between his lungs.

He took this for a panic attack. It was not.

Bernice came back in, carrying a shot glass of tequila. She put it down on the card table. 'Cristián?' she said,

26

seeing his eyes distracted, bright sweat standing out on his forehead.

'WHO ARE YOU?' he shouted, standing up like a spring uncoiling. 'WHO?'

The shot glass fell off the table and spat onto the rug. The phone rang.

For a moment Bernice sat in her chair, horribly torn between Cristián, the phone and the tequila.

Then the Mexican shot across the room to the phone. '*¿Diga? ¿Si?*' he yelped into the receiver. 'What? What? Wait a moment, will you?'

He held the phone out at arm's length. Bernice took it from him, feeling his forehead. He was burning hot, and his eyes were glazed and blank. Cristián's cheese had slid right off his cracker.

'Hello?' she said.

The morgue attendant looked around. What was he doing here?

He blinked hard, as though someone had been shining a bright light into his eyes. He was in the psychiatric wing of the hospital. 'How appropriate,' he said out loud. It had been a strange pair of nights. Perhaps he had spent too long watching over the dead.

There was a thick electric feeling in the air – he had felt it in the mountains, in the green jungles. A storm was coming. The small hairs on his arms were standing erect. He could hear voices, and there was a light – one of the cell doors was open! According to the signs, this area was for those who required permanent care.

What was going on?

A little quiver of fear went though him as he went to the door, irresistibly attracted. He had never been into the chronic wards before, though he had sometimes heard the sounds ... Visions of horror films danced in his head. He had to look.

Seated on the floor of the padded cell were a little pale man (*where have I seen him before?*) and an Indian who was presumably the cell's occupant. That was an educated guess, based on the fact that the Mexican was wearing a strait-jacket. *Perhaps*, thought the attendant, *I should ask for the name of his tailor.*

They sat face to face under the naked lightbulb. The madman's eyes were very wide, and his gaze was held by the visitor's. It was unusual for an Indian to have blue eyes.

'Can you remember, Feliciano? Can you remember that day, that moment?'

'No.'

'Come on, I know you're in there.'

'No.'

'You remember it clearly. Far too clearly.' The little man's voice was equal parts compassion and anger. 'It plays over and over again inside you.'

'No.'

One part of the attendant's mind knew that he ought to stop this, whatever it was. He ought to challenge the little man, raise the alarm. Another part was fascinated by the one-sided conversation, wondering what secrets might be hidden behind the mask of madness. A third part of his mind was screaming at him to run away before something unspeakable happened.

'You're in there, Feliciano. Behind the Blue. I see you, even if no one else can.'

'No.' A single tear meandered down the Indian's cheek. 'No.' He leant forward until his head was resting on the visitor's shoulder. It was the only gesture he could make.

'Tell me,' said the Doctor.

'May your heart open!' pronounced the madman, his voice muffled. 'May your heart draw near! You bring me torment, you bring me death.'

The Doctor's face creased in intense concentration as the madman spoke. 'I will have to go there where I must perish. Will you weep for me one last time? Will you feel sad for me?' The words degenerated into sobbing.

'Where must you go?' said the Doctor.

With the suddenness of a snake striking, the madman sat back. '*Otiquihiyohuih,*' he snarled, with a smile.

The Doctor grabbed his shoulders. 'Who are you?' he shouted. 'Who?'

The lightbulb swelled into brilliance and exploded. The attendant screamed in the darkness. A great hot wind rushed through the cell, pushing him off his feet. He scrambled in the dark for the door, the floor, but there was only blackness, and he was falling.

There was the smell of flowers and blood. And then there was silence.

Chapter 2

Nine-tenths Below the Surface

It took Benny a moment to identify the image, a half-remembered picture from some ancient film.

The respirator clung to Ace like a facehugger.

Benny had parked Cristián in bed and grabbed a taxi, alarm crawling through her in waves. She didn't want to leave him alone. She had to leave him alone. He was scared of hospitals and he was looped, his eyes careering all over the place. She had left him in his bed, babbling in Spanish and *Nahuatl*.

Now she found the tears trying to crawl out, and forced them back down. You're in charge, it all depends on you: squeeze out questions, intelligent questions, instead of salt water. 'What happened?' she said.

The medic was harassed, her greying hair wriggling out of its bun. 'We don't know yet,' she said, standing by the bed like a mourner at a grave. 'I've ordered a CAT scan for the morning. Possibly some sort of epileptic episode.'

'She doesn't have epilepsy,' said Bernice.

The woman tilted her head, non-committally. 'The scan will tell us if there's brain damage or a tumour.'

Brain damage or a tumour. 'Where was she when it happened?'

'A hotel up on Guatemala Street. I'm sorry, you'll have to excuse me.'

Benny nodded.

Ace the tough as leather, Ace the invincible. Ace with her head on a thin hospital pillow and a plastic mask on her face, wired to machines that squiggled and bleeped. It was too early in the game for things to be this bad.

She wanted to stay next to Ace's bed. But she had to find the Doctor. Whatever in hell was going on, she needed to find the Doctor.

She found him in the basement.

She had been wandering in a shocked daze through the hospital, trying to remember where the entrance was. Somehow she'd ended up on the lowest floor, in dimly lit corridors, her footsteps echoing horribly as though something were following her. She had already passed a door marked with a red *stop* hand. The morgue.

A sneakered, ponytailed intern was pushing the gurney. The Doctor lay on it, partly covered by a white sheet. They had already put one of those plastic tags around his toe, labelled *John Doe* in smudged blue pen. A single trickle of blood had run down from his scalp, across his left temple.

Benny stretched out a hand, but the intern grabbed it before she could touch the Doctor. 'What are you doing down here, Señorita? Did you know this man?' she said around her chewing gum.

Benny the tough as leather, Benny the invincible, caught the edge of the gurney, found herself kneeling beside it, gripping the frozen steel for comfort. 'This can't be happening,' she protested weakly. 'Oh God, this isn't happening.'

There were footsteps, echoing in the dark tunnel. The intern looked up. 'Don't you people know this area's off limits to the public?' she said, irritated.

Benny raised her head. It was Cristián.

He pushed past the intern, put his left hand on the Time Lord's face and said, 'Wake up.'

The Doctor's eyes snapped open, bright blue and alert. '*Otiquihiyohuih*,' he said. 'I've just been having a little think.'

Benny yelled. The intern fainted.

Ace found herself being examined by a horrible face, a face like Cristián's, but horrible, painted half blue and half

31

black, white teeth standing out against the coloured lips. The face was surrounded by hair bleached white with time. He was saying something to her, some word that she couldn't understand.

'Who are you?' She couldn't speak properly – there was something on her mouth. On her mouth and nose, blocking out the air. She clawed at it. 'Get it off,' she muttered.

The mask came away from her face, and she gulped air that tasted of disinfectant. 'Medic,' she said weakly.

'I'm here,' said the Doctor. He looked up at Cristián. The Mexican looked grim, his arms folded. He was wearing a black coat over his pyjamas.

Cristián shook his head. 'It is gone,' he said. 'Whatever it was, it's gone.'

Ace said, 'Hey, Doc, you look like I feel.'

'How do you feel, Ace?'

'Like a pile of shit. What the frag happened?'

Benny rolled her eyes. Ace was going to be just fine.

'Booby-trap,' said the Doctor. He glared at the grey-haired medic, who scuttled to check on her next patient. 'Meant for me.'

'The hotel,' said Ace. 'Somebody knew you'd come snooping around eventually. So they left a bomb behind for you to find.'

The Doctor nodded. 'A telepathic bomb. A pool of psychic energy. Just waiting for a trigger.' Suddenly he took her hand, squeezed it. 'I told you to leave the research to me.'

'It's a trap,' said Bernice. 'The whole situation is a trap. Doctor, we can't stay.'

Already Ace was swinging her legs over the side of the bed. She was wearing a murky green hospital robe, open down the back. Cristián blushed delicately and retreated. 'Where the hell are my clothes?' said Ace. 'For that matter, where the hell is my gun?'

'Ace!' said the Doctor. 'We had an agreement!'

Ace reached for the bedside table, discovered her shades, and pushed them onto her face. 'Let's get the frag out of here.'

* * *

The morgue attendant probably would have seen the joke. He might even have laughed. But all he did was lie there, staring up at the ceiling.

The Doctor put a finger to his lips as he led them through the morgue. Cristián's eyes were raking the floor, the ceiling, the rows of metal wash-basins against the wall, anything but the work-benches with their heavy burdens. Benny took his arm. He was shaking all over, as though he'd used up all his courage in just coming to the hospital.

The Doctor stopped short, looking at his handiwork: the attendant and the madman, lying side by side on the metal benches, with those ridiculous little tags hanging from their toes.

'They had no idea . . .' he breathed. He reached up and plucked a piece of broken lightbulb from his scalp. 'I wonder if it would have made any difference?'

'Not knowing why they were dying?' said Ace. 'Doesn't matter now, does it?'

The Doctor shot her a glance. 'I just don't like running away,' she said.

The Time Lord put his hand on her shoulder, looked into her eyes. 'Hey!' she protested. 'What are you doing?'

'There's a word you want to say, Ace,' said the Doctor firmly. 'What's the word?'

She tried to pull away, but she couldn't unlock herself from his eyes. 'No way,' she snarled.

'Say the word, Ace.'

Her lips twisted, and she gagged, as though there were something inside her throat that was choking her. Her face tried to move in three directions at once.

'Spit it out,' said the Doctor.

With a convulsive shudder, she said, '*Tlax* – urgh! *Tlax-caliliztli!*'

The Doctor let go of her shoulder. 'Here,' he said, giving her his handkerchief. Ace realized that her nose was bleeding.

'Now,' said the Doctor, 'where would a nice girl like Ace learn a word like that?'

* * *

33

The *pesero* smelt exactly like every other taxi in the world: cigarettes and vinyl and people. Ace relaxed into the mundaneness of the VW wagon. The seat was soft and cool against her back. In the rear vision mirror, the Doctor looked extremely serious.

'Whatever the Blue touches,' said Cristián from the back seat, 'it leaves fingerprints behind.'

Benny took a deep breath and said, 'Why did those two others die, and not you?'

The Doctor folded his arms tightly. 'If someone swung a punch at you, what would you do?'

'Duck?'

'I ducked. Mentally. They didn't.'

'The booby-trap,' said Ace. 'All that energy – it came looking for you.'

'That's why you survived,' said the Doctor. 'But it left its fingerprints behind.'

Ace wiped cold sweat from her forehead. Fingerprints in her brain. She looked sideways at the driver. The *chilango* was dutifully ignoring them.

'Enough of this,' said the Doctor. 'I think it's time we left Mexico City behind.'

Benny sat up. 'Where are we going?'

'Tenochtitlan,' said the Doctor.

'This thing, this Blue thing,' said Cristián. 'It's bigger than Mexico. It's everywhere. It was in London and New York. It's bigger than places or times. If you're running to Tenochtitlan to get away from it – '

'But I'm not running away from it. I want to look it in the eye.'

The *pesero* pulled up at the mouth of an alley. The TARDIS was half-hidden under the awning of a disused building. The Doctor paid the driver while Ace and Bernice and Cristián stood looking at the police box.

'The Aztecs,' said Ace. 'They were the ones who did a lot of open-heart surgery, right?' Cristián said nothing. In his pyjamas, he looked like a sleepwalking child.

The Doctor discovered the TARDIS key in his hat and

unlocked the vehicle, whistling. 'Come along.' They followed him in.

A moment later, Cristián came running back out, breathing hard. He leaned his back on the blue box, clutching his good hand to his chest.

'Cristián?' The Doctor put his head outside the TARDIS. 'What's the matter?'

'I can't,' he said. 'I can't handle any more.'

Bernice pushed past the Doctor. 'Haven't you been in the TARDIS before?'

Cristián shook his head, eyes firmly closed. 'It's – it's – '

'Don't say it,' said the Doctor.

'But it's – '

'Don't say it,' said Benny.

'It's bigger on the inside!' Abruptly, Cristián burst into tears. 'I'm *scared* of travelling through time. I've read stuff. I know what happens if you tread on a butterfly, if you say the wrong thing to the wrong person. What if I kill my great-great-grandfather or something? I can't go. I can't.'

'It's not as simple as that,' said the Doctor, but Cristián had collapsed into Bernice's arms, a sobbing, exhausted wreck.

'We can't take him with us, Doctor,' said Benny gently, stroking the man's hair. 'He's been through too much already.'

The Doctor screwed up his face in irritation, but he nodded. 'All right, everyone. Conference.'

'You've got visitors, Prof,' said Robin, putting his head around the door. The honours student vanished again. Professor Fitzgerald put down the *Journal of Mesoamerican Antiquities* and pushed an enormous pile of papers into his top desk drawer.

'Good morning,' said the Doctor, breezing into the room. 'Got a minute?' He was followed by Bernice, who held a clipboard.

'Good Lord,' said Lawrence Fitzgerald. 'I never thought I'd lay eyes on you again.' He stood up and leaned over the

35

desk, shaking the Doctor's hand heartily. 'Not after that bother with the Egyptian government.'

'Yes, well, I'm sure that's all been forgotten about,' said the Doctor. He pulled up a chair, looking around Fitzgerald's office. 'This is Professor Summerfield, my associate. You've brought the mess with you, I see.'

Fitzgerald laughed. He was a wiry Englishman in his fifties, with teeth which appeared to have been fitted at different angles to one another. 'You didn't come here to compliment me on my tidiness.'

'No, I didn't. I wanted to ask you some questions about the Great Temple.'

'Not really my department.' Fitzgerald sat back in his chair, steepling his fingers. 'I'm only here to give some lectures on Egyptology. Adds a bit of spice to their usual archaeology courses – nothing but Aztec, Maya, and Inca all year round.'

'But you would have access to records?' said Bernice. 'Details, trivia, the sort of fiddly information that never turns up in the journals.' She flipped the pages of *Mesoamerican Antiquities*.

Fitzgerald leant forward, encompassing them both in his unblinking stare. 'You're on to something again, aren't you?'

The Doctor smiled and put a finger on the side of his nose.

'What is it you're after?' said Fitzgerald, delighted.

And in his flat, Cristián Alvarez hugged his arms to himself, watching the sky lighten. He was safe for the simplest of reasons. He hadn't set the trap. He wasn't the bait. He wasn't important at all.

Nowhere, Nowhen

It was like diving into water. A cosmic splash, and they were away, plunging into the Vortex that surrounds and permeates space-time.

The Doctor sat by the side of the swimming pool, in

a relaxed half-lotus, hands curled into a *mudra*. He was surrounded by plants, in a cloud of sweet, dense alien scents.

The pool was one small advantage of his new-old TARDIS. He had been obliged to jettison the original TARDIS' pool when it had begun to leak into the co-ordinate circuitry. This time he'd tracked down the problem before it had begun and mended the equations that formed the water filtration system. But that was the delight of mathematical realities; they were easy to understand, easy to control.

And what about *real* reality, Doctor? What about that?

Cristián had been repeatedly affected by some force outside his control and understanding. He was sensitive to the push and pull of the hidden web accessible only to the telepath and the mystic.

Ace had also been caught up in that web. She had been assaulted and then simply thrown aside, the threads of her mind still twisted together with its strands. With whoever or whatever the weaver was. If he had not intervened, wiped out those Blue fingerprints . . .

But she was free now. The question was, was he?

So he ranged his own mind, looking for anything out of place, anything that might have been left behind. Alien seeds planted in his inner garden.

He opened his eyes. Nothing. Not a thing.

You'll have to do better than that, he told his unknown opponent.

With a tremendous splash, Ace dived into the pool. She skimmed the bottom like a seal, eyes closed, listening to the echoing silence of the water.

Moments like these were precious – a few seconds to catch your breath, to pick up the pieces. The odd thing about time travel was that you never seemed to have any time.

She broke the surface and trod water, pushing the sodden hair out of her face. They'd really been chucked in the deep end this time, hadn't they? And now they were on their way back to visit the Aztecs. No offence to Cristián, but Ace was not all that crash hot on meeting the original Mexicans. She didn't know too much about them, except about the sacrifice. And she was not going through the human sacrifice thing again.

What she did know was that they had an enemy, and that they'd (a) find out who it was and (b) sort them out.

She wondered who or what it was. But as the Doctor had once put it, the possibilities were endless.

She surfaced again, flicking water at his shoes.

'We had an agreement,' he said.

Ace screwed up her face. 'It was only a little gun.'

'We agreed. No combat suit, no weapons. No heavy metal.'

'And what about the trap?'

The Doctor held her gaze. 'How much good did your little gun do you?'

She plunged back under the water. Enjoy the quiet while it lasted.

And so they sailed on through the Vortex. Through an endless pulsing web of space and time.

Chapter 3

Sun King

Tenochtitlan, 1487

It was hot in the city of the *Mexica*. In the marketplace, sweat streamed down the faces of merchants, jammed side by side from one wall of the sacred enclosure to the other, each one sporting a halo of customers, all haggling at full speed. There were feathers and precious stones, skins of jaguars and deer, fruit and grain, wood and honey, rabbits and ducks, fish and fowl. And there were the slaves.

The sound of chisels rang out over the enclosure. The stone-workers called to one another, hurrying. They had a task to finish, perhaps the most important in their lifetime. The Great Temple – the very greatest temple – was to be dedicated in three days' time. And if they did not complete the final work, well, they could see the slaves' cages in the marketplace.

Inside one of the cages, Iccauhtli was waiting to die. He sat hunched over in the low wooden pen, his arms wrapped around his knees, keeping his eyes to the ground. He wore nothing but a breech-cloth and a wooden collar. No more the finery of the nobleman's son for Iccauhtli.

It had been his own fault, of course. The punishment was perfectly justified. He had made a mistake in the drumming, losing his grip on the stick at just the wrong moment, so that it clattered across the wood and to the ground, making an ugly, random sound like hailstones. Such errors were to be expected in the school. But not in the emperor's palace, during his coronation. A wrong note was as dangerous as a mis-recited prayer.

At least they were going to kill him. It might not be the Flowered Death, but it was the next best thing to dying on the battlefield. And he had hated being a slave.

He wondered if his father and his brother might visit the marketplace. Even if they spotted him in the dense crowd, they wouldn't speak to him, of course, they'd pretend he wasn't there. There was no reason for them to share in his shame. The thought that they might be there, looking, was too much for him. Hurriedly, he glanced around the market.

It was because of this that he didn't miss what happened next.

The TARDIS landed where it had been, minus five hundred and seven years. It stood in the sun for a few moments. The virtual paint peeled a little bit more, imperceptibly. Then, with a wriggle that would have put the best morphing program to shame, it transformed itself into a stone statue with a faceful of teeth.

The Doctor and Ace emerged. They were covered from top to toe in hooded cotton robes. The design was not pure Aztec, but with so many foreigners about in the city, the Time Lord didn't expect anyone to notice. He glanced at the baleful idol his TARDIS had become and grinned at it, irreverently. The swimming pool wasn't the only thing he'd repaired.

It was the noise which struck Ace first – a blend of drums and human shouts, the long *Nahuatl* words running together in a rhythmic pattern. Everyone seemed to be talking at once; they were awash in the sound of barter and gossip. A macaw squawked somewhere nearby, its electric blue and red plumage catching her eye as it shimmered in the heat.

Each merchant had a blanket, or a collection of blankets, and their wares were arranged with geometrical tidiness. Grains formed squares of red and black and

40

white. Different kinds of fruit were separated into neat piles. How did they keep it all in order with everyone so close together, treading on one another's toes? Ace imagined one person falling over and knocking everyone else down like dominoes.

She could smell meat cooking, and something else that reminded her of the pancakes in Cristián's flat. Suddenly she realized that she hadn't had breakfast. 'Doctor,' she said, but the Time Lord was gazing around the market-place, lost in memories hundreds of years old.

She tugged his sleeve. 'Earth calling Gallifrey. Listen, how about some Mexican take-away?'

The Doctor produced a small bag from inside his cloak. Ace drew its strings and sniffed. 'Cocoa beans. Barter, right?'

He nodded. 'I think we ought to stay together.'

'Too right.'

Ace went up to the nearest merchant. He was stewing something in a big earthenware pot. 'Um,' she said, hoping he couldn't see her clearly inside the cloak. 'What are you selling?'

The Aztec grinned broadly, and lifted up a rolled tortilla filled with the stuff in the pot. 'Frogs with green chilli,' he said.

Someone screamed in Ace's ear. She whirled around, grabbing at her hood to make sure it stayed in place.

'Yahhhh!' shouted the boy. 'Big lock of hair on the back of the head!'

She caught just a flash of his face as he pushed roughly past her. He was dressed in a breech-cloth and a white cape, and his naked chest was splattered with blood.

He was just one of a gang of young men, all dressed similarly. Each carried a long wooden blade like a narrow cricket-bat. The edges were studded with ragged chunks of black volcanic glass. They jeered and leered at their rivals: another group of youths whose skin had been painted a dark colour. They screamed and shouted back, waving their swords. Then the groups were gone, pushing and shoving their way through the hubbub of the market.

'Big lock of hair?'

'He didn't see you,' murmured the Doctor. 'It's an insult. True warriors have their children's lock of hair cut off.'

'And they were true warriors?'

'Some of them were – warriors in training. The priests have the body paint. Otherwise, there isn't too much difference. The knights are chosen from both the warriors and the priests.'

'I need *Jane's Book of Aztecs*,' said Ace.

The Doctor nodded towards a man bending over a wooden box. Ace did a double-take. The man was dressed as a giant cat – no, a jaguar. He wore a padded jaguar-skin suit, and a helmet made from the head of one of the big cats. His impassive face looked out from beneath the jaguar's snarl. He was awful and magnificent, and he obviously knew it.

'The warriors and the priests are rivals – at least, the younger ones are,' the Doctor was saying, as though he were speaking to himself. 'And the jaguar and the eagle knights are sometimes rivals. The Aztecs are intensely competitive. It begins at the moment they are born, and it continues throughout their life: the litany of duty, of correctness, of doing what you're supposed to do. Every warrior wants to die. They live for it.'

Nearby, drums were beating softly, as a man half-sang and half-recited, gripping his feathered cloak.

'May your heart open!
May your heart draw near!
You bring me torment,
You bring me death.
I will have to go there,
Where I must perish.
Will you weep for me one last time?
Will you feel sad for me?
Really we are only friends,
I will have to go,
I will have to go.'

42

The jaguar knight had moved aside, and she could see into the cage. 'Is he a sacrifice?' she asked quietly.

'No,' said the Doctor. 'He's a slave. But . . .'

'They sacrifice the slaves?'

'They paint by the numbers. The priests won't just snatch you off the street and tear out your heart. They sacrifice only the correct people in the correct way.'

What does it take to distract the marketplace? What could draw the Aztecs' attention away from the merchants, the mock battles, the shouts and songs?

The Doctor simply took his hood off. He heard a drum clatter to a standstill, heard a merchant shout in surprise.

He looked around at the crowd, his face expressionless, neither hostile nor welcoming. His pale face, his blue eyes. The Indians stood with surprise graffitied across their faces. Only the ringing of tools on stone did not stop, echoing out across the sacred enclosure.

This, thought the Doctor, *is the way to make an entrance.*

He smiled, took out a trio of red globes, and started to juggle.

Crack.

Iccauhtli was trying to see what the crowd were looking at. He started at the sound next to his ear.

It took him a moment to realize what was strange about the girl. Her *chocolatl* eyes might have suited an Indian, but her skin was as pale as a cloud. And she was knocking the rocks off his cage.

There was a massive stone at each corner – three now. She glanced around at the mesmerized crowd, and with a casual motion, she shoved a second stone off the top of the cage. *Crack.*

'What are you doing?' whispered Iccauhtli, barely able to believe his eyes.

'You're coming out of there.'

'I can't! I'm a slave!' protested the Aztec. 'I'm supposed to be in here.'

43

'You want to be dead?' she hissed, peering at the crowd from inside her hood. *Crack*.

Iccauhtli gave this a few seconds' thought. 'No.' He was a little bit surprised to hear himself say it.

'Then help me get the lid off this thing.'

Iccauhtli uncurled himself and stood up, stretching muscled legs. The fourth stone hit the ground, and the lid followed it. *Crack*. CRASH.

He stepped out of the wooden cage. Ace grabbed his arm and started running.

'Well,' said the Doctor, tucking the red spheres into his sleeve. 'Thank you very much for your attention, ladies and gentlemen. Must be going.'

He moved forward a little, curious to see if the crowd would part around him. It didn't.

'Who are you?' boomed the jaguar knight. The crowd did move aside for him; the cat-face towered above them as it stalked towards him.

The Time Lord knew exactly why he had their attention. He was not going to do anything as tedious as pretending to be a deity. 'I'm not *atlaca*, if that's what you're thinking,' he said. 'I'm just a traveller. Here for the festival. The dedication of the temple.' He smiled broadly. 'I hope I didn't frighten anyone.'

The knight turned on his heel, angrily, the *Mexica* getting out of his path as he walked disdainfully away. The crowd took their cue from him, moving away from the Doctor, their faces turned towards the musicians, the macaws, anywhere but the scary stranger. They were not cowards. Fear was for barbarians and foreigners.

There was a shout, and the Doctor saw that the empty cage had been discovered. 'Stage one,' he muttered under his breath. He hoped that his directions had been clear enough.

Ace was lost.

Iccauhtli was precisely no help. She had never seen anyone look so guilty as when she'd got the collar off him;

44

it was as though he expected lightning to strike him, or something. She looked at him, trying to see Cristián's genes in his face. 'Okay, I give up,' she said, leaning against the wall of a house to get her breath back. 'Which way to the palace?'

'The palace?' said Iccauhtli. He looked around. 'This way.'

He pointed, but he didn't move. 'Come on,' said Ace, taking his arm again.

'Wait,' he said. 'Are you – why are you doing this?'

'You didn't want to get carved up, did you?' she said testily.

'It's the will of the gods,' said the slave. 'Of the Lord of the Close and Near.'

'Yeah, well, it's not your will, and it's not mine either.' She peered at his puzzled face. 'Waitaminute. You don't think I'm a god?'

Iccauhtli sort of smiled. Ace rolled her eyes. 'You didn't mention this, Doctor,' she said aloud. 'Look, sunshine, I'm just a human being, all right? I just want to get you to the palace, because the Doctor said that slaves get sacrificed, but slaves who make it to the palace go free, and what this has to do with what happened to us in 1994 I have no idea, but until we sort you out I guess I won't know, so get it into gear!'

She gave him a shove to get him moving again, and this time he followed her, shaking his head as though there were an insect in it. Authority figures, right? All she had to do was shout loudly enough, and he'd do whatever she wanted.

The Doctor had replaced his hood and was strolling the streets, anxiously looking for his misplaced companion. Presumably, if she really lost her way, the Aztec would be able to fill in the gaps in her mental map. Assuming that he was willing to co-operate. He might well have been looking forward to an honourable death under the knife.

He had quite forgotten what an extraordinary people they were. Beauty and horror, Susan had said. They built tremendous buildings, they made floating gardens, they surrounded themselves with feathers and flowers and poetry.

And they slaughtered thousands of people in war and on the altar. Hundreds of thousands, by the time Cortés arrived to slaughter *them*. They tore out the hearts and burned them, peeled off the skins and wore them, ate the best parts of the flesh.

Somehow it seemed logical that whatever had assaulted them in 1994 might have sprung from this archetypal horror. There was a feeling in the air like the fizzing of sherbet, the tang of the approaching storm. He wondered if the Aztecs felt it as well.

There were four men standing on the narrow platform at the top of the pole. Ace saw its base first, surrounded by a knot in the swirling crowd, their faces trained upwards in anticipation. As though they were waiting for a suicide to jump.

Four suicides. Ace's mouth opened, but she didn't know whether to shout a warning or a plea or just a shout. Each of the men wore a plume of white feathers on his head, and wings of large feathers on his arms. They were athletes, heavily muscled, standing with straight backs against the burning blue sky.

The crowd stepped back. As one, the suicides leapt off the platform.

Ace didn't manage to look away – and then she saw that each of them had a rope tied to his legs. They spun around the pole, descending in rapid, violent spirals, their arms outstretched like the wings of eagles. It was bizarre, and beautiful, and over in seconds, as the eagles hung limply from their ropes, swaying gently back and forth.

Someone's hand descended on her shoulder. She didn't bother to jump. 'There you are, Doctor.'

'How's your friend?' he asked, examining Iccauhtli from within the hood of his robe.

'Fine. We got lost.'

46

'For goodness' sake, the palace is just outside the sacred enclosure!'

'Well, your directions weren't very clear!' she snapped, trying to catch a glimpse of his face. He was obviously agitated about something. 'Is everything all right?'

'Not until we get to the palace. We're virtually on top of it. Come on.'

It was a magnificent, weird procession, making its way slowly through the garden. Not a step was out of time, not a gesture out of place.

The emperor wore three cloaks, all richly embroidered, one over the other in a layered display of opulence. The face below the feathered diadem was impassive, almost emotionless, gazing around the garden with the absolute dignity of the absolute ruler. He was freshly returned from his two-year campaign to capture sacrifices for the dedication. Renovating the Great Temple was always the first act of a new emperor.

With him walked a handful of the nobles, including old Tlacaelel, to whom they all owed so much. It had been Tlacaelel who had inspired the holy wars, the sacrifices, who had devoted his life to furthering the glory of the Aztecs and of their emperor. The great Ahuitzotl, eighth *tlatoani* of Tenochtitlan and the greatest of their generals, rarely made a decision without consulting his trusted Tlacaelel, much as the *tlatoanis* before him.

There were judges and officials, and their wives; a party of perhaps a dozen, privileged to take the evening air with the mighty Ahuitzotl. And there were guards – the mightiest of the jaguar and eagle knights, just as privileged to be protecting their *tlatoani*.

A few of the party were not *Mexica*, but nobles from rival cities, secretly invited for the festival. They walked with heads bowed, hearts affected by the glory of Tenochtitlan. Just as they should be.

Not one of the party had any idea as to the eventual fate of the Aztec empire. As far as they could see, there was no reason that its glory should not expand forever and ever. It

47

would be Ahuitzotl's successor who would learn the lesson, thirty years later.

The *tlatoani* looked up at the sound of rustling in the garden. He wondered for a moment if one of the animals from his zoo had got loose.

Then the three fugitives appeared, as if from nowhere. The two groups stared at one another for a moment, in absolute surprise. The knights brandished their weapons.

The history books do not record what happened next, and this is not very surprising. After all, it was the wise and mighty Tlacaelel who rewrote the Aztecs' past, so that the people might not believe they were descended from barbarians. And Tlacaelel would have made certain that the records omitted the sight of the powerful Ahuitzotl, eighth *tlatoani* of the Aztecs, on his knees before a short white man, a woman, and a slave.

'The god Quetzalcoatl,' said the Doctor, 'is not due to return until the year One Reed.'

Ce Xochitl inclined his head. 'Perhaps the emperor thought you had arrived early.'

'But you don't think I'm a god, do you, Ce Xochitl?'

The aged judge sat back in his wooden chair, regarding his pale-skinned visitors. 'I think you are the man who saved my son's life.'

The Doctor smiled graciously, and Ace resisted the urge to kick him under the table. He hadn't rescued Iccauhtli entirely out of humanitarian motives. *Human*itarian, ha! He'd made himself an ally. And quite a powerful one.

Ce Xochitl had been one of the emperor's group when they'd come crashing out of the trees. He and the slave had gazed at one another, unable to speak or move. The other nobles had gasped or put their hands to their faces, looking to the knights to protect them.

And then the emperor had knelt down. It was an ego-boost, all right, having a king kneel in front of you. And a relief. When the knights had lifted their swords, she had thought *this is the end of the line, all change*.

The Doctor, of course, had taken charge of the situation

– after all, he was the one everyone thought was Quetzal-whosis. God knew he probably was. He had turned out to be weirder people.

So now they had a friend; a friend who owned an enormous mansion with a garden in the middle and a flock of slaves. Like all the men, Ce Xochitl wore a breech-cloth and a robe; Ace had worked out that the more elaborate the robe, the more important the wearer. When he sat down at the table, he had turned the cloak around to the front, so that he looked as though he were wrapped in a blanket. His hair was just beginning to turn grey, bound neatly back from a striking face with large, dark eyes. She could see the resemblance between him and Iccauhtli.

The ex-slave had been hungry and exhausted; the judge's slaves had brought him wildfowl and tortillas, and then he'd curled up on one of those flat little mattresses and started to snore. She'd realized he was sixteen, perhaps seventeen. The Aztecs grew up fast.

She thought it was a little strange that Ce Xochitl had slaves of his own.

What she had not seen, in the emperor's garden with its exotic snakes and its scented flowers, was the wise and mighty Tlacaelel watching them as they departed, his dark eyes reflecting the deepening blue of the sky. '*Otiquihi-yohuih*,' he whispered into the evening.

The sun had gone down, leaving the canals and the flowers steaming with the heat they'd soaked up in the day. The air was sluggish and humid, but at least there was no smell of petrol, no fumes to hide the burning stars. The Plough hung over the Great Temple.

Ce Xochitl walked with the Doctor. The crowds had retired to their houses for the night; but the chisels were not still, ringing out over the market. Their metallic rhythm joined the beating of drums and the chanting of songs in the temples. None of them were as tall as the Great Temple.

The temples might have been buried under Mexico City, but the market-place had survived. Somewhere around here, hundreds of years in the future, Cristián Alvarez would sense the temple's re-emergence – and find himself caught up in the nightmares of the Hallowe'en man.

Now, wasn't that an interesting pair of coincidences.

'You must have come very far for the festivities,' said the judge. He walked in slow, sedate steps, his every move elegant with the programmed grace of the nobles. 'I have dealt with traders from hundreds of miles away, and yet I've never seen your likeness.'

'Oh yes,' said the Doctor vaguely. 'I've come quite a distance.'

'Surely not merely for the good deed of rescuing my son.'

The Doctor looked at the Aztec, smiling a tight smile. Ce Xochitl was not missing anything. 'I'm curious,' he said. 'About the festivities. About *tlaxcaliliztli*.'

'The nourishment of the gods? You must speak to my other son. Achtli is a novice priest – soon to serve at the new temple, to his honour. I have some little knowledge of the Lord of the Close and Near, but my son can tell you of his many manifestations.'

'The new temple,' said the Doctor. 'It's not so much new as improved, is it?'

'It is the same site of worship that the *Mexica* founded when they settled here. Then it was a modest hut of straw. Each emperor in turn has added improvements to the temple. In four days we will dedicate the newest structures to Huitzilopochtli.'

'Your chief god?'

The judge paused. 'Your knowledge of our religion is imperfect,' he said gently. 'The left-handed hummingbird is the patron of our nation. It was he who led the *Mexica* to this place, who caused the first temple to be built. It is he who leads us into war. Who makes us strong, glorious.'

'And who needs nourishment.'

'Yes.'

'More and more every year.'

'Yes.'

'His appetite increases every year.'

50

'If we do not feed the gods, they will die, as any man might die if food is withheld from him. Huitzilopochtli is the sun. Without the precious liquid, there will be nothing but night.'

'And who fed the sun before the Aztecs? And who will feed it after you're gone?'

Ce Xochitl breathed a long sigh into the perfumed night. 'These are not questions which concern me. You must speak to my son – or one of the older priests.'

'I spoke to an Aztec priest once,' said the Doctor. 'He believed that the sun would shine and the rain would fall without the shedding of blood. Has it ever occurred to you that the reason the sacrifices are made is to dispose of foreign warriors taken captive in battle – and to cause more and more battles to be fought?'

'I cannot speak of such matters,' insisted Ce Xochitl.

'In four days, the Aztecs will kill twenty thousand people,' said the Doctor. 'Twenty thousand warriors and slaves. Their hearts will be torn out on the altar at the top of those stairs. Their blood will be smeared on the mouths of the statues, and what's left of their bodies will be thrown down the stairs.' He grabbed the judge's wrist, and pressed the man's palm against his own heart. 'Feel that? It's no different to any of those twenty thousand hearts.'

Ce Xochitl said, 'The gods exchange their stores of food for human blood. That is their covenant. If we starve them, we shall surely starve ourselves.'

'What will happen when you run out of foreigners?' said the Doctor. His blue eyes burned into Ce Xochitl. 'Can your glory, your conquests go on forever?'

The old man opened his mouth, as though to say yes, to say no, to bless the Doctor for his insight, to curse him for his blasphemy. At last, the judge said, 'I do not understand.'

The Time Lord sighed. He was fighting against a lifetime of conditioning, fighting against an entire way of life. He would have no more success in making this man understand him than Barbara had in swaying the entire Aztec people.

'Forgive me,' he said firmly. 'I was speaking out of turn.'

Ce Xochitl nodded graciously and stepped past him. The old man had already put the discussion out of his mind.

The Doctor looked up at the Great Temple. It was a massive pyramid-shaped shadow against the night sky, blocking out the stars behind it. Here and there red flames licked the blackness where the sculptors continued their work.

Four days. Twenty thousand sacrifices.

That was a lot of *tlaxcaliliztli*.

If Ce Xochitl had looked back, he might have seen his strange guest start to shiver, his blue eyes locked on the temple. He could not move. He shook with the revelation.

The temple was *looking* at him.

Chapter 4

Pronounced Weet-Zeelo-Potch-Tlee

'He underestimates me.'

The priest nodded sympathetically. He adjusted his cloak, throwing a glance at his fellow.

'Or perhaps he just overestimates himself.'

The priests started walking, and Bernice found herself striding swiftly to keep up with them. 'It's not as though I can't keep up with him,' she explained. 'He thinks he's the only one who can understand the situation. He thinks he's the only one who's been uprooted, who's seen every side of life.'

They crossed a bridge. A frog splashed in the marshy water below. 'Here I am, thirty-two years old, perfectly capable of looking after myself. I can think, I can even fight.'

There was a massive building ahead, some sort of ziggurat, a great sculpted serpent wriggling at its base. One of the priests took her arm with a black-painted hand, and she leaned on his muscular bulk. 'He wants to do all the thinking. All the fighting. Does he think he's God's police? Or is it just a bad dose of the messiah complex?'

She smelled flowers and fresh-cut stone, and something else, something metallic, as they began to ascend the steps of the pyramid. The steps were slippery, and the other priest had to take her arm to help her up. 'Maybe he's just trying to protect me. Can you believe it? Protect me? He's trying to protect me.'

They were almost to the apex. There were two small

53

stone houses on the flat top of the pyramid. Each was flanked by a huge statue of an idiot-faced man. The sun was going down, throwing burning orange light over the houses. The colour floated on the waters of the lake.

At the front of the shrines was a great chunk of stone like a truncated, blood-stained bed. The priests led her to it, her shoes slipping in the precious liquid. 'One day they're not going to fall for his tricks, his clever strategies, you know. They're not going to join in the game. They'll just crush the life out of him.'

They laid her down on the stone. She felt the liquid soaking through the back of her shirt as strong hands gripped her wrists and ankles, bending her uncomfortably backwards. Above her, a statue snarled at the sunset, gripping a banner in one stone hand. Bright feathers moved in the warm breeze at the top of the pole. Distantly, she could hear chanting in a language that sounded like falling rain.

There was another priest with a knife. His hair was long and white, bone-white and glistening in the dimming light, and his face was painted half blue and half black. He smiled at her with pearly white teeth. He held a stone knife that had a little face on it, a toothy mouth and a beady white eye that looked down at her.

He said something to her in the language like rain.

Benny jerked awake and discovered she was lying on the kitchen floor. She'd rolled off the mattress, got tangled in her blankets. The lino was cold under her cheek.

She sat up, banged her head on a chair, and managed to stop herself from swearing loudly. The luminous dial of her watch told her it was three a.m. The absolute nadir of the circadian cycle.

Tomorrow – this morning she'd be off to the Institute for some more research. Bernice had wanted to make a side-trip to 1978, to check out the actual date of Coyolxauhqui's discovery for themselves. But Cristián wasn't going anywhere in the TARDIS, and besides, they'd surely be able to find out more from the sixteen years of research that had followed.

Research. She was the archaeologist. She was the one

who should have had a joyride back to ancient Mexico. But the Doctor had elected to leave her behind, sifting through dusty records. Surely she'd be more help, more use in the past. It wasn't fair.

Childish, childish. Ace couldn't do the research Benny was going to have to do. And there was no reason to think that 1994 would be any safer than 1487. And anyway, Benny always worked better by herself.

At least Cristián hadn't had any more . . . fits. She was starting to recognize the signs of his panic attacks: he went quiet, his breathing was a little faster, he couldn't pay attention to what you were saying. Sometimes his hands shook, just enough that you could notice. It happened every few hours.

She tried to imagine being frightened all the time, and couldn't do it. It conjured up images of cowardice, and Cristián wasn't a coward, he was just ill. Bernice knew what fear was, from nervous anticipation right up to the extraordinary cold sensation of knowing you were about to die . . . though of course she never did die. Not yet. Fear was a cool brushing on the backs of the knees, a tightness in the throat, the physical reaction of the animal. Something to be ignored or pushed down, the way you might set aside the symptoms of a cold when you were trying to work.

There was, of course, a different kind of fear, the kind that visited you at three in the morning when you woke up with a start and realized that one day you were going to have to die.

She wondered if the Doctor was ever afraid, in the same way that human beings were afraid. Musing on this point, she rolled over and went back to sleep.

Ace came awake in a moment. She stretched her back against the rough mat, half-covered by the Doctor's white jacket, smelling earth and smoke, tortillas browning on the stone.

The house had surprised her with its sophistication: plastered walls, wooden beams in the roof, perhaps two dozen rooms looking onto the garden courtyard in the centre. Warm daylight leaked in under the belled curtain in the doorway.

She got up and went through her morning exercises, stretching and bending. A slave, carrying Aztec garments, watched her slow-motion dance in puzzled silence. She smiled, took the clothes, and shooed the woman away.

A sleeveless blouse, and a sort of wrap-around skirt. Maybe not.

She'd come prepared: a duffle bag with clean clothes and a few creature comforts, soap and toothpaste and sunblock. There was usually the chance they'd be away from the TARDIS for an extended period of time. She pulled on yesterday's blue jeans and a Cure T-shirt, put on the Doctor's jacket, and followed the smell of breakfast. Probably babies on toast.

She passed the Doctor's room on the way. He was sitting up against the wall in the lotus position, eyes one-third open, staring at the floor as though it were the most interesting thing in the universe. She left him to it.

The Doctor heard her leave for the dining room. He heard the distant throb of drums and the call of the flutes. But he couldn't hear what he was listening for, the elusive whisper that had spoken to him from the temple.

It had been the same sensation he had tasted when the trap had been sprung in 1994. He'd felt it, just for a second, before his mind disappeared like a turtle into its shell. The Blue. The thing that had driven Cristián insane. The thing that wanted to . . .

Kill him?

The temple had wanted to grab him like a lost child and hold onto him forever.

The feeling was diffuse, powerful, not the directed clarity of true telepathy, but just ripples in the ether, spreading out to touch the minds that could sense them.

It might be nothing more sinister than a natural pooling of psychic energy – like Saul the talking church, who had been brought into consciousness by generation after generation of worshippers.

It was a good working theory. Now all he had to do was see if the facts fitted it.

The Institute's archive was a great dark hall, kept at a constant three degrees Celsius. After the swelter of the Mexican noon, it was positively arctic.

Fitzgerald was looking very archaeological in a tawny jacket and white T-shirt. His long face grinned toothily at Bernice as he indicated a two-storey-high wall of files and wide, flat wooden drawers. 'Aztec records,' he said.

'Where do I start?' said Bernice, looking glumly up at the mountain of documents.

'Depends on what you want,' Fitzgerald went to the nearest drawer and slid it open. He extracted a large yellow book, printed on glossy paper, and unfolded part of it. 'A codex,' he explained. 'One of the Aztecs' religious or historical books. A reproduction, of course – the originals are in the Special Documents Section.'

The book, full of starkly coloured figures, unfolded like a screen. 'They were on their way to an alphabet – phonograms mixed with ideograms. Here, you see, a Spanish cleric has kindly interpreted.' He ran his thumb down a wide column of handwritten blue text on one side of the page. 'And there's an English translation running in a narrow band across the bottom. So there's your primary source material.'

Bernice nodded, more impressed with twentieth-century archaeology than she had expected. 'How many of these books survived?'

'Not many. The conquistadors burned a lot of them – especially those to do with religion. They had special orders to destroy anything heathen. The Spanish translations always have a strongly Christian flavour – all the Aztec gods are lumped together as "the Devil", and so forth.'

'Right. I'm especially interested in the Great Temple – ancient as well as modern records.'

Fitzgerald moved along the wall until he came to a bulky filing cabinet. 'Here we go. The '78 people weren't the first

57

to find the temple, you know. There was Gamio in 1913, and Cuevas found a bit of the stairs in 1933.' He slid open a drawer and pulled out a fat file. 'But the proper excavations didn't begin until they found Coyolxauhqui.'

Fitzgerald snapped on a desk lamp and spread out the photos on the wooden surface. 'Charming little lady, isn't she?' Coyolxauhqui lay in a circle of stone, a demon-faced woman, her head and limbs disconnected from her distorted body. 'After their hearts were removed, the victims were sent tumbling down the stairs into her hard embrace. As soon as the archaeologists got a look at this, they knew they'd found part of the temple of Huitzilopochtli.'

'Weet-Zeelo-Potch-Tlee,' said Bernice, trying to get her mouth around the word. 'The sun god?'

'Well, yes. Though the Aztecs' gods are far more complicated than the Egyptian ones – they had a hideously complex religion. Huitzilopochtli was the Aztecs' personal deity. Their mascot, if you like. He killed his sister Coyolxauhqui when she plotted against him. She was a night deity, and he represented the sun – so it was an allegory for the perpetual return of the dawn, the triumph of light over darkness.'

'Hmmm,' said Bernice. 'What I ideally need to know is whether anything unusual happened when the relief was found. Any peculiar events, any strange objects ... anything at all out of the ordinary.'

'Curse of the mummy's tomb, you mean?'

'The Aztecs didn't make mummies,' said Bernice.

'I know, I know,' laughed Fitzgerald. 'But after Egypt ... I just wondered if you were after some more of the Doctor's von Daniken stuff. Little green men.'

Bernice shrugged. 'Any planet in a well-populated galaxy will have traces of extraterrestrial contact. That's a given of archaeology.'

Professor Fitzgerald shrugged with his face. 'The Egyptian government won't let me back in to take a look at the Sheta-Khu'u site, you know. Apparently there's a military blockade around it.' He went back to the filing cabinet. 'Look, you can have a rummage through all these records –

it's a complete inventory of the items removed from the temple.'

Bernice gave the man her best smile as he departed, wearing the quizzical expression she had seen on the faces of many people who'd encountered the Doctor.

Right. The temple. What was so important about it?

Ace yelled and brought the sword around. Iccauhtli caught it with his shield, the obsidian blades sticking in the wood, and twisted his club between her ankles. Back-pedalling, she tripped, laughing. 'Good!' she shouted. 'Let's start again.'

The Doctor stood with Ce Xochitl, watching the mock battle. The judge was in full regalia – a patterned cloak, golden plugs inserted into his nose and lower lip.

The Time Lord reached up and extracted his jacket from the flowering tree where Ace had hung it. 'Would it be possible for us to visit the sacred enclosure?' he asked.

'I must go to court today. There is a great deal of work to be finished before this old man can join in the festivities. But I will accompany you to the temple precinct, and request that my son Achtli be released from his duties to speak with you.'

'You have befriended me,' said the Doctor. 'Thank you.'

Ace and Iccauhtli circled one another. Freed of his slave status, the judge's son had tied his hair up into a warrior's topknot, and painted a single black stripe across his face. He wore only a purple loincloth and a pair of sandals. 'They are not ill-matched,' Ce Xochitl said, polite surprise in his voice. 'I have never before seen a warrior who was a woman – or a doctor who was not a woman. You must have come from further away than I thought.'

'I'm glad that, despite our differences, we're able to understand one another. Thank you for all your help – and for your hospitality.'

Ce Xochitl nodded politely. 'Take care she does not damage you,' he called to his son, laughing.

'Enough of this,' spat Iccauhtli, throwing down his sword.

* * *

The Great Temple rose like a geometric mountain from the sacred enclosure. The Doctor shaded his eyes with his hands, trying to guess its height. Perhaps two hundred feet. The view from the top must be spectacular. Briefly spectacular.

'Indiana Jones, eat your heart out,' said Ace. 'Are we going to take a look at the top, then?'

'There's only one way to get to the top of those stairs,' said the Doctor ominously.

Huge carved stone serpents curled at the base of the mammoth staircase, leading up to the hidden top of the solid pyramid of stone, where the twin shrines of Tlaloc and Huitzilopochtli sat side by side. A river of black stain ran down the steep steps.

The sacred precinct was a vast square of stone built on the firmest part of Tenochtitlan's muddy island. Yesterday the market had been here; now the farmers and artisans had gone home again, and only officials and priests stalked the stucco paving, intent on their preparations for the next day's dedication.

'Reminds me of Uruk,' said Ace. 'Could we be dealing with another Ishtar? Some alien or other mucking up Earth's history?'

'Possibly. Possibly.' The Doctor seemed agitated. 'It is a capital mistake to theorize before you have all the evidence. I'm hoping Achtli might be able to provide us with some.'

Ace watched a priest strut by, his body painted jet-black, his hair matted with blood and ashes. 'Meeting one of these blokes up close should be a real joy. I hope he's brushed his teeth.'

'Perhaps you could lend him your toothbrush.' They exchanged glances. 'I wish you'd leave your little anachronisms behind.'

'What, the premature discovery of dental hygiene might wreck Aztec society?'

'No, but lipstick and sunglasses certainly attract a lot of unnecessary attention.'

60

Ace decided to change the subject. 'How often have aliens interfered in Earth's history, anyway?'

'Very often. There were the Osirians in Egypt, the Exxilons in Peru, Scaroth all over the place. The Timewyrm, of course, and various Dalek sorties, and – '

'And you're Merlin. Great. Why do these bug-eyed monsters always pick on Earth?'

'Bug-eyed monsters?' said the Doctor, with mock indignity.

Ace nodded at Ce Xochitl, who was coming towards them across the precinct. 'Achtli will be able to return home this afternoon,' the judge said. 'He must return to the temple in time for tomorrow morning's ceremony, but you may speak with him until this evening.'

'Excellent,' said the Doctor. 'Thank you once again, honoured judge.'

'You have befriended me, honoured midwife,' said Ce Xochitl.

Ace looked at the Doctor. 'Midwife?'

'Healer,' he translated. 'Curer. Stop laughing.'

Achtli followed the streets beside the canals, watching the canoes go by in slow motion. He felt so light, as though a gust of wind might blow him into the air, rolling down the canal like a petal on the breeze.

Children scurried out of the way of the young priest, watching with round and respectful eyes. He was painted black, his hair was a bloody penitential mass. His legs and ears were marked with deep scratches, the result of years of blood-letting with cactus thorns, feeding the gods. His cloak was feathered and he carried his tobacco pouch at his side. He was a person of importance, one of the scribes of the temple of Huitzilopochtli.

When he closed his eyes, he saw coloured patterns wheeling in the redness. He paused on a bridge, feeling dizzy, feeling as though he were tumbling down a slope and nothing could break his fall.

His old home swam into view, its blank-faced walls looking onto the canal where he'd splashed about as a child.

61

Mother had been dead for fifteen years now. She had perished on the battlefield of childbirth, taking her third child with her.

It wouldn't be long before Achtli would be finding his own paradise.

The slaves met him at the door to the courtyard. 'The *Ticitl*, the foreign midwife, is waiting for you in the room put aside for parties,' they said. Achtli nodded, acknowledging their fawning greetings.

In the courtyard, his younger brother was fighting with a woman.

The priest watched as they circled and wheeled in the slow-motion dance of practice combat. The woman's skin was pale as bone, and her clothes were like nothing he had ever seen before. His father's description had underemphasized the weirdness of his visitors.

'*Otiquihiyohuih!*' Iccauhtli exclaimed, stopping the fight. The warrior-woman leaned on her sword, regarding him strangely. 'You've worn yourself out coming here to visit us.'

'I hope I'm not distracting you from the important things you must have to do,' said Achtli, who was still looking at the woman. When he spoke the scars on his tongue became visible.

'You're in good health?' asked Iccauhtli.

'Our Lord is kind to me,' said Achtli. 'And your own fortunes?'

'One can never tell,' said Iccauhtli. 'Father says I should be able to go back to school. I'll continue my warrior training. He's organizing a feast for the teachers. To help them make up their minds.'

Achtli nodded, pleased, his head ringing giddily. 'You'll make a fine warrior, my brother. Your luck is shifting at last, eh?'

'I'm very grateful to the Lord of the Close and Near,' Iccauhtli said.

Achtli clapped him on the shoulder. 'Give my best wishes to our father, then.' With a final glance at the strange woman and her sword, the priest went into the house.

The stranger sat on a reed mat, drinking *chocolatl*. It took Achtli's eyes longer than usual to adjust to the gloom inside the house. The foreigner looked up as he came in, putting down his bowl of drink.

His eyes were blue.

'*Otiquihiyohuih*,' said the midwife. 'You have expended a great deal of breath in coming here to see me.'

'Please don't get up,' Achtli said faintly, automatically. 'I don't want to distract you from the important things you must have to do.'

'On the contrary, I've been eager to meet you. I hope you're in good health?'

'I am enjoying the beneficence of our Lord. I hope your fortunes are good.'

'Ah well,' said the Doctor. 'You never can tell.'

'No, you can't,' said Achtli. He took the obsidian knife out of his tobacco pouch and moved forward.

Chapter 5

Into the Fire

'As well as being the god of sun and war, Huitzilopochtli was the personal deity of the *Mexica*, the denizens of Tenochtitlan. However, to think of Aztec gods as separate entities is to miss an important feature of Aztec religion. The gods blurred into one another like hues on a colour wheel, each one an aspect of the others. One school of Aztec philosophy had it that there was only one deity, a single androgynous god with multiple faces.'

Bernice turned the page of the textbook. She'd been reading for hours, soaking up the details of Aztec society. There didn't seem to be any aspect of their lives that wasn't affected by religion – birth, death, school, agriculture, the market, war. The magical calendar spun its double wheel, churning out dates that were lucky or unlucky. The gods controlled every event, every person's destiny. It was the sort of fatalism that was perfect for a warrior culture.

'This single god was divided into a male and female aspect, and this pair, the Lord and Lady of Our Duality, had four sons, the four Tezcatlipocas. The White Tezcatlipoca was Quetzalcoatl, a white-skinned, bearded god who was overthrown by the Black Tezcatlipoca and exiled across the ocean. It was prophesied that he would return in the year One Reed – 1519, the year of Cortés' arrival in the New World.'

Tough luck for the Aztecs, who'd mistaken the invaders for returning gods. If they hadn't dithered over Cortés' apparent divinity, they might have wiped out his tiny force.

As it was, they waited long enough for the conquistador to ally himself with their enemies.

The Red Tezcatlipoca was the god of spring, Xipe Totec, who went about wearing a human skin as a sort of overalls. And the Blue Tezcatlipoca was the Aztecs' patron, Huitzilopochtli. 'Gotcha, Mr H. Let's see. Huitzilopochtli's name is variously translated as Left-Handed Hummingbird, Blue Hummingbird, Hummingbird Wizard. The name is composed of two words, *huitzilin*, hummingbird (literally *thorn-jingle*), and *opochtli*, left.

'The hummingbird was the emblem of the warrior; those who died in battle were reincarnated as hummingbirds. Each of the four Tezcatlipocas watched over one cardinal direction. To the Aztecs, the universe was facing west, so the south was on their left. Hence the real meaning of Huitzilopochtli's name: Southern Warrior. It is not unlikely that the god is a combination of the deity Opochtli, and an actual Aztec chieftain.' So he was real. The god of war was real.

The stranger moved with surprising grace and speed. He caught Achtli's hand in a tight grip, twisting.

The priest cried out, wrenching himself to one side to free his weapon, striking at the seated man with his knee.

In the courtyard, Iccauhtli lunged for the door. Ace grabbed his arm. 'Stay put,' she hissed.

The Doctor had rolled to his feet, dodging the blow. Achtli pulled off his cloak, letting it fall to the floor, balancing on the balls of his feet as he judged where next to put the knife.

A wave of anger crested through him, so strong and fast that he found himself leaping forward without consideration for skill or elegance. The foreigner took his elbow, so that Achtli's knife-hand was held uselessly behind his opponent's back.

With a roar, Achtli twisted his foot between the stranger's ankles and brought them both crashing to the floor. He wrenched the Doctor's head back and pressed the obsidian blade to his throat.

That cool sky-blue gaze burned into Achtli's eyes, an impossible colour and depth . . .

'Tradition has it that the Aztecs left their original home, Aztlan, somewhere to the north of the Valley of Mexico, in the year 1168. They spent a century and a half as nomads, following the magical idol of Huitzilopochtli which spoke to the priests in dreams.'

Bernice yawned, scratching her fringe. She had pages of notes and a stiff neck. And she was disappointed that, after ploughing through Aztec history for hours, she hadn't come across a single reference to the Doctor's original visit to their civilization.

She doodled a doodle on her notepad. From his description, she was pretty certain he'd turned up during the drought of 1454, when the Aztecs had been busy sacrificing humans to Tlaloc. The Rain God and Huitzilopochtli shared the Great Pyramid, their shrines built side-by-side on the top. 'After many adventures in the wilderness, and many attempts to settle down, only to be driven out by the locals, the Aztecs came at last to a small marshy island in Lake Texcoco.

'While the priests watched, an eagle flew down out of the sky and perched on a great cactus. When it saw them, it bowed its head. And the idol of Huitzilopochtli called out, "Oh *Mexica*, it shall be here!" '

So they'd built their city on the lake, dredging up mud and silt to make floating gardens, building causeways to the shore and aqueducts to bring in fresh water. For a century, they'd been the ruling power in Mexico, their empire stretching from shore to shore, fifteen million human beings under the Aztec yoke.

And in 1519, Fernando Cortés and six hundred Spaniards had destroyed them almost completely.

'How completely?' said Bernice aloud. Had something survived? Something from Tenochtitlan, crushed beneath the weight of Mexico City, that was still alive, still here?

Achtli found himself slumped against the wall of the party

room. The Doctor was standing over him, holding his knife. The young priest closed his eyes, seeing colours snake before him in the darkness, and waited to feel the bite of the blade.

He heard the warrior maid say, 'Why'd he try to kill you?'

'Tlotoxl tried to test Barbara's divinity with poison,' said the *Ticitl*. His voice sounded like a conch-shell inside Achtli's head. 'The gods can't be killed.'

Achtli opened his eyes, squinting, as the warrior knelt down beside him. Cold sweat broke out on his forehead, and he realized that his shoulders were trembling. He gulped a breath.

'Doctor,' said the warrior, 'this guy's comfortably numb.'

'Mmm.' Achtli felt the rim of his eye gripped. Tears pooled as the Doctor peered into his dilated pupil. 'Have you been eating mushrooms, Achtli?'

The priest pulled his head away from that *atlaca* gaze and nodded sharply. Everything about the stranger was so . . . strange: the clothes, the pale skin, the foreign voice, the eyes. If he were not a god himself, he was a manifestation, a splash of sacred colour spilled into the picturebook of the ordinary world. 'He's marginally telepathic,' the *Ticitl* told his warrior, incomprehensibly.

'Like Cristián?'

'Apparently psychic sensitivity is floating around in the Aztec gene pool.'

'But drugs normally suppress psychic ability,' said Ace.

'Yes, as does anything which interferes with the normal activity of the brain – in this case, with the serotonin metabolism. But the native Americans have a long tradition of using hallucinogens for religious revelation. Who told you to come here with your knife, Achtli? Was it one of the priests?'

'The Blue,' said Achtli. '*Xiuitl*. The mushroom told me.'

'It's no use talking to him while he's got his reindeers hooked up, Doctor.'

The *Ticitl* was shaking his head. 'What did the mushroom tell you?'

67

'I hear it singing,' said Achtli. 'Always singing. In the temple, in the mountains. The gods let flowers fall onto the earth, they're our songs, lasting only as long as a blossom.' He giggled. 'On snake mountain, on the way to Tula . . .'

'What's that?'

There were all sorts of records and rumours of lost Aztec treasures: mostly gold and precious stones, things that had been stolen by conquistadors or archaeological poachers. Many of Cortés' men had drowned in the marsh, weighed down by their plate mail and the gold they were carrying.

Bernice flipped through a photo album of the Institute's collection: earrings, lip and nose plugs, statues, obsidian clubs and arrow-tips. From time to time, Mesoamerican treasures turned up on the black market. When the Institute could, it quietly bought them. How many works of art had ended up as gold bars?

Among the many items said to exist were half a dozen codices that would more clearly explain the Aztecs' religion; human-sized golden statues with gems for eyes; whole warrior costumes preserved intact; mysterious weapons of war. There was never any specific evidence, no location or seller mentioned – just the rumours.

Bernice closed the photo album and rubbed her weary eyes. She hadn't come much closer to solving the mystery. Now all she could do was wait for the Doctor and Ace to return.

And if they didn't?

She wondered if Spanish were easy to learn.

'Coatlicue became magically pregnant when a ball of hummingbird feathers fell out of the sky near her,' Achtli was chanting, almost inaudibly. 'She was sweeping, cleaning the temple, and she tucked the feathers into her skirt. When she looked again, they had vanished. When Coyolxauhqui learned that her mother was pregnant, she became so jealous that she gathered together her brothers,

68

the stars of the southern sky, and they resolved to slay Coatlicue.

'But Coatlicue's brother helped her escape to snake mountain, and her unborn child spoke to her from the womb, asking his uncle how close the pursuing army was, telling his mother, "Don't be afraid; I know what to do." '

'A telepathic foetus?' whispered Ace, but the Doctor waved her silent.

'When Huitzilopochtli was born, fully formed but for his withered left foot, he put on his battle gear. He picked up his feathered shield, he painted his face with children's paint, he wore plumage on his head. On his left foot he wore a feathered sandal. His legs and arms were painted blue. And he picked up the *Xiuhcoatl*, the turquoise serpent.

He struck his sister Coyolxauhqui with the *Xiuhcoatl*,
Send her tumbling down the mountain:
He cut off her head
And left it lying on the slope of the snake mountain.
Her body went rolling down the hill
Her hands fell here,
Her legs fell there.'

Achtli blinked sleepily. 'Enough of this,' he said, ending his tale.

'Like a sacrifice tumbling down the steps of the temple,' said the Doctor. 'The Great Temple represents the snake mountain. And during Huitzilopochtli's annual festival, they hurl a burning paper serpent down the steps. The *Xiuhcoatl*. A ray of the sun.'

'What is it?'

'Just a weapon,' said the Doctor. 'Just a weapon.'

The sound of the stoneworkers had stopped at last. Tenochtitlan was subdued, waiting. Tomorrow morning the great dedication would begin, the consecration of the greatest temple the Aztecs had ever built. The slaves and the captives were enjoying their last night, as the old women washed their faces, cooing to them like mothers, feeding them blood and cactus wine to give them courage for the dawn.

In the coolness of the evening, Ce Xochitl returned to his house, to discover that his sons had taken off their jewellery and washed away their paint. They stood in plain cotton cloaks and simple sandals, waiting for their father.

'*Otiquihiyohuih*,' said Iccauhtli. 'Father, with your permission, we must take a boat onto the lake tonight.'

Ce Xochitl looked from one to the other. Achtli looked unwell, his eyes cast to the ground. 'What of your duties in the temple, my son?'

'I may not be able to return to the temple, father,' said Achtli. 'I have tried to kill the *Ticitl*.'

Ce Xochitl turned his shock into a graceful movement of his hand, a stylized gesture of surprise. 'For what reason?'

'Father,' said Achtli, 'you know that for many years I have been able to see the world behind the pages of this book, to take a glimpse of those gods whose painted figures we are. Now the god who paints me has set me on a path of his choosing. First to slay the *Ticitl*, now to follow him. For a true god cannot be slain.'

From the shadows behind them came the Doctor and Ace, dressed for the journey. 'I have saved one of your sons, honoured judge,' said the *Ticitl*, his unnatural eyes glittering in the torchlight. 'Now let me try to save the other.'

Ce Xochitl knew that what was taking place was beyond his understanding. Reality was slippery, the gods were fickle – might not a man be wealthy one day and a slave the next? He bowed his head, determined to accept the divine intrusion into his life with proper humility. 'Follow where your visions lead you, my children,' he said quietly. 'And I will pray for you both.'

He laid his hands on their heads.

Bernice found Cristián in his pyjamas, watching the soccer in Spanish with Ocelot in his lap.

He smiled at her tiredly, turning down the sound with a

remote. Ocelot chirped, batting at her bag. 'Behave, animal,' said Cristián. 'How went your researches?'

'Well,' she said, taking out her bulging notebook. 'At least it's possible to research the fifteenth century in the twentieth.'

'You're disappointed not to have had a closer look.'

'After reading about your ancestors all day, I'm not particularly keen on inviting them round to tea. No offence.'

Cristián massaged Ocelot between the ears. 'It must seem like a backwater of history, this little city in this little year. Very boring, for an archaeologist who has all of history at her disposal.'

'No, no.' Bernice sat down on the floor, sorting out her pieces of paper. 'People think history is made up of battles and catastrophes. It's really made up of the ordinary lives of the people who were there. Televisions, and grocery shopping, and – ' she waved a sheaf of papers. 'Photocopying. The archaeologist's job is to piece together that day-to-day life.'

The Mexican grinned at her, his face lighting up with the sudden smile. 'Then, Professor Summerfield, may I offer you a traditional late twentieth-century evening of pizza and rental video?'

Bernice nodded with mock seriousness. 'Thank you, Señor Alvarez. I have only one question.'

'*Sí?*'

'What's a pizza?'

The canoe cruised softly through the shallow water. It passed floating gardens, squares of piled mud and silt with corn growing in tidy rows. Fish broke the surface from time to time, with a *pop* and a *splitch* as they disappeared again. Frogs sang in low voices along the distant bank.

Achtli stood in the prow, holding a wooden torch, looking out over Lake Texcoco as Iccauhtli paddled the vessel north. Ace and the Doctor sat in the back. She had wrapped a coarse blanket around her shoulders. There were weapons and torches stored in the bottom of the boat.

The Doctor pointed out distant lights to the east.

71

'Texcoco,' he said. 'One of the cities in the Triple Alliance. Can you see the hills?'

'Only as silhouettes.' The night was brilliant with stars, the Milky Way a solid band of smudgy white winding its way across the highest point of the sky.

'There'll be priests on each of them,' said the Doctor, 'keeping a watch over the Aztecs' lands. Always the threat of invasion, the threat of war. The world is a flat disc ending at the seas, with fifteen hundred cities conquered or waiting for conquest.'

Ace shook her head, letting her hair fall down out of its ponytail. 'Is the water safe?'

'Yes.'

She lay back in the boat, letting her hand trail in the lake. 'Always the threat of war,' she said. 'Not so different from the world I knew. Before the time-storm, when the world ended at the edges of Perivale, there was always someone fighting. The Iranians and the Iraqis on telly, or the Protestants and the Catholics, or me and my mum . . .'

'But in your time, there were peacemakers as well. The Aztecs have no word for pacifist.'

'But what do they do when there's no one to fight?'

'They organize battles between the allied cities – the Flower Wars. The warriors fight amongst themselves, and the priests stop the battle when enough prisoners have been taken for sacrifice.'

'That's always the excuse, isn't it? Sacrifices have to be made.'

'You tell me, soldier.'

'Tlash-cal-ill-iz-tlee.'

Bernice checked the word against the pronunciation key. '*Tlaxcaliliztli*. Nourishment, specifically, the nourish-ment of the gods with human blood.'

She rummaged through her accumulated photocopies. '*Ixiptla*. Ee-sheep-tla. A representation of a god. *Ixiptlas* were everywhere in Aztec religion, from the little statues of the gods kept in the peasants' houses, to the human god-

72

representations who were pampered and slaughtered by the priests.'

She dug out another article. There was a reference to someone called the Perfect Victim, the *ixiptla* of Tezcatlipoca, who lived as a nobleman for a whole year, followed everywhere by his attendants and his pleasure girls.

'The *ixiptla* was an earthly representation of the god,' she told Ocelot, who was watching her from the kitchen floor. 'The priests often dressed as gods. In some ceremonies both the sacrificial victim and the sacrificing priest were dressed and adorned as the deity.'

Ocelot kept rubbing against her legs under the table, making it difficult to concentrate. 'As a physical manifestation of a hidden force, the *ixiptla* made it possible for the common people to see and understand their gods.' She picked up the little animal and studied it critically. 'I'm trying to work,' she explained to it. 'Go and catch a mouse, or whatever it is you do.'

She put Ocelot on the floor. The tabby promptly jumped onto the kitchen table and sat on her photocopies, meowing. 'Grief!' she said. 'How do you switch these things off?'

She rummaged in the cupboard until she found a tin with a cat on the label. 'I hope that means cats are supposed to eat this,' she told Ocelot. 'It could be embarrassing if it's a relative of yours.' A thought struck her. 'Hey, cat? How do you open this thing?'

The phone rang.

Bernice looked over her shoulder at it. She put the tin of cat food on the floor, leaving Ocelot sniffing uselessly at it. Uncertainly, she picked up the receiver, and said, 'Hello? Yes?'

'You must return at once to the hospital,' said the voice on the other end. 'There's been an accident. Señor Alvarez is – ' *Click*. Dead. The line was dead.

Bernice just stood there, looking at the phone.

In the kitchen, Ocelot stood on the table, his fur sticking out like porcupine quills, and hissed and hissed and hissed.

Fitzgerald hung up the phone. The phone box was a

73

rectangular island of yellow light, a fleck of civilization in the darkness. Stay inside, and you had access to people, to help, to the world. Step outside, he thought, and you were back in the jungle.

The jack-handle was weighty and hot in his hand. He saw the light go out in the apartment above, and stepped out into the jungle.

The luminescent dial of Ace's watch told her it was around midnight, local time. She had been snoozing for the last few miles, just listening to the night sounds.

'This is the right place,' said Achtli, very softly.

'Have you been here before?' asked the Doctor, his voice coming out of the dark.

'Not by boat, or by foot,' he said. 'But I know, I feel . . .' He looked around. 'The same feeling that the mushrooms give me is here. In the air and in the water.'

Ace folded away her blanket and picked up the weapons they had brought.

'I've heard about this place,' said Iccauhtli, taking his sword from her. 'It's said that anyone who comes here dies. Quickly or slowly, at once or many years later.'

'Oh great,' said Ace. 'Why didn't you mention this before?' Iccauhtli didn't answer, but she knew why: he didn't want them to think he was afraid.

The brothers hauled the canoe onto the shore. Except for the frogs and the wind, it was completely quiet. The Doctor held the torch, standing at the centre of a pool of reddish light. 'Have many people come here, Iccauhtli?'

'I don't know,' he said. 'I've just heard the stories – the place where no grass grows, a cave or a place in the hillside that's been cursed by the gods. One story says that an unfaithful priest fled here and was finally caught and slain on the hill.'

'It's not far from here,' said Achtli. 'Not far.' The hill loomed above them, another dark shape in the dark night.

Then, with a cry like a wounded bird, the bandits attacked.

74

Iccauhtli shouted as the figures came out of the darkness. He blocked a blow with his sword as Ace snatched up a weapon for herself. She caught a flash of the Doctor's face, heard Achtli cry out, saw the torch whirl and land on the grass, sputtering in the wetness.

Someone rushed her, and she brought the sword up between them, seeing a glitter of red light off the attacker's obsidian knife. She snapped her foot up into her assailant's groin, hearing a satisfying yelp, and danced backwards, swinging the sword in a mighty arc to smack into his side.

He screamed. She roared, wrenching the weapon free, feeling blood spatter onto her face. Someone was shouting her name, but she couldn't hear anything except the battle.

The lift smelled of hot oil and cigarettes. It groaned tiredly as it crawled towards the lobby of Cristián's block of flats.

The doors opened with a mechanical sigh. Benny hurried into the lobby, noticing for the first time the tacky orange carpet, the Smokers Please thing, a spot where the striped wallpaper was peeling. She remembered Cristián's comment about the hideous decorations in hotels.

Suddenly, for no real reason, she had an overwhelming sense of homesickness – for Beta Caprisis, for the cool friendliness of the forest outside the Academy, even for Heaven before it became hell. For familiar places that didn't even exist yet. She was cut off, lost in an utterly alien city where she couldn't even speak the language.

She chewed her left thumbnail.

Someone tackled her from behind.

She yelled and hit him with the frying pan in her right hand again and again and again and again and again.

Chapter 6

Instant Zen

Two torches flickered on the ground. Only the legs of the combatants were visible – and Ace's wounded brigand, on his knees in the intermittent red light, one hand clamped against the gash in his side.

One of the robbers jumped at her. She turned, bringing the sword up to his knees as she side-stepped his clumsy blow. There was an almighty *crack* as wood and obsidian connected with bone. The brigand lost his balance and fell, blood streaming from his fractured knee.

So far, the battle had taken four seconds.

Ace reached into her jacket, pulled out the .357 Magnum she had brought with her, and pointed it at the fallen robber.

Impossibly, in that impossible second, it went *click*.

For the first time she registered the sound. Someone was shouting her name. Hands closed around her gun-hand.

Impossible.

The Doctor, still holding onto the weapon, looked her in the eyes. Her face caught fire, as though that gaze was peeling back the skin, seeing through to the bone. Searching for something.

'I took the bullets out,' he said.

Ace snarled and wrenched herself free, looked around, looking for anyone else who was still standing. She made out a figure stooping for one of the torches – Iccauhtli, his torso splashed with scarlet. He held an impressively gory club. After a moment, Achtli picked up the other torch.

The brothers were looking at her with round eyes. They had never seen anything like her. And they had no idea what she had been planning to do with that oddly shaped lump of metal.

Cheated! She had been cheated! The fight-flight response was only just kicking in, the sweet singing of power in her heart and in her limbs. But the battle was already over, the excitement was already ebbing. The two brigands were whimpering like chastised children.

'Throw it into the lake,' said the Doctor.

Ace fingered the trigger of her useless weapon.

'Do it!' he roared.

She turned and hurled the Magnum into the water, almost before she knew what she was doing. It made an ugly, heavy parabola before hitting the surface with a dull splash. *Let the archaeologists work that one out.*

The Doctor was still watching her, his eyes meaningless highlights in his shadowed face. *Good soldier*, Ace told herself, *following orders*.

She wished she had thrown it at him.

Cristián fumbled open the door of the apartment block with his elbow, carefully balancing in a cardboard stack one Hawaiian pizza and one extra-hot pizza with jalapeño peppers.

That initial relief – that now the Doctor was here, everything would be okay – was coming back to him. He was feeling good; nice company, nice food, a general sense of all that responsibility having been lifted from his shoulders.

On the floor of the lobby, Professor Bernice Summerfield knelt next to the body of a man whose face had been hammered in with a large, flat metal object.

'Mother of God,' said Cristián. There was a ghastly stain leaking from the man's face onto the orange carpet.

He took a step forward. Bernice half-raised the frying pan, her eyes wild. There were bits of grey hair clinging to the metal.

Cristián dropped the pizzas.

* * *

The jungle pressed in around them, a tangled mass of shapes. Now a gnarled tree limb was caught in the torchlight, now a bat flew across the face of the moon. Ace could only see three or four feet ahead of her. Most of the time, she kept her eyes on the path, stepping over rocks and roots. The world formed a sort of black tunnel, the torches ducking and weaving through it, defining its borders with their shadowy light.

They travelled in silence. The Doctor was at the rear of the party, moving through the blackness as though he could see in the dark. She could feel those eyes of his burning into her back, the way they had sometimes burned into her when she was younger and more foolish. The 'gaze'.

It had been a fight. In a fight, you use the best, the most effective weapons available. If the sword hadn't been handy, she would have drawn the useless Magnum first. And if she had done that, she'd be dead now, her skull split open by an Aztec club. How'd you like that, Mr All-Powerful Time Lord?

And the Doctor hadn't tried to stop Achtli and Iccauhtli from dispatching their opponents. He hadn't said a word to them about it, just left those corpses lying in the jungle, as if they'd be a useful marker for finding the boat again.

There was no way it was coincidental that those robbers had turned up, right here, right now. They'd been sent by the enemy, sent to kill them before they could muck up anything important. The Doctor hadn't even let her question them, just sent the survivors slinking away with a glance. For all the Doctor knew, they might have gone for reinforcements, or be stalking them through the jungle at this very moment. At the very least they might have pinched the boat.

Achtli stopped, the red point of his torch hovering nervously. 'It's here,' he said, very quietly.

The Doctor passed Ace without a glance, taking something out of his pocket, a snub-nosed shape that might have been mistaken for a gun. It made a familiar crackling noise, like beetles underfoot.

'The three of you will be staying here,' said the Doctor. 'I won't be very long.'

Iccauhtli and Achtli instantly sat down, holding their clubs in their laps. They beat the torches against the ground until they went out. A moment later, for want of anything better to do, Ace joined them on the dewy grass.

The stones of the Great Temple hid things. Rubies and jade and every kind of gem had been thrown into the mortar. After all, since such treasure belonged to the gods, wasn't it only right to use it in their service?

Huitzilin hid in the stones, embedded in the rough cement. He hid in the carved snakes that jutted from the base of the temple, in the tiny offerings under the floor of the pyramid, the delicate jade fish and the necklaces of carven shell. He was in the sculpted eagle that rested in front of his sanctuary at the top of the pyramid.

Huitzilin reached for himself, dragging the lost pieces back to the centre. He was leaking out between the stones, he was dripping in fat splashes from the beak of the eagle, he was running down the steps in a thin film of Blue. He snatched at himself, crying out, holding on, holding on.

He was coming unglued. He needed nourishment.

The Doctor moved through the blackness without a sound, listening with his ears and with his mind. There was a thunderstorm feeling here, the same sense of anticipation he had tasted in Tenochtitlan.

And there was a lot of radiation. The closer he came to Achtli's cave, the stronger the reading from the radiation detector, clicking rhythmically in his hand. He stopped, fished in his pocket for anti-radiation pills.

He came to a place where the trees had stopped growing, and the ground crunched underfoot, bare of grass. Unlucky Aztecs had visited and had left with their DNA smashed apart, dying quickly with their hair and teeth falling out, dying slowly as their bone marrow grew out of control. Even with the pills he couldn't stay for long.

The cave was a simple breach in the hillside, just the sort

of place a group of wanderers might rest on their way to a new home. The Doctor took out his pencil-torch. A single beam of whiteness stabbed into the heart of the cavern.

The cave couldn't be more than twenty feet deep; there were a few pools on the floor, the gentle tap-tapping of water as it dripped from new-born stalactites. No animals, of course.

He walked into the cave without hesitating. If this were a trap, it was long overdue to be sprung. And he wanted to be back in Tenochtitlan in time for the dedication. The bloodthirsty anticipation sizzling in the city's air could only match that auspicious event.

Bloodthirstiness.

He had seen it on the face of his companion as she whirled in the uncertain torchlight, her Aztec weapon dripping with the precious liquid. Ace the fighter, and more: Ace the killer.

He had searched her eyes for a flicker of the Blue horror, expecting to find that influence again, soaked up into her mind like coloured ink into a white carnation. But he hadn't found it. The Ace who had wielded the sword, pulled the trigger, was his Ace.

He was going to have to do something about it.

His torch-beam flared on metal.

He traced the shape, carefully. A jagged edge, a ragged curve. The chunk of silver lay against the wall of the cave, a meaningless shape, perhaps as large as a hub-cap. He turned the form around in his mind, trying to make sense of it.

The metal curved slightly outwards. He did not dare come too close, or touch it; the radiation detector was screaming. He ran the torch at random over its surface, until he found a black line, a curve, a series of dots . . .

It suddenly fell into place.

He was looking at a ruptured fuel pod from an Exxilon spacecraft, a sphere containing an opaque tube of plutonium. Even with the metal torn, the force-field would have held the radiation in. But once its power source had begun to run down . . .

He could imagine the artefact as part of the Aztecs' baggage as they meandered down from the north: a holy relic, part of a spaceship that had crashed or been abandoned. The interference of the Exxilons had been essential in the development of the Inca, whose civilization had peaked around the same time as that of the *Mexica*.

How long ago had the spacecraft broken up – or been disassembled? Had the Exxilons also performed their experiments on the Aztecs, and if so, why was there no other evidence of it? Was an alien even now manipulating the Indians, manipulating him?

He found he was sinking his teeth into his bottom lip. It was like finding all the pieces of a jigsaw puzzle, and not knowing what the picture was meant to be.

And the cave wanted him to stay.

Its walls curved over him and around him like loving arms, wanting to hold him, hold him like a lost child and never let him go.

Iccauhtli said, 'So then Chief Coxcox praised his soldiers, and said, "The Aztecs are cowards, none of these captives are theirs." But then he saw that thirty of the captives had only one ear. Coxcox said, "Why is each captive missing one ear?" And the Aztecs reached into their packs and showed that they had cut an ear from each warrior they had taken in the battle. In this way they proved that they were the bravest of all.'

'Right,' said Ace. Achtli was nodding, with a broad grin on his skinny face. The tale was obviously an old favourite.

The little group fell silent for a moment, each one listening for the Doctor's return. Achtli shuddered, sensing something his companions couldn't. Ace found herself thinking of Preston, his little world stained forever by the Hallowe'en Man.

She thought of all the stains on her own life. She thought of Mike lying like a shattered doll on the stairs of his house, the splintered banisters strewn across the floor. She thought of the sound Daleks made when you killed them,

81

the organic hiss of a shattered carapace, like the noise of chips in hot oil.

Stained.

Achtli was touched by that nameless Blue horror, as Cristián had been. As she had been. She remembered spitting out that awful word, a word she couldn't remember how to pronounce. They were all being progressively contaminated by the whatever-it-was.

She didn't feel any different . . . at least, she didn't think she felt any different. How had it been for the Hallowe'en Man, in those last desperate minutes, alone in the crowd – clutching his gun?

His gun.

A tiny noise made her spring into a crouch, before the brothers could react. 'Doctor,' she said.

She thought about it later, curled up in the canoe, wrapped in the patterned blanket, her head resting on her folded arms. The Aztec brothers were silent, Iccauhtli once more rowing the boat with strong strokes.

'Our weapons,' the Doctor had said, 'are not our own.'

They had walked perhaps twenty feet ahead of the others. Ace found herself stumbling, trying to keep up. 'What did you find in the cave?'

'The Hallowe'en Man was a tram,' he said, his voice coming out of the forest in front of her. 'He was just following the rails that had been laid down for him. Think about the weapon, obtain the weapon, use the weapon.'

Was this a lecture, or was he just thinking out loud? 'Those same rails may have been laid down many, many times. Here we are, in 1487. Columbus is five years away, Cortés thirty. Your ancestors have just finished fighting the Wars of the Roses. There are five centuries between us and the Hallowe'en Man. Five centuries disturbed by . . .' His voice trailed off, and for a moment she could have believed he had melted into the trees.

'What did you find?'

She stopped suddenly to avoid walking into him. He was standing still, facing her, blocking the path. 'Whatever it is,'

82

he was saying, 'it's interested in death. Quite interested. And it likes weapons.'

'My gun,' said Ace. 'You don't want it to turn me into another Hallowe'en Man.'

'No,' he said. 'You're perfectly capable of doing that to yourself.'

With speed that surprised even her, Ace belted him.

He didn't lose his balance, though his head moved with the blow, snapping to one side.

'If you see what I mean,' he had said.

Achtli huddled in the bottom of the canoe, shivering all over. 'Can you feel it?' asked the Doctor quietly. The priest nodded. 'So can I,' sighed the Time Lord.

'Look,' said Iccauhtli. 'You can see the fires on the top of the temple.' He pointed at the red beacon in the distance, looking out from Tenochtitlan in all directions, penetrating the night.

'It must be almost dawn,' the priest said. 'They'll already be preparing the sacrifices.'

'How will it be done?'

'Altars have been provided for the two visiting kings. Old Tlacaelel will sacrifice at the altar of the sun. And the mighty Ahuitzotl has the place of honour at the top of the Great Temple, killing men for Huitzilopochtli.'

'You're not going to do anything about it, are you?' said Ace, without opening her eyes.

'Any suggestions?' said the Doctor.

'You'll just let them all die. All twenty thousand.'

'Yes, Ace. I'm going to let them all die.'

She opened one eye. Did he look pale, or was it the torchlight? There might or might not have been a bruise forming across his left cheekbone. Did he bruise? She couldn't remember.

Hitting him had been easy, so easy, so very sweet.

'What will I do?' he said, and he wasn't really speaking to her. 'Will I run to the temple, shout for them to stop? Will I cast down their civilization, kill their gods, wipe them from the face of the earth?'

Achtli was gazing at him with calm terror, quite certain that he could do what he said.

'It's already written in the book of history,' he continued. 'Painted in the records. Nothing I can do or say is going to change it. But there's something else here, something that isn't in the book, or wasn't the last time I visited. Things have changed. Something's wrong. Someone's interfering. I need to find a way to read between the lines . . .'

'Run to the temple,' said Ace. 'Shout for them to stop.'

The Doctor's expression said *make up your mind*.

'War's different. This is – murder. Suicide. I don't know. Stop it.'

'Achtli,' said the Doctor, 'when do you best perceive the Blue?'

The young priest said, 'We have a law that drunkenness is punishable by death. Only the very aged may drink cactus wine, except on special occasions.'

'Why is that?'

He raised his hands in a gesture, as though trying to frame the meaning of what he was explaining. 'The gods are wild and fickle, always looking for ways to break into the world. Every aspect of a person's life is touched by the brush of the *atlaca* – their birth date, their good fortune, their fertility, their death. What hope do we have of keeping the supernatural away?'

'By keeping it well-fed,' said Ace.

'By not providing it with paths into our world. A hungry god may strike down the crops, strike down a human being. Our sacrifice keeps the gods at arm's length, reminds them of their duty to us.'

'But the drunk provides a path for those gods to enter the world.'

Achtli nodded. 'The cactus wine, the morning glory seed, the mushrooms – they are the causeways along which Huitzilopochtli can journey into Tenochtitlan. They are the smoky mirror we can use to see his world more clearly.'

'Now I see through a glass darkly,' said the Doctor. 'Achtli, I'm going to need your help. We've got to penetrate this veil of Blue. No more mysteries and hints. I want the truth.'

The priest nodded, his eyes very wide. 'I know where we can buy dried mushrooms. We'll need honey to cut the taste.'

'Hey, Doctor,' said Ace, 'just say no.'

He scowled. 'It is what I came here for.'

'What, a spot of instant Zen?'

'No,' he said testily. 'I told you. To look the Blue in the eye.'

Ace dreamed.

She dreamed she was back in her combat suit, its black material clinging to her arms and hips, blaster holstered at her side. Her name blazed on her back in bright letters, a challenge, a shout to the world. She smiled, pulling the gun out of its holster.

It formed the end of a long chain, starting somewhere in her hindbrain, tracing down through her neck, circled by the stiff collar. The line moved down through her arm, through her hand, along the barrel of the gun to its business end. Her business.

She blew the Aztec's face off.

Inexplicably, the blaster fired bullets. Skin and muscle peeled back in a double wave, the skull shattered in two, revealing soft throbbing brain between the man's hollow eyes.

He grinned at her with the face of death. He was wearing a business suit, and she could see the pinstripes running down his shoulders, down his chest beneath the spattering of pink. 'Well done,' he said. 'You deserve a promotion.'

He put a decaying hand on her slick black shoulder, and corrupting matter formed a smear on the material, like a medal or an extra stripe.

She stepped back, tugging at the collar, wondering why she couldn't get the suit off. With a guttural cry she tore it loose from her shoulder, but it had sunk half an inch deep into her skin, ripping loose the flesh from the bone as she pulled it away.

She stared at the mass of meat and white bone, blinking rapidly, unable to understand why she felt no pain.

'You see,' said the boss, 'we're the same underneath.'

Taking care of business.

The Great Temple hummed to itself, a silent, electric song like telephone poles whispering to one another. Everything held its breath.

At the base of the temple, the sacrifices were waiting. They wore only their loincloths. Some were defiant, some were petrified, many of them were drunk, and all of them were waiting.

The queue stretched back from the temple, stretched through the great courtyard of the sacred enclosure. The line twisted through the streets of Tenochtitlan, over the bridges, across the canals. Along the white stretch of causeway that shot across the marshy waters to the bank. Halfway around the lake.

The kings of the Triple Alliance put on their finest cloaks, their golden lip-plugs, their golden ear-plugs, their golden nose-plugs, their arm-bands and their anklets. The priests put on the garb of the gods they represented. Together they ascended the pyramids, sedately moving up the steep, steep stairs, their sandalled feet crunching on the dried blood.

And then they waited.

And the temple hummed to itself. Waiting.

'Psilocybe mexicana,' said the Doctor. He held the tiny umbrella up to his face, turning it slowly. *'Teonanacatl.* The flesh of the gods.'

As good as his word, Achtli had returned to the house with a pouchful of the magic mushrooms. They were small, fawn-coloured and shrivelled, with a long, thin stem.

'I'm not so sure about this,' said Ace.

The Doctor and Achtli laid the mushrooms out on the mat between them. The very first glimmerings of dawn were beginning to touch the ground in the courtyard. As one of the city's important officials, Ce Xochitl had already departed to prepare for the ceremony.

'Sure about what?' said the Doctor, examining another of the mushrooms.

'Well.' Ace chipped a bit of plaster off the wall with her thumbnail. 'What's in those things, anyway?'

'4-Phosphoryloxy-NN-dimethyltryptamine.'

Ace put the structure together in her head. 'Something like LSD.'

'Psilocybin. Nothing I can't handle.'

'Oh yes?'

'Humans have very poor control over their biochemistry.' He looked up at her. 'There's nothing this drug can do to me which I don't want it to.'

'And you reckon if you eat that, you'll be able to see it?'

'See what?'

'The Blue. Our enemy. Whatever the hell it is that's going on.'

The Doctor nodded.

'The thing that drove Cristián out of his mind. The Hallowe'en Man, the thing that made him shoot all those people.'

The Doctor nodded.

'Look,' said Ace. 'Are you sure you want to muck about with it?'

'Well,' said the Doctor, 'this is the thing that drove Cristián out of his mind. This is the thing that made the Hallowe'en Man shoot all those people. We have to find out what it is. I have to know.'

Great, thought Ace. *Wonderful. Shit.* 'Where does that leave Achtli?'

'I want him as my co-pilot.'

The Aztec said, 'I'll follow wherever the mushroom leads.'

'Do I get some too?'

The Doctor raised his eyebrow at her. 'I want you and Iccauhtli to keep an eye on things. Whether our "brigand" friends have reported in or not, someone's bound to be curious.'

Unexpectedly, he held out his hand to her, and unexpectedly, she took it. 'Don't leave us, Ace,' he said.

They gripped one another's hands for a moment, and then she went outside the house with a sword, to join Iccauhtli in keeping guard.

It wasn't until much later that she realized he had been saying goodbye.

Bernice screamed.

It was a wail of horror and outrage, the wordless sound a child makes when it's really hurt itself. Her back arched and she came up from the gurney, clawing at the arms and hands that held her down and pushed needles into her skin. Someone was strapping her limbs to the metal trolley.

Cristián saw it all in slow motion, the way he'd seen the Hallowe'en Massacre, detail after detail stored away to be replayed at leisure. He stood several feet from the trolley, and he was the only thing in the room that wasn't moving.

Bernice tore both arms out of the restraints, and now she was shouting, 'Yes! Yes! We are the same underneath!', and it didn't mean anything, anything except that she was sick.

The pair of paramedics who had brought her in were standing around, looking like they wanted a smoke. Their faces were hostile blanks. They were used to collecting the victim, not the assailant. She had reversed the natural order of things.

Cristián had caught a glimpse of Fitzgerald's face as they zipped up the black plastic shroud. She had smashed him apart, as though once she'd struck him she couldn't stop, smacking the non-stick frying pan into his face until there was no face at all.

Now they'd managed to tie her down, and she was still shouting. Half of it was *Nahuatl*, stuff he couldn't understand. The other half was just gibberish.

'Take the suit off,' she gurgled. 'You young idiot! Take it off, take it off!'

Ignored by everyone, Cristián quietly started to cry.

* * *

88

Achtli was shivering all over like a wet cat. He fidgeted and swayed.

The Doctor sat perfectly still, his left foot on his right calf, his back straight as a ruler. His eyes were barely open.

The initial effects of the drug were unpleasant, but they'd pass. His stomach hurt. He couldn't feel his fingers or toes. He was aware of the phosphoryl group being knocked off the psilocybin, converting it to psilocin, the psilocin's false messages confusing the signals of his natural neurotransmitters.

Ace was right: normally neurotoxic substances inhibited telepathic efficiency, just as they interfered with all of the brain's activities. But for some reason, the hallucinogen was increasing his perception of the Blue. It was something in the air he could taste, a hue in the shadows, something that had definitely not been there on his last visit.

But he still couldn't see it clearly.

Normal thought couldn't catch it, except as a glimmer, out of the corner of the mind's eye. But the drug broke down normal thought, normal perceptions, tore down the walls.

The walls of the temple were crumbling, tumbling, opening to reveal whatever was inside.

And again he felt that longing, that clutching. The Blue wanted him, *him*. The trip was a trap.

He laughed shortly. Achtli started, breaking into a sweat.

The warriors were dressed in their finest. Their hair was coiffed backward and up into the warrior's ponytail; their faces were ornamented with jewellery and paint, their cloaks were richly woven. They walked in sandalled feet until they came to the house of Ce Xochitl, the judge.

There were six of them, some of Tenochtitlan's finest. They had nothing to do that day, and there'd be plenty of time to see the gory spectacle at the temple precinct; it was going to take days to slaughter that lot of prisoners, days.

So they went to the house of Ce Xochitl, the judge, where they found the white-skinned warrior maiden and one of the judge's whelps, leaning on their swords in the dusty street.

'Skirt and blouse,' called out one of the warriors. The woman watched them coolly, as though they were no one, peasants.

Oh, and she was a sight to see: no make-up and jewellery for this woman, but foreign clothes, sandalled feet, a warrior's shield and sword. Did she think she was Coyolxauhqui, the fighting woman who had been brought low by their god?

'Hey, skirt and blouse,' the warrior said again, 'why stand there in the dust with that little boy?' Iccauhtli bristled. 'Little boy with a big lock of hair on the back of the head. Were you too frightened to drag a captive down?'

The woman didn't move, didn't even seem to be listening to them. 'She's got skin like an axolotl,' one of them joked. 'Pale white axolotl. Hey, little axolotl! Don't stand there. Come with us, and we'll give you cactus wine and mushrooms. You can dance for us.'

Iccauhtli looked from the warriors to Ace. Against half a dozen experienced fighters, he wouldn't last a minute. But she – at that moment, watching her stare down the warriors as though they were children, he believed she could kill them all with a blow of her sword.

'Come with us, skirt and blouse.'

'I'll come with you,' she said. Her voice silenced them, and they waited, clutching their weapons.

And she screamed, 'All the way to hell!'

Inside the house, Achtli was leaning against the plastered wall, yawning uncontrollably. Tears kept rolling out of his eyes. He could hear every sound – his own cheek scraping against the plaster, distant drums, the scuffling of feet and shouts outside the house. He heard his brother cry out, heard a scream of rage.

He heard the ragged breathing of the *Ticitl*. From time to time he remembered the little man, opened his eyes to chart his progress through the Blue shadows.

The Doctor lay on his side on the reed mat, curled up like a child, hands pressed against the cold floor. His eyes were open, and he was seeing, *seeing* . . .

The queue moved slowly, shuffling forward like people at a bus stop. The priests flanked the first of the victims, a Huaxtec taken in the rebellion, the scars still livid on his legs and arms. Together they walked to the top of the stairs, carried forward by destiny as much as anything, by the weight of the queue of twenty thousand pressing at their backs.

The Huaxtec's breath was taken away by the view of Tenochtitlan, spread out among the waters of the lake like a great flower of humanity. He saw the crowds looking up at him, their faces an anonymous blur of expectation. He saw the line of sacrifices stretching into the distance, a skinny finger pointing at the temple. Pointing at him.

Five priests took him and bent him backwards over the killing stone, holding his wrists and ankles, pulling his body into a taut arch. The emperor himself stood over him, holding the fat stone knife. They looked at one another.

Without further ado, the emperor smashed the knife into the Huaxtec's chest. There wasn't even time to cry out before the blade plunged through skin and fat and muscle, shattered his ribs.

The emperor pushed a muscular hand into the Huaxtec's chest, past the jagged ends of bone, and ripped his heart out with a single violent tug.

Someone pushed their hand in through the Doctor's face. He convulsed, mouth open. He squeezed his eyes shut, but patterns of blue and red and yellow screamed across his field of vision.

This was much too much. This was out of control. It was time to metabolize the psilocin, turn the poison into something harmless, time to come back from the trip.

He tried.

Nothing happened.

The fingers touched the whorls of his brain, intolerably.

He ran to the temple and shouted for them to stop.

* * *

The humming of the temple had become a strident buzzing, and the Blue had leaked between the flagstones, colouring everything.

Ahuitzotl wrenched another fluttering heart free from its sinews. Huitzilin felt it as though it were his own heart, his back arching as he clutched the edge of the altar with intangible fingers. His teeth were bared in a rictus of glory as death drenched him.

'Again,' he said.

Another victim topped the steps, was pushed onto the altar. Perhaps this one saw Huitzilin's face before he died, his mouth gaping with surprise as the blade shattered his body, his heart shuddering in horror as it met the daylight. Huitzilin grinned invisibly at the dead face, meeting those glazing eyes in the seconds before they lost the world.

'Again,' he said.

Another victim, his body criss-crossed with battle scars, let himself be dragged onto the stone. He stared stoically at the sky as the emperor sliced him open. Death exploded out of him, showering Huitzilin like blood. He opened his mouth, tasting it, spiced with despair and with pain.

'Again,' he said.

The children and the chickens squawked and fled as the warriors ran through the streets. The fighters screamed and yelled, their blades whirling like great wings.

Ace had lost track of the battle, lost track of her surroundings, everything but the moment. She cried out in awful pleasure as she slammed her weapon into the leg of one of the warriors, saw him fall. She grabbed his hair and dragged him shrieking out of the battle, tumbling through the dirt. He slid down the muddy side of a canal, landed in the water with the filth and the fishes.

Something hit her, feeling like a bomb exploding in her side, but it didn't matter. She yelled, gloriously, stepping aside and swinging the sword sideways to connect with the warrior's head. He fell without a word, and the fighters stepped over his stunned form.

Oh, the details of the battle were unimportant. At these

moments, she was a hand inside a glove, and for once the glove wasn't too loose, wasn't too tight, but fitted perfectly. A human hand inside the glove of battle, reacting with perfect speed, pure grace. There was no memory, no worries about the future, there was no self-doubt or anger or pain.

Taking care of business.

The street rippled under the Doctor's feet, washing up and down like waves. Sometimes the ground seemed close, sometimes far away. Time was slowing down to the consistency of treacle.

He stumbled and he swayed, but somehow he kept moving, drawn towards the temple like a marionette dragged through the dirt by its strings. From time to time he cried out in alien words, and any Aztec who saw him thought he was mad or a sorcerer or a god and left him alone.

He could almost see it – almost see it –

At the four temples the kings were smashing through chest after chest with their heavy stone knives. The hearts they tore loose they held up to the burning sky, blood seething down their arms, and then they hurled the quivering organs into the hollow back of the eagle statue, its body sizzling and smoking as the hearts burned.

The priests lifted the shattered bodies and hurled them down the steps, bouncing and tumbling, their arms and legs spinning randomly like the spokes of a broken wheel. Cheekbones and fingers snapped on the hard stone.

At the base of Huitzilopochtli's temple, the bodies smacked into Coyolxauhqui. Her hard stone body embraced them for a moment before they were dragged away by the priests to be cut into meat.

And the queue kept moving forward.

And the Doctor saw it all.

'Don't you understand what you're *doing*?' he shouted, but his words were turning into coloured fish and floating away. 'Don't you understand what it is you're *feeding*?'

And the queue kept moving forward.

* * *

She had dragged four of them down, screaming. Two had fled.

Ace felt herself gliding down from the high of combat, felt the strength starting to leave her arms and legs, became aware for the first time of the blood washing down her side, the insistent ringing in her ears.

Where was Iccauhtli?

Glorious.

No sign of the little warrior. Her side was throbbing in time with her head.

'Dear God,' she said. 'I left him. I left the Doctor.'

She dropped her sword and bolted back through the streets, leaving a trail of red.

Bernice screamed, 'Stop it! Stop it!'

Or perhaps her mouth opened, silently battering the hospital walls with her horror. She moved against the sheets, her wrists pinned to the cold metal by the restraints. Cristián did not wake up.

She needed to get up, to run away. She had to deliver her warning. She pulled on the restraints, the rough straps cutting into her wrists.

'Be quiet,' said a cool voice in her ear. Non-existent fingers ran themselves over her forehead, her shoulders. She shuddered and gulped.

'Be quiet, Bernice. Be quiet.'

Doctor? Is that you?

But there was only the sound of traffic and air-conditioning, and Cristián's quiet breathing, oblivious in the cool darkness.

He pushed through the crowd at the base of the temple, pious faces twisted upwards to the sky like sightseers at a suicide. He pushed through the wall of human flesh, the line that stretched across the stone floor of the temple precinct. No one took any notice of him.

'Stop it!' he screamed, as time slowed down to a standstill. The line hovered in mid-step. 'Stop it, stop it!'

He found himself looking up at the temple, to the side of the frozen queue.

SOMETHING WAS WALKING DOWN THE STEPS.

At first it was just footsteps without feet, just the fact of walking with no one to do it. But as he watched, as frozen as the other sacrifices, the truth began to be painted in.

Huitzilin was a ghost, an image smeared in the air. He was tall, and muscular, and dressed as an Aztec chief should be, in gold and feathers. His smile was white. His hair was long and white. His eyes were Blue.

The Time Lord's head snapped up, his body held rigid, his eyes and mouth wide with horror. A single drop of blood traced its way down from his nose as something inside him broke.

A flower of Blue exploded into blossom deep within his chest. Its petals unfurled, and each of the petals was a flower, unfurling its own petals, and each of those flowers was made out of *flowers*, and each of those *flowers* was made out of *flowers*, and each of those *flowers* –

He fell sideways, making no attempt to catch himself, head and shoulder smacking hard into the stone. Blood was coming out of his ears and his nose. His eyes were burning, blazing, *seeing*, seeing at last, seeing. . .

'*Sing for me,*' *said Huitzilin.*

The Doctor screamed.

Ahuitzotl smashed the knife into his victim.

The Doctor screamed.

Ahuitzotl smashed the knife into his victim.

The Doctor screamed.

Ahuitzotl smashed the knife into his victim.

The Doctor

Second Slice

I have yet to see any problem, however complicated, which, when you looked at it the right way,
did not become still more complicated.

                                      Poul Anderson

Chapter 7

And the Smile on the Face of the Tiger

Over the Atlantic, 1994

Macbeth hated flying.

He smiled cheerily at the flight attendants and nodded at his fellow passengers. But as soon as the plane dragged itself into the sky over Heathrow, he pulled down the blind, hiding those two alarming little puncture marks in the glass of the window, like a tiny vampire bite.

He had a pair of seats to himself – it was the off season, and he was leaving the English weather behind. He pulled off his shoes, balanced his Scotch on the aisle seat's tray, and opened his black leather briefcase.

Macbeth was tall and red-headed, with a speckling of red stubble just starting to crawl across his square chin. His nose had been broken some time in the past, lending a hint of thug to his face that was belied by his tidy speech, the Glaswegian accent kept rigidly under control.

Macbeth's stomach did something odd as the plane levelled out, giving the hair-raising sensation that he was suddenly falling. He gripped his whisky and spread out the files he'd brought.

The first was a neat folder of newspaper articles from the cuttings service. Eyewitness reports of the Hallowe'en Massacre – plus half a dozen tiny news items, a scattering of unrelated events. A riot in an asylum. The sudden deaths of a group of Indian midwives, cause unknown. The abrupt closure of a Mexican university's research project on dream telepathy. All dated October 31, 1993.

The clipping from *Fortean Times* featured an article on the asylum riot. Apparently its timing had coincided perfectly with the massacre – they were calling it the one-minute rebellion. Two attendants had been attacked, a dining hall had been smashed up, four patients had died suddenly. Cause unknown.

Nothing new to Lieutenant Macbeth, formerly of UNIT, who had seen the same thing happen in 1968.

He'd been there from the beginning, when the United Nations were looking for ways to deal with extraordinary events. Alien invasions. He'd stayed in London when the Yeti took over, taking holiday snaps and trying to rearrange his world view. All those hints of extraterrestrial visitors, all the rumours and confused reports, all the charlatans and nutters . . . and then they were face-to-face with genuine ETs in the London Underground.

The next file contained a hastily photocopied death certificate, Doctor Sullivan's name inscribed across the bottom in a square hand. Sullivan had been one of those men closest to UNIT's little secret. He seemed to have vanished altogether.

RSM Benton had chased Macbeth off his used car lot. Corporal Bell had been promoted to captain and had ended up brain-damaged in a car accident. Captain Yates, who had retired under odd circumstances in the mid-seventies, wouldn't speak to anyone.

But he had managed to find one of Sullivan's nurses. Bugger the Secrets Act, she told him over tea and scones, they'd killed that poor man. She spoke of secret tests and strange technology, and how Doctor Sullivan had made her write 'heart attack' on Hubert Clegg's death certificate, even though she was sure he'd been the victim of some kind of experiment.

After Macbeth and UNIT had parted company, he'd still kept an eye on their activities. In fact, he had rather more information about them than they'd be comfortable with. Paranormal researchers had all sorts of ways of finding things out. There were those mysterious evacuations of London, the prison riot, something chemical in Wales, something nuclear in Cornwall, the *church* they'd blown up, for Chrissake.

Ancient history. In the paranormal, there was always this week's special flavour – crystals or levitation, synchronicity or Atlantis, Space Alien in Love Triangle with Two-headed Woman.

Christmas 1968 had been his last chance to dip his toes in the ocean of the unknown before UNIT had thrown him out. Now he hovered on their fringes, picking up scraps of information, never coming quite close enough to find out what was going on.

Scraps of information wouldn't be enough this time. '68 was happening all over again, down Mexico way. And this time he was ready for it.

Mexico City, 1994

Someone nudged Cristián's hip with their foot. He muttered into the pillow, breaking away from dizzying dreams where he listened to *Magical Mystery Tour* and watched TV and wasn't afraid of anything.

He jerked awake, pulse pounding, and forced himself to breathe slowly while his heart went through its early-morning aerobics. 'Señor Alvarez,' said the nurse standing over him, 'you can't just lie about on the floor like this.'

Cristián wriggled his arms out of the sleeping bag, looking up at Professor Summerfield's bed. 'How is she?' he asked.

'She's sleeping,' said the nurse. 'Her EEG's almost back to normal. Now, what about getting up off the hospital's nice clean floor?'

Cristián struggled out of the blue bag, scratching at his face and scalp. He didn't think the floor was that clean.

He gripped his top lip with his bottom teeth and blew out a sigh through his nose. Professor Summerfield looked very peaceful. In the morning light, the whole room seemed different, back in the real world. *Her EEG's almost back to normal* . . . was she going to be all right? Was everything going to be all right?

He stumbled into the green hallways of the hospital and bought plastic-flavoured coffee and a dry pastry from a vending machine. He stumbled back into the hospital room. Had she moved? He watched her while he ate, the coffee searing the roof of his mouth.

'Who am I?' she said.

He nearly choked on the pastry.

'Just kidding,' said Bernice, as Cristián spat crumbs into the waste-paper bin.

'I can't think of many things worse,' she was saying, glancing around the room, 'than waking up in hospital without knowing why.' She looked him up and down. 'You're not really holding up your end of this conversation, you know.'

'*¿Como esta?*,' he managed at last.

She shrugged, shoulders moving against the pillows piled up under her head. 'Much too healthy to be in here.'

'What is the last thing you remember?'

She stared at the air for a few seconds. 'It's a bit of a blur, really. Nightmares. Lots of nightmares. Before that . . . you went to get the pizzas, didn't you? Don't tell me I'm allergic to pizza.'

'What were your nightmares about?'

Bernice shook her head. 'Cristián, what happened to me?'

'I, um, I don't know. But the nurse says you're all right now. We'll ask the Doctor about it, when he gets back.'

'The Doctor.' Bernice's forehead creased in the tiniest of frowns. 'Cristián,' she said, 'something's happened to the Doctor.'

They exchanged glances, and what frightened Professor Summerfield even more than her sudden premonition was the fact that Cristián believed her.

102

Ace sat cross-legged on the floor of a room in Ce Xochitl's house. She felt nothing at all.

They had laid the Doctor out on one of the sleeping mats, gently arranging his hands by his sides. She had wiped the red streaks away from his face, soaked his burning forehead in cool water from the canal. His blood-spattered jacket and tie were rolled up in her duffle bag. There was nothing she could do now but wait and watch.

A curing woman and a soldier with nothing better to do had carried his limp body through the streets to the judge's house. The curer had fussed over the shallow wound in Ace's side, left behind some herbs for the Doctor's fever, and beetled off without asking any questions.

Ace waited through the afternoon and into the long shadows of the evening, listening to the mayfly flutter of his breath.

Iccauhtli was dead. He had drowned in a canal after a warrior had split his ribcage open. Achtli was dead. His eyes had bled all over the floor. The Doctor was dying. His forehead was so hot that Ace could feel the fever in her fingertips from half an inch away.

Yeah, if this were a plan, it was a right cock-up.

She gently levered open one of his eyelids. The pupil was shrunk to a pinprick of black. The blue of his iris glittered unnaturally, too bright. She let the lid close again.

Had he expected her to leave him? She had mucked up his smooth-running plans more than once, going off when she should have stayed put, staying put when she should have gone away. Telling people things they weren't supposed to know.

Whatever had happened to him, she would have tried to stop it. She might have mucked up his plan. So maybe she was supposed to go off and get in a fight, after he'd taunted her about being a soldier. Supposed to leave him to the Blue.

What was she supposed to do now?

Whatever the Aztecs wanted in the way of funeral arrangements, that would be fine. She'd seen too many corpses to bother about just one more, even this one. And then she'd try to learn the local language, perhaps find some work, if they'd let a woman into the army. Perhaps she'd be able to leave a message for Bernice, in some carving or scroll that wouldn't be discovered until the twentieth century.

It was just the beginning of a new chapter. Ace's life came in two pieces, Perivale and After Perivale. Even when she'd walked out on the Doctor, it had just been a lull in the action. She'd still been in space, the world beyond Perivale. His world.

She remembered when they'd first met on Svartos, that thrilling offer of a chance to hitch-hike the galaxy. She had felt incredibly lucky, really privileged. It hadn't been for a little while that she'd sussed out the situation: the Doctor always had a travelling companion. There were rooms full of dust and memories, little knick-knacks and clothes and things that the others had left behind. He'd been playing this stupid game for centuries before he met her.

When the stakes got high enough it was easy to concentrate on saving everybody, and forget about any one person. But that was what chaos theory showed, right? It was just as bad to destroy a single person as it was to destroy a whole planet. Even when that person was you. Especially when it was you.

She wrung out the cloth and dipped it in the cool water, wiping away the fine sheen of sweat from his forehead. His hair was wet with it. It was weird, seeing him like this, totally vulnerable. Sometimes she forgot he was flesh and blood. Sometimes he seemed to forget that too.

They had that in common. Ace had seen death on the grand scale; she had made the dead and mourned the dead, in numbers. They were like Aztecs, the Doctor and her; they had got used to death by being constantly surrounded by it. Warriors had control over death; they gave it, and they could choose when to die, instead of waiting by the fireside for old age or bad luck to come and get them.

When she had run away from him on Heaven, it had been the worst thing she could think of to do to him, the worst possible punishment for his sins. He wasn't scared of monsters or pain or dying, he was scared of being alone. She imagined him travelling through the blackness at the end of the Universe, every sun and planet and life-form withered away to nothing, leaving him travelling, travelling alone.

That was what dying would be like.

If he were going to die, he wasn't going to die in the dark by himself. Whether or not his plan had screwed up, she'd sit here and hold his hand, if that was all she could do, and they'd wait together to see what happened.

Macbeth sat in the foyer of the police station, his yellow teeth clamped around a duty-free cigarette, and glowered at the young policeman behind the counter. The *chilango* ignored him as best he could, busying himself with rearranging the paperwork on his desk.

Macbeth picked up the newspaper – two days old, with the crop of circles left by coffee cups imprinted across its surface. A cursory glance revealed nothing of interest. He could read fourteen languages with varying degrees of accuracy, and speak enough of six to get by – another handy attribute for the researcher of things beyond mortal ken.

Mortal Ken, thought Macbeth as he dropped ash on the paper, wouldn't even have noticed anything strange was going on in Mexico City. But he recognized the pattern. Sudden hospitalizations. Outbreaks of violence – or in this case, a single outbreak of violence.

As usual, he hadn't been able to get funding, not so much as a free plane ticket. The UFO people thought the whole thing was irrelevant, the telepathy people were busy trying to get their own funding for the Shuttle experiments, the bloody Skeptics had their usual deal going: proof first, money afterwards. He'd even called Scotland Yard's Paranormal Investigations Unit. Graham was sympathetic, as always, but about as useful as a bent spoon.

So he'd hocked some junk and got himself over here, leaving a number of projects half-finished: tracking down that sorcerer in Liverpool; trying to catch the Skeptics making Mandelbrot-shaped crop circles in Yorkshire.

He looked over the top of the newspaper as the police chief appeared, grasping the envelope of goodies he'd sent in to tempt the man out. *El Jefe* was looking worried. Good. He had every reason to be.

In his office, the police chief spread out the fragments of paper on the table. A note scribbled in Macbeth's angular handwriting; a couple of newspaper clippings; a forged UNIT pass.

Macbeth turned the chair around as he sat down, leaning his bony elbows on the back. The effect was that he loomed over *el Jefe*, a short man with rounded features. 'Well?' he said. 'Am I right?'

The Mexican eyed him with open suspicion. 'I don't understand how you know so much,' he said, 'but there's one incident . . .'

'Tell me about it,' smiled the Scot.

The Chief pulled out a manila folder and passed it across to the researcher. 'I have to warn you, that material's confidential,' he said, as Macbeth turned the folder around. 'Anything in that file mustn't go beyond this room.'

There were typed reports, photos of evidence – and another photo that made the blood in Macbeth's ears pound like heavy industry. 'Where is she now?' he managed, turning the snapshot around so that *el Jefe* could see it.

'In hospital,' said the chief. 'She's being watched. We haven't decided whether to charge her yet.'

'Let her go,' said Macbeth.

The chief raised an eyebrow at him.

'Let her go, but let me follow her. We'll see what she's up to, eh?'

'I don't think I can do that.'

Macbeth reached out a long arm and picked up his UNIT pass. 'I think you can. And I can guarantee you – UNIT's the only hope you've got of sorting this mess out.

Let me have it, Chief. Give me all your problems. I'll solve them for you. Starting with her.'

The chief stared at the photo of Bernice. 'Lieutenant Macbeth,' he said. 'Exactly what is it you want from us?'

At the Institute, the doors were locked.

They tried phoning. When Bernice said who she was, they hung up.

They tried ringing up the universities to get a visitor's ass.

They tried calling the journalists at Cristián's paper, to see if one of them could get in.

'This is not good,' said Bernice, curled up on Cristián's sofa. 'None of this is good. They've built a wall around the place. The lights are on but nobody's home.'

Cristián sat on the floor and looked glum. 'They are very organized, whoever they are,' he said. 'An academic institution like that should always be accessible in one way or another.'

'We can try some of the historians at the universities, then,' said Bernice. 'Or perhaps we'll just wait until all the excitement dies down.'

'*Sí*. I still don't understand why the police didn't give us more trouble.'

'Do you know, when you speak English, you have a London accent.'

Cristián said, 'I lived in St John's Wood for six months. That's when the photo was taken. I studied English at university, but I learnt how to speak it in London.'

'What were you doing in England?'

'Seeing the world.' Cristián's smile drained off his face. 'What are we going to do if the Doctor doesn't come back?'

Benny shrugged in irritation. 'He'll come back. He always comes back.'

The Doctor opened his eyes and stretched. It was morning; pale yellow light leaked into the room from the courtyard, colouring the shadows.

Ace was lying near him on the cool floor of Ce Xochitl's house, her duffle bag stuffed under her head, her body curved into a comma. 'Wake up, sleepyhead,' he said cheerfully.

She sat bolt upright, her hand moving automatically to a holster that wasn't there. She pressed her palms flat against the floor and stared at him.

'Good morning,' he said.

'What's the last thing you remember?' she said.

Slowly his face went blank.

'Where's Achtli?' he said.

From the doorway, the judge Ce Xochitl said, 'My sons are dead. Get out.'

'Ce Xochitl – ' began Ace, but the Doctor touched her arm.

'We're going,' he said, very quietly. 'No more words.'

'You can't smoke in here, señor.'

'*Lo siento*,' said Macbeth, stubbing out his cigarette on the wall.

'Can I help you at all?'

The intern came out from behind the desk, folding the downy arms that protruded from the short sleeves of his uniform. A no-nonsense man. 'I was looking for someone who would take money in exchange for information,' Macbeth said, straight-faced.

The intern ran emotionless eyes over the foreigner. 'You are from the press?'

'Yeah,' said Macbeth. 'The public has a right to know, eh?'

'Right,' said the attendant.

'For a while now,' said Macbeth, 'strange things have been going on in your hospital. Electrical failures. Odd behaviour from the mental patients.'

'Nothing strange there, señor.'

'Things going missing and turning up where they're not supposed to be. Perhaps even mysterious deaths.'

That caught the man's attention. 'If you know all this,' said the attendant, 'what more do you need to find out?'

'Details,' said Macbeth. 'Dates. Paperwork. And there are some photos I want you to look at.'

He pulled a snapshot out of his pocket and held it up.

The man's expression was delightful. Macbeth wondered if that was what he'd looked like when *el Jefe* had shown him the police photo. 'Have you seen this man?' he grinned.

'*Sí*,' said the attendant. 'I think he killed a friend of mine.'

'Is that so?' said Macbeth. 'Anything else?'

'Yes,' said the attendant. 'He walked out of the morgue.'

Macbeth's mouth came slightly open. He lowered the arm holding the photo.

Ace followed the Doctor through the streets of Tenochtitlan. The air was thick with the sour smell of rotting blood. They passed small groups of people leaving the city, their servants carrying bedding and cooking utensils on their backs. They would return when the killing was over and the air was clear again.

At the temples, the sacrifices were into their third day. A pall of quiet hung over Tenochtitlan, as though the city were exhausted, waiting to rest once its duty was completed.

They walked in silence for a while, Ace trying to cold-start her mind. Not only was the Doctor not dying, but it was as though he had never been ill.

At last she asked, 'So, what happened?'

He turned around to look at her. 'You tell me.'

'A couple of bystanders brought you back to the house.'

'Before that.'

She blew out a breath between her teeth. 'Iccauhtli and I got caught up in a fight.'

He nodded, eyes troubled. 'So you don't know what happened. You didn't see.'

'Doctor, if you don't know what happened, no one knows what happened.'

She reached into the duffle bag and brought out his jacket. He took it from her, looking at it curiously, as

109

though it were an old photograph that he couldn't quite place. Speckles and splashes of blood ran down the left lapel and shoulder. His hands wrung the material, wanting to extract the memory.

'I haven't learnt anything,' he said. 'All I've managed to do is kill Iccauhtli and Achtli. And almost you.'

'You what?'

'That wound in your side,' he was saying, and Ace glanced down at the bandaged cut, invisible under her jacket. 'You might have been killed fighting those warriors.'

She shrugged. 'They weren't anything to write home about. Anyway, they came to kill you.'

'Yes,' he said. He looked around at the street, the water, a stray chicken flapping in the morning sun. 'Enough of this. We're going back to Mexico.'

'Are you all right?'

'All right? Me? Yes. I'm fine. Why shouldn't I be all right? It's everything else that's wrong!'

He gestured with the bloodied jacket at the universe in general. 'The time is out of joint. Someone has interfered again. Something's changed. Something *changed*. And I can't remember. I can't remember what.'

It was a fine afternoon in Mexico City, sunlight filtering through the dusty air. The TARDIS ground into existence in the alleyway, startling a stray dog. It went off yapping to tell its friends.

Ace had showered and pulled on jeans and a denim jacket. She had been surprised by how cool it was in Mexico. When she was ready she meandered back up to the console room, where the Doctor was standing with a glum look on his face. He had taken away his jacket and tie and cleaned them somehow-or-other.

'How is she?' Ace asked.

'Sulky,' said the Doctor. 'Very sulky!' he shouted at the console, flicking a bit of dust off one of the controls.

Oh, great, he was seriously worried. She could ask him about it, of course, for all the good that would do her.

110

Keeping the lid on was a bad habit that he needed to lose. Sometimes, though, he just wanted her to work things out for herself.

She had already come up with two more nasty possibilities. Had he cut some kind of deal, and was faking amnesia? Had someone done something to him, and then wiped out the memory?

She eyed him, looking for little changes, anything that might give away his mental state. She had to be ready in case anything major was wrong.

The Doctor marched out of the TARDIS. Ace gave the console an understanding pat on her way out.

Outside, the TARDIS shimmered once and stayed in its police box configuration. The Doctor scowled, looking as though he wanted to kick it. 'Cristián's flat.'

'Is he?'

He turned his gaze on her, and she found herself being scrutinized with that alien intensity again. *What are you looking for?*

She pulled out her sunglasses, flicked them open, and slid them onto her nose, matching his blue stare.

After a moment he turned to hail a *pesero*. But she'd seen it, just for a second: there was something wrong, and the Doctor didn't know what it was.

Yeah. The situation was bad this time.

She followed him to the taxi, her teeth massaging her bottom lip, and wondered what she was going to do about it.

Macbeth watched them go.

He clutched a half-eaten take-away taco in one hand, fingers shattering the fragile shell into flak. Red hair clung to his forehead, sticky with sweat, trying to climb into his eyes. He pushed it out of his face, leaving behind a streak of tomato sauce.

He and the TARDIS faced one another across the alley-way. A couple of laughing children raced between them, their shouts echoing from the decayed surfaces of the buildings.

Mortal Ken might have looked for a rational

explanation for the presence of a London police box in a Mexican alleyway. Hank Macbeth had his explanation ready-made.

He came closer to the thing, letting go of the forgotten taco. He tripped over a trash can lid that was lying in the dust. The clattering split the air.

He put his face close to the police box, and listened.

After a moment, he heard it. The humming.

He sat down in the dust, his heart stammering and chattering, all the pieces of the puzzle falling into place.

And deep inside him, something Blue was itching, something Blue was wrapping itself around him like a shroud. It was possible, even probable, that he was not aware of it. But the Blue was there, an unnatural colour, a spreading stain in the soft greyness of his brain.

He checked in his pocket for his gun. It was still there. No mysterious forces had spirited it away.

This time he would be able to wrap everything up neatly.

They sat on the floor of Cristián's apartment, eating take-away and feeling drained.

The Doctor sat with his back to Cristián's lounge, arms resting along the seat. 'You first,' he said.

Bernice and Cristián started talking at the same time. The Indian broke off, looking around agitatedly.

'Fitzgerald tried to kill me,' said Benny levelly. 'I killed him.'

'She was ill,' said Cristián. 'She was having fits, calling out meaningless things. When she awoke, she was sure that you were in danger.'

'The worst thing,' said Bernice, 'is that I don't remember any of it. It feels as though someone's dusted the black-board. Nothing left but smudges.' She pressed tense fists against her eyes. 'Did you do any better?'

'No,' said the Doctor.

Ace chewed slowly on a burrito, not sure of whether she should add to that.

After a bit, the Doctor went on. 'Some sort of psychic force is operating in the general area of Mexico City.

Something which certain people of Aztec blood can sense. Something associated with mass killing.'

'So you haven't learnt anything more than we already know.'

'What we've learned,' said Ace, 'is that we're up to our collective arse in crocodiles, and we have no idea how to drain the swamp.'

'Do you know,' said the Doctor, 'two years ago the Russians took a survey of what frightened them the most. It wasn't winter or economic collapse. It was vampires. Specifically, vampires that lived on life energy. Psychevores.'

Ace picked up another burrito. Bernice said, 'Mind eaters.'

The Doctor let his head tilt backwards onto one of the cushions until he was staring at the ceiling. Bernice looked at him oddly as he said, 'There are many and varied creatures which feed on the mind. The Mara fed on raw emotion. The Fendahl sucked souls whole.'

'Are you saying that's what we're up against?' said Benny. 'A mind vampire?'

'Or many mind vampires. Or something completely different. It's entirely possible that the event which affected me in Tenochtitlan was simply a massive psychic discharge – a natural, meaningless event.'

'Affected you?' said Bernice. 'What happened?'

'I've no idea,' he said, bringing his head down to look her in the eyes. 'I've lost about twenty-four hours. *Tabula rasa.*'

'This vampire,' said Ace. 'Can you shoot it?'

The Doctor waved a hand at her, agitatedly. 'It's only one theory. What was Fitzgerald hiding, what was it you weren't supposed to find out? Why'd he help you and then try to kill you? We need to go back to the Institute.'

'Did the Aztecs have vampire legends?' Benny wanted to know. 'I don't recall any from my readings.'

'There were undead,' said Cristián. 'Ghosts of women who died in childbirth.'

'There might have been records which were destroyed,'

113

said Bernice. 'Most of their religious writings were burned.'

'Yes, very convenient,' said the Doctor. 'What does survive?'

'The Florentine Codex has a whole volume devoted to the *atlaca*, the inhuman,' said Benny. 'Other bits and pieces. The Institute will have all sorts of stuff. If only they'd let us in there!'

'We'll have to let ourselves in, then.'

Cristián looked alarmed. Ace grinned around her burrito.

The Doctor was an extraterrestrial. He was also a criminal. He had killed the morgue attendant and one of the patients, for whatever reason – perhaps they'd found out his secret. His companion had killed Professor Fitzgerald.

The UNIT people spoke of him like some harbinger of doom. When he was around, people died, people's gardens up and killed them.

Macbeth drove in a rental station wagon through thick and angry Mexico City traffic. The sky grew dark. He had everything he needed.

He flashed his faked ID to the guards, parked in the Institute's lot. It was on his instructions that they'd blocked Professor Summerfield's access; she wasn't what he wanted. He wanted the man himself.

He wanted a little word with the extraterrestrial who posed as a human, the real-live interplanetary monster doing God knew what amongst them while the military bowed and scraped and no one *did* anything, and he also wanted a word about that girl he'd shot dead in 1968, her dark hair whirling around her as she fell, mouth open in a frozen circle of surprise.

The Doctor and Bernice were making a rough map of the Institute in the kitchen, talking in low voices and scribbling on a bit of butcher's paper. Ace and Cristián played draughts in the lounge.

'That sixth sense of yours,' said Ace.

Cristián looked at her over the board. He was old enough to be her father. When he had first met her, he had been young enough to be her brother. She was as timeless as an image captured on videotape. She also played draughts very badly.

She said, 'We met a guy in Tenochtitlan who had the same kind of psychic thing. He could sense the Blue.'

'Yes?' Cristián was interested. 'There were other people with it?'

'Probably still are. The Doctor says the gene was scattered through the Aztec population.'

'But nearly everyone in *la Republica* has some Indian blood.'

Ace shrugged. 'It's just the luck of the draw. Most human beings have latent psychic powers. They don't usually work. In the future – in the future more people have learned how to use them. They can bring them out with drugs.'

There was something sharp in her voice, as though she were remembering something from the future, and Cristián didn't ask her anything more about it. Instead he toyed with the new idea, that he might be normal, that he might not be alone.

After a bit, Ace said, 'So, about your sixth sense.'

'You're clean,' he said.

Their eyes met over the board. 'I can't sense the Blue coming from you. I think. If that's what you're asking. Bernice too.'

Ace nodded coolly. 'Cheers, Cristián. What about the Doctor?'

'Oh,' said Cristián. 'Yes, of course.'

'Good,' said Ace, taking his last draught. Cristián looked blankly at the empty square.

In the kitchen, the Doctor had drawn a little blue X on the map. 'Here there be TARDISes,' he said. 'That puts us next to the Special Documents Section.'

'What exactly will we be looking for?'

'Anything. Everything. Things Fitzgerald might have

115

been hiding from you. Cristián can be our bloodhound, sniffing out the Blue . . .'

'Doctor,' said Bernice, 'do you think we're all right?'

He carefully smoothed the paper of the map. 'What are you asking?'

She sat back in the wooden chair. 'I keep thinking about this book I read once, about the people of a country town, knocked out for twenty-four hours – '

' – and when they woke up, the women were carrying *The Midwich Cuckoos*,' said the Doctor.

Bernice shuddered, really shuddered. 'Cuckoos. What if we're the nests? Did something leave a message while we were out?'

The Doctor reached out and spread the fingertips of his right hand on her forehead. They stayed like that for a few seconds, their eyes locked together.

He snatched his hand away, as though he'd touched something hot. 'Nothing that shouldn't be there,' he murmured.

'And what about you?'

'I am perfectly all right,' he said. 'There is nothing wrong with me. Believe me, I've looked, I've checked, and I can't see anything out of place.'

'When I first met you,' she said quietly, 'you were playing a game.'

'I'm not playing one now,' he said. 'Trust me, Bernice, I'm not.'

But he'd just been in her mind, and he knew she didn't trust him.

The Special Documents Section was suddenly filled with a noise: the arrogant music of equations shoving aside the particles of the air, of engines grinding unhealthily as they dragged the TARDIS into reality.

There were eight guards in the building, as well as four postgraduate students and an academic working late. Of these, two guards and one of the students heard the noise of the TARDIS's arrival. The student put it down to the noisy plumbing. The guards did what they had been told and stayed put in their little glass booth. Waiting.

Out of the TARDIS came Ace, in black, Bernice, in black, Cristián, in dark purple, and the Doctor, still in his white clothes. Bernice eyed him in irritation – he virtually glowed in the dark. He grinned back at her, as though to say, 'Which of us looks least like a thief?'

They were in a long hall, as much a display area as a library. Glass cases, softly lit by fluorescent bulbs, lined the walls of the room. There were more of the giant filing cabinets that Bernice had seen earlier, plus reading desks and bookshelves and a neon SALIDA sign dotting and dashing in a meaningless red morse.

The Doctor strolled up to one of the glass cabinets and peered into it. It contained two fragile Aztec books, long screens of yellow paper unfolded to expose the illustrations. Purple handwriting meandered down the sides of the Aztec drawings, ran between pictures of kings and gods. The conquerors trying to make sense of the conquered.

Cristián stood in the middle of the room, head turning slowly one way and then another. 'Something,' he said. 'Something locked away.' Ace came and stood next to him, silently offering moral support. It had taken him hours to build up the courage to get in the TARDIS; even a short hop through space had freaked him out. She looked around as though she might be able to see what he was seeing.

As the Doctor knelt by the cabinet, something went *click* next to his left ear. He ignored it for a moment, intent on his study of the codex.

A cool circle of metal pushed into the skin under his ear. 'Stand up slowly,' said a voice very quietly. The Doctor stood up slowly.

He saw Cristián and Ace looking at him, their mouths open. Ace was tensing, wondering if she could safely retrieve the gun tucked into the back of her jeans.

'I don't want you to do anything unexpected,' said the

117

voice behind him. 'And neither do you. I'd be perfectly happy to shoot your head off. All right?'

'Who are you?' said the Doctor.

A heavy grip spun him around, and he found himself looking up at a six-foot-tall redhead with murder in his eyes and a .45 calibre pistol in his hand.

'Well, that leaves me none the wiser,' he told the stranger.

'Now *that*,' said Macbeth, 'is just adding insult to injury. *Don't* pretend you don't remember me. What the hell are you doing in here, eh? Finishing up your business with Professor Fitzgerald?'

'Who the hell?' whispered Ace, glancing at Cristián. The Indian shook his head.

Macbeth's gun hand jerked up to cover them. 'Shut up,' he snarled, 'you just shut up! I'm the one with the gun here, and I'll tell you when you can bloody well talk!'

This was the point at which Bernice put her hands on either side of his neck and pressed. Macbeth said, 'Yrkrkrk – ' and dropped the gun, sagging gracelessly against the glass cabinet.

The Doctor caught the weapon as it fell, looked at it bewilderedly, and handed it to Bernice. She stood back from Macbeth, keeping the gun trained on him. The big man was rubbing his throat, his head bobbing about dazedly.

'Well, that was a nice brief crisis,' said the Doctor. 'Perhaps you'd care to explain yourself, Mr . . .?'

Macbeth brought his knees up, hugging them to him, looking up at the Doctor with undiluted hatred. 'Lieutenant Macbeth. Formerly of UNIT. And you can all go to hell.'

'Name, rank, and serial insult,' observed the Doctor dryly. 'Right. Make yourself comfortable, Lieutenant, we'll sort you out in a moment.'

Macbeth struggled to his feet, moving slowly, keeping his eyes on Summerfield. Even in the half-light he could see that she hadn't aged, not one bit, not a single wrinkle. Jesus. How'd she managed that?

They'd stuff him into their flying saucer and no one would ever see him again. Or maybe they'd just shoot him here and now.

Bits of panic dropped into him like stones into a pond, spreading fat ripples through him. You've really, really mucked it up this time, MacB. Mortal Ken might have had the sense to leave well enough alone and ship his arse back to Glasgow.

Oh well, at least he'd get to see what the inside of a UFO looked like.

Shit.

'Here,' said Cristián.

He was standing next to one of the glass cabinets, a high thing like a lecture stand enclosing a single tattered piece of maguey-fibre paper. The Doctor crossed to the cabinet. 'Let me see,' he said, leaning over the glass, and began to read.

Slow motion:

The Doctor turns sharply away from the cabinet, his hands coming up to his face. Cristián takes a step back from him, startled by the suddenness of the movement.

The Time Lord stumbles and overbalances, landing on the polished wood on his side, fists pressed to his eyes. Cristián kneels beside him. There is blood coming out from behind the Doctor's fingers.

Cristián's head snaps up. 'Oh God,' he says. 'Oh God oh God oh my *God* – '

A wind starts blowing, cold and fresh, lifting Ace's hair away from her shoulders.

Macbeth explodes.

It's not a horror movie explosion, with his skin rupturing and skull shattering and one of his kidneys striking the ceiling. He just vanishes, howling his surprise, in a coruscating fountain of Blue light, a violent up- and outrushing of energy.

'He's *here*!' screams the Doctor, hands jerking away from his bleeding eyes.

Ace is slapped backwards by the shockwave, DMs skidding on the smooth floor. Somehow she keeps her

119

balance. She reaches under her jacket and snatches out the gun.

The SALIDA sign sizzles and bursts. The lights in four of the cabinets buzz and shatter. The glass above the single page explodes outwards in a glittering shower. Hard rain falls on Cristián.

Bernice steps backward, mind frozen, looking up at the thing Macbeth has become. She recognizes it from the painted books.

The image is ghostly, like a cheap hologram, a series of outlines in the air – hands, eyes, feathers. Intangible. The colour boils, seething Blue. Sketch feet step towards her as the wind whips her clothing, smelling of blood and flowers.

'No!' screams Cristián. 'No!' He reels backwards, finds the cabinet, tears the page out of it. The frail paper bends and rips in his hand.

Huitzilopochtli the war god turns aside, gliding towards him, a bitter wind sailing across the floor.

Ace fires again and again and again, the gun kicking against her palm as the creature crosses the room. But the bullets just keep going, flaring in the fountain of light for an instant before they pass harmlessly through.

The Doctor wails, '*No!*'

'This is what you want!' Cristián shouts, holding out the page. 'Come and get it!'

He bolts for the exit.

Huitzilopochtli comes and gets it.

Chapter 8

The Cat in the Hat

Benny's mind snapped back like a rubber band.

On the other side of the hall, Cristián was lying on the floor, the Doctor kneeling next to him. Ace stood over them, her gun arm hanging loosely by her side. There was no wind, no noise.

Benny bolted over to where they were standing. Her shoes skidded unexpectedly on the wooden floor, and she looked down stupidly. Ice. A thin slick of ice had formed on the lino.

There was something terribly wrong with Cristián. It was as though he were underwater: she couldn't see him clearly, couldn't make out the outlines of his face, his hands.

She knelt down beside the Doctor. There were streaks of blood on the Time Lord's face, like crimson tears. Cristián was speaking in a hoarse whisper.

'The page,' he said. 'He wanted the page.' He was clutching a handful of ashes in his good hand. 'He came for the book. It's dangerous. Dangerous.'

'What did he do? What did that thing do?' said Bernice.

'Please,' said Cristián. 'Help me.'

The Doctor reached out and smoothed the hair away from the Indian's forehead. He let his thumb and forefinger sit together on the skin above Cristián's eyes.

They stayed like that for a few seconds. The Doctor's face changed, his eyes closing into a tight squint of pain.

Cristián relaxed, his fist opening, letting the ashes slide onto the frozen surface of the floor.

With a sparkling motion, like flashes on the surface of a pond, Cristián dissolved away. The Doctor's hand passed through him until it came to rest on the icy wood. And then he was gone.

The lights slammed on, flooding the hall with searing brightness. Someone shouted in an adjoining room. With a convulsive movement, Bernice hauled the Doctor to his feet, and half-dragged him to the TARDIS. She heard Ace following behind as she pushed the shivering Time Lord through the doors, but she just kept walking, opening the internal door, ignoring the sound of dematerialization as she walked and walked, wishing her mind would switch itself off again.

London, December 20, 1968

At first, Hank hadn't been too sure about the uniforms, the ranks, the whole military bit. He wasn't a soldier, he was a psychologist, and he wasn't about to shoot anyone.

But the set-up was perfect. Decent funding, at long last – no more palm readings to support the hobby, eh. Access to all sorts of files and reports that the army had squirrelled away. A goddamn genuine alien invasion to worry about.

Macbeth grinned at himself in the glass of the train window. He planned to be the Intelligence part of the United Nations Intelligence Taskforce.

It hadn't been immediately easy to convince UNIT to establish their Paranormal Division. It was a spoilt field: trying to find genuine paranormal phenomena was like searching for the proverbial needle, having to sift through a haystack of astrologers and fake gurus and clairvoyants who dialled up your Great-Uncle Dieter on their telepathic telephone and then couldn't answer the questions you asked in German.

But after the Yeti had come, the military's minds had been blown wide open. If hairy robots could take over

London, anything was possible. Their research had been ruthless and flawless; they'd discarded thousands of hopefuls and nutters and come up with a handful of people with demonstrable psychic talents – nothing spectacular yet, but it was all consistent and replicable. And it all came under the aegis of the Official Secrets Act.

And in the meantime, Hank Macbeth had followed up a few leads, found out about the operation, and landed himself on their doorstep with the twin observations that he knew exactly what they were up to and that he needed a job. They'd checked his academic qualifications and made him a lieutenant the next day.

The Paranormal Division was small, but it was organized with military efficiency – four lieutenants, fresh from university; twelve lab assistants still struggling through degrees in psychology or physics; six honest-to-God psychics. Macbeth could talk to them for hours, and he had done, hearing the stories again and again – how they'd hidden their powers away, how they'd been frightened and lonely, how much better they felt now that they knew they weren't alone. Oh yeah. They were cattle, bloody cattle, and God knew what the army were going to do with them.

MacB, in the meantime, had other fish to fry. If UFOs and psychics were real, reasoned the UNIT people, what about other phenomena? They'd put him in his civvies and dispatched him to investigate, of all things, a haunted house.

He was carrying a big leather briefcase, packed with haunting goodies – string and chalk and glue, plaster of Paris, big camera. He hadn't done too many ghosts, though there had been that flat in Piccadilly – at least before the media got hold of it, and the landlady started to get calls all day and night from people wanting to see the spectre . . .

No more of that amateurish stuff, freezing his brass monkey in someone's garden waiting for the poltergeist in the potting shed to turn up. Thank Christ. This job was a simple one: pop round to a house in St John's Wood, introduce himself, and keep an eye and ear out for what the neighbours had reported: strange noises, stranger manifestations, and Things that Went Bump in the Night. Though given who lived in the flat, he could already guess why they were seeing things.

Ace's body was furiously at work on the machines, muscles stretching as she moved weights in endless, repetitive patterns. Her mind was moving slowly, separated from the gym and the exercises. She was trying to find a shape.

She remembered a book the Doctor had given her about optical illusions, full of straight lines that looked crooked and crooked lines that looked straight. There was a picture made of blobs labelled *What is this*? She stared at it for an hour before she'd worked it out, leaving the book on her dresser while she perched on the bed ten feet away. Seen from a distance, the meaningless blobs had resolved themselves into a photograph of a shark. Spotting the shape. Pulling it out of the background.

The enemy was hidden, moving underneath the water, surfacing from time to time in ways they'd couldn't predict. When Bernice had come close to finding that book, he'd had Fitzgerald try to kill her. When Fitzgerald had failed, the enemy had made Bernice kill him: dead men tell no tales.

What did he want? Was he after something that only the time travellers could provide? Or was he just a hidden canker that didn't want to be brought out into the light?

Canker. They were all contaminated. Only poor Cristián had come through it, pushing aside his fear at the last moment. And then the psychevore had eaten him whole. How the hell had it done that? It hadn't just swallowed his mind, it was as though it had stolen away his entire existence. No more Cristián, no more tears.

That was the shape of what they were facing. An enemy who knew what they were doing, who stayed hidden until he was ready to strike, and who could erase them from the face of reality with a touch.

And you couldn't shoot him.

So she'd just have to think of something else.

Her routine was finished. It had burned off part of her

anger, but mostly it had just made her tired. She wandered out of the gym and threw herself into the pool, still wearing her leotard, and allowed herself to sink to the bottom, blowing out a lazy stream of bubbles.

After a bit she hauled herself out and crouched next to Bernice, who sat with bare feet in the water, one arm wrapped around a pot-plant as though it were her best friend. A near-empty bottle was tucked into the plant's soil. Bernice stared into space as Ace extracted the bottle and sipped from it.

They just sat there for a bit.

At last Benny said, 'He asked us for our help. And we killed him. What did we do wrong?'

'It was his call,' said Ace. 'It was a good call. He saved your life. That was pretty tough of him.'

'If only the Doctor had done something.'

Ace looked up, across the pool. After a moment, Benny followed her gaze to the Doctor. The Time Lord was standing there with his hands in his pockets, watching them, trying to decide whether he should say something or not.

'We have to go.' His voice was hesitant. 'We'll be landing soon.'

'What's the point?' said Bernice. 'Cristián's dead.'

'Cristián's not dead,' said the Doctor. 'Not now. We have to go and find him.'

Benny peered blurrily at the Doctor. 'What're we going to do?' she said. 'We screwed up. Cristián died because we screwed up.'

'Cristián Alvarez,' said the Doctor, 'is not the be-all and end-all of this situation. Something is happening which is much larger than Cristián Alvarez. He's dead in 1994. It is now 1968, and it is snowing outside, so bring something warm.'

'Something's changed,' said Bernice, her eyes locked on the Doctor's.

'No,' he said. 'Someone's changed something. We need Cristián's help to find out what.'

Cris' feet start to tingle, tingling inside his shoes, until the itching drives him crazy and he sits down in the snow, fumbling with the laces. His head is spin dizzy and his fingers are fizzing worse than his feet.

He stumbles off down Baker Street, past the place where the Apple Boutique used to be, with its rainbow cosmic guru colouring the building wall. The snow kills the buzzing in his feet as he tracks around a broken bottle.

A London bus goes past, its horn sounding a single blast that makes Cris' brain feel as though it's trying to crawl out through the top of his head. He feels a sudden intensity, lodged between his lungs, a star brighter than the Three Wise Men saw. He puffs out a great breath. That's what he's looking for.

Some woollen-coated woman gives him the eye as he drags himself onwards. Maybe he shouldn't have left his shoes behind; someone will steal them. She's probably thinking of rivers of blood, trying to work out what race he is. Her eyes say, you see all kinds around here, with those hippies just moving in and taking the place over. Maybe she's a landlady, likes to throw people out after the police come.

Mother of God! What's happening to me?

The burning in his chest spreads down the back of his neck, driving him on, past the entrance to the Tube and through a gate. The sounds from the station feel like pins and needles inside his head – someone shouting the evening paper, the rush and whoosh of conversation as the crowds come and go, the rumbling of the trains themselves, like the earth clearing its throat.

His hands shake. He holds them up to his face, flicking his black hair out of his eyes. My hands are shaking. My eyes feel like they're coming out of my head. How can I get away, get away from this?

He stuffs his trembling hands into his pockets. Don't let them see, don't let anyone see. The burning feeling is growing, pushing through him in waves, like the train crowd, coming and going. He tries to concentrate on it, tries to make out its outline, its shape, but his head is spinning all over the place.

I hope I don't throw up. Throw up in the snow. My God. Mother of God.

He's been walking for hours, for hours now, how long has he been walking? St John's Church is an improbable angular shape in the dusk. His feet are too far away, like when Alice was wondering whether she'd have to mail instructions to her feet to get them to walk around . . . is that right? Am I walking the right way, walking home? No. Home's in Mexico. Or . . . home's in . . . where am I, anyway?

Somebody's coming. Like in that song about Santa Claus. Someone's on their way . . .

He looks into the glass window of a shoe shop, at dummies in hip clothes, smiling out at him. His body is all wrong, all the wrong shape, too tall, his fingers are the wrong length. The dummies don't look all stretched out. It's someone else's body he's looking at. Not his.

He should stand still. He should stand perfectly still, hold himself in place, or his arms and legs might ribbon away on the cold wind, his fingers stretching out over Notting Hill Gate and trailing into the Thames.

The burning fills up his head. He opens his mouth as though to tell the snow about it, shouting *It's here, it's here*! But the shouting is only inside his skull.

He's been running. His feet are bleeding! His feet must be bleeding. He tries to look down at his feet, tries to turn his head and open his eyes. But it's like in a dream where you're at school and you have to look at the blackboard, have to look, but you can't open your eyes because you're actually asleep. Sleeping with your eyes closed.

The Blue Meanie is chasing him. What'll it do when it catches him?

Tears thump against the inside of his eyes, two thumbs pushing against the cold jelly inside. The need to cry makes a leaping motion inside his chest, but everything's frozen, frozen in place, and his face is wet and he can't feel his feet, a million miles away.

They've found him! They've caught him!

Someone is standing over him, he sees those feathers

127

and freaks, just loses it, screaming and screaming get away! Get away! The Blue crests over him like a manic wave and he screams and screams.

Something cold presses against his wrist. If I could move my hand, if I could get away –

– away –

'Who are you?' Cris gulps, and it's the first thing he's said aloud.

'Hold still, Cristián.' They're gripping his wrist, putting that cold thing on it. 'You're going to be all right.' The sky leaps over him, impossibly high behind the stranger's face. All shadow in the Blue light, no features, only those eyes looking down at him.

Cris screams again.

'Go on, you get out!'

Elizabeth threw a dish at Macbeth's head as he retreated backwards down the steps. John took her shoulders from behind, gently. 'Just leave us alone,' he instructed the straight, around his cigarette. 'You haven't even got a warrant, so just take a walk.'

'Whatever you say,' said MacB, wondering if the woman had any more missiles hidden in her shabby clothing. He turned to go through the gate.

'Jesus,' said Lizzie, watching the straight depart.

John passed her the cigarette. 'It's cool, it'll be cool.' He was wearing a moth-eaten fox coat over a bright orange kaftan. It hurt Lizzie's eyes to look at it.

She dropped the cigarette in the snow and swore. 'Where the hell is Cris? What if he gets arrested?'

'Yeah, what are they going to do to him? He's not carrying anything. Just be cool.'

'Hey,' said Lizzie.

Coming through the freezing night were four people, one of whom was Cris. He was being half-carried by two of the weirdest-looking women that Lizzie had ever seen. Cris looked at them blearily over the fence. 'Did anybody find my shoes?' he shouted.

'Hey,' said Lizzie again, as a short man pushed the gate

open and trudged up to them through the snow. He was wearing white, not much for the cold weather, and a squashed-looking fedora hat. Someone else trying to invade their space –

'It's all right,' he said, 'I'm the Doctor. He's coming down now. We'd better get him inside.'

'Okay,' said John. Lizzie twisted up her mouth, but John said, 'He's a doctor. Come on in.'

The two women dumped Cris on the sofa and then just looked at him. He was skinny and eighteen, long hair matted over his face, big eyes squinting up at the wicker shade over the front room's light. He wore ragged denim. His naked feet were desperately pale around the toenails.

The older woman was staring around at everything, smiling crazily. She started to ask a question, but the cat in the hat put a finger to his lips. 'Socks,' he told John, peeling the chlorpromazine derm from Cris' wrist. 'And something warm to drink.'

Lizzie hugged herself, saying nothing. The Doctor looked up at the black woman. Her eyes flicked away from him, moving over the flat, obviously unhappy with this new intrusion.

The front room was almost bare; an old milk crate supported a bowl of fruit, a couple of mattresses were stacked against the wall. There was a small record player and an asymmetric stack of LPs. It looked as though they had just moved in, or that they were ready to leave again at the drop of a hat. The air was rich with the smells of cooking and incense and marijuana.

'Hippies,' said Bernice, grinning like someone who had just discovered a new species of butterfly.

'Yeah,' said Ace.

'Where'd Cris go?' asked Lizzie.

'We found him on Primrose Hill,' said the Doctor, 'in the snow.'

'Told him he needed a co-pilot,' said Lizzie. 'He's new. Doesn't know how much it can open out your head.'

'How much did he take?'

'Just one tab. But he always gets his mind blown away.

It'll be better when he gets more experienced.' Lizzie sat down on the sofa and put Cris' feet in her lap, starting to rub his toes, until the Doctor gently restrained her. 'Just let them warm up slowly.'

Molly came into the room, bearing a pair of thick socks. The plump woman took one look at the Doctor and froze, sort of hovering in place, her fingers kneading the socks convulsively. On the sofa, Cris started, nearly pulling his feet out of Lizzie's lap.

Lizzie gaped at Molly. Molly gaped at the Doctor.

John came out of the kitchen, put the cup of tea down on the floor, and extracted the socks from Molly's grip. 'Go back inside.'

Molly continued to stare at the Doctor, who raised an eyebrow at her, rummaging through his mental filing system to see if he recognized her. John took her arm and turned her around. 'Go back in, Molly,' he said firmly.

They got Cris sitting up, ensconced his feet in the socks and put the cup of tea into his hands. He sat there dopily. Lizzie kept looking at John, trying to catch his eye.

'I want to thank you very kindly for bringing Cris home,' began John. 'Most people around here would have left him where he was lying. Or ripped him off.'

The Doctor shrugged companionably. 'We're not from around here. As a matter of fact, we've only just arrived in London.'

'Got somewhere to stay?' said Lizzie, too quickly, and John silenced her with a sideways glance.

'Well, yes,' said the Doctor. 'Just up the road.'

'I hope you'll do us the kindness of coming to our Christmas party tomorrow night,' said John evenly. 'Our Happening. To say thank you, you know. Cris should be okay by the morning.'

The Doctor smiled, and there was a peculiar strain in his smile, as though he'd rather be burning the house down. 'We'd be delighted.' He looked over his shoulder at his companions, whose faces both said *what's going on here then*? 'What time?'

'Any time,' said John smoothly. 'Any time you like.'

Chapter 9

Number Nine

Macbeth was stomping along an icy sidewalk, gnashing his teeth on an unlit cigarette. He was out of matches. Stomp, stomp, stomp.

'Do you want a light?' said a miniature voice beside him.

He stopped dead, managing at the last moment to prevent himself from slipping on the pavement. He pushed his hands into his pockets and grimaced at the five foot two woman. Molly peered up at him, one rounded hand holding out a spluttering match. She wore a leather jacket, the sleeves adorned with stripes like the plumage of a short, plump bird. She wore a single necklace of artificial pearls over her orange and purple shirt, half-tucked into her ragged jeans.

When his scowl failed to vaporize her, Macbeth inclined his body until the chewed cigarette met the tiny flame. Almost immediately it blew out as winter whipped a handful of garbage and snow along Abbey Road.

The hippie blinked at the charred splinter she was grasping. 'I need to talk to you,' she said.

Molly was delighted with her free coffee. So delighted that Macbeth shrugged and ordered her an entire English breakfast: bacon and eggs and sausage and squashy tomatoes and beans and ... he chain-smoked queasily, watching her eat.

When she started to slow down, he stubbed out his

cigarette in the cold remains of her coffee and asked, 'All right. What is it you want to talk about, eh?'

She squinted at him in belated suspicion. 'How do I know you're really an investigator, then?'

Macbeth sighed and passed across his UNIT ID card. Molly took it in buttery fingers and held it up to her nose, squinting in the flickering café light.

'I like your first name,' she said firmly.

Macbeth raised both eyebrows.

'It's better than Molly, anyway.' The hippie held onto the card, as though for security.

'I'm not properly in the army, you know,' said MacB, scrounging around in his head for what he knew about hippies, which wasn't much. 'I don't know how to use a gun or anything.'

'They're doing weird stuff in my flat, Lieutenant,' said Molly. 'Was that what you came to investigate?'

'I came because your neighbours complained.'

Molly's shoulders slumped in disappointment. 'The neighbours are always complaining. This is my third place in two months. We're trying to be really quiet this time. Nobody wants to be on the street in winter.'

MacB nodded in his best sympathetic manner. 'What weird things are happening in your flat, Molly?'

'Two of us,' she said, chewing her bottom lip as though to keep the names from spilling out, 'are – well, a lot of us are into alternative religion, right? Lizzie's reading *Zen and the Art of Archery*, and John's sort of into Stonehenge and that.'

'What about you, Molly?'

'I'm a Christian.' She waved her pearls at him, and he saw the little plastic crucifix in amongst the colourless beads. 'No denomination or anything, no church. Just Christ.'

Macbeth couldn't help the laugh. 'You're a Jesus freak.'

'Yeah,' said Molly. 'Jesus was the original hippie. All his followers going around in the desert and getting hassled by the Establishment.'

'Why no church?' asked MacB, genuinely curious.

'I used to be really keen on it.' Molly drew faces in the condensation on the window. 'I used to go two, three times a week. C of E. But after a while it really started to get my back up. All those sermons about sex and getting married. I thought, I don't need some old man telling me this. Real religion comes from here.' She thumped herself on the chest. 'I've got Jesus to tell me what's right and what's wrong. So I struck out on my own.'

Macbeth blew out a long sigh. 'Sounds like me. I got ripped off by so many people. I thought they could really read minds, or tell the future. I chased around from one uni project to another.'

'That's bad,' said Molly. 'The occult's really bad for you.'

'Yeah, well, it was bad for my wallet, anyway. I remember the day I caught one guy cheating on his Zener cards. Before that I'd been able to fool myself that there was really something in it. Then it all came tumbling down.'

'What did you do about the cheating cat?'

MacB grinned. 'He claimed he couldn't help cheating, because his powers weren't working that day and he didn't want to disappoint me. I told him I couldn't help punching him in the nose.'

Molly didn't laugh. 'Some of the people at the flat are into occult stuff, astrology and things. Lizzie reads about human sacrifice.'

'You sure it's not just morbid curiosity?'

'Did you see that little fellow when, er, when you were splitting?'

'Coming up the path with the two women and the overdose?'

'That was Cris. He's always blowing his mind. I won't touch that stuff. Anyway. Lizzie and John have been going on about how the healer becomes the warrior, and how they were waiting for someone, waiting for the healer to show up, waiting for jingle-jangle ... and it's got something to do with Cristián's fits ... and I keep having these dreams ...' She took a shuddering breath and started to cry. 'The healer becomes the warrior.'

133

Macbeth said, 'I'll bet your parents blamed you when things got broken or went missing.'

Molly sniffed. 'What d'you mean?'

'Things moved when you were around. Vases fell off tables. When you were angry, the phone rang sometimes, but no one was there.'

Molly's mouth was as open and round as an O. She fingered her crucifix.

'Mmm,' said Macbeth. 'Tell me about your dreams.'

Molly told him. MacB asked, 'Is that the same as when you're, ah, tripping?'

'I don't take acid any more,' she said again. 'There was one really good trip at the beginning, one real blast into the arms of God. And then all it did was make me sick. All I saw was blue and cobwebs.'

'Blue, eh,' said Macbeth, as though this held some mystical significance of which he was aware.

Molly's voice sank to a whisper. 'You want to know what the really weird part is?'

'I do,' said MacB.

'I dreamed that little man.' Molly's voice was almost inaudible. 'And I dreamed one of the women he has with him.'

Macbeth nodded sagely, trying to disguise the fact that his heart was racing. *It's the real thing*, he thought, muddledly. 'Are you the only one who has these dreams?'

Molly shook her head. 'I think Cristián has much worse dreams. That's why he's always having these terrible trips. I mean, you're supposed to get used to acid after a while.'

'Your friends don't want me around,' he said. 'How can I find out more about whatever they're doing?'

'They've got stuff in the basement,' said Molly. 'They don't let anyone else down in there. But I went down there once when they were out. I could leave the window open, you could come in and have a look . . .'

Bernice began to ascend the pyramid. The air was hot and close, smelling of flowers and fresh-cut stone, and something else, something metallic. She was speaking to the priests who helped her up the slippery steps. Her voice echoed away in the hot wind, incomprehensible.

The pyramid's top was flat, its broad back supporting two stone houses, flanked by huge statues of idiot-faced men gripping tall banners of feathers. The plumes danced in the wind, tracing coloured curves against the searing blue of the sky.

At the front of the shrines was a great chunk of stone like a truncated, blood-stained bed. The priests led Bernice to it, her shoes slipping in the precious liquid. 'One day they're not going to fall for his tricks, his clever strategies, you know. They're not going to join in the game. They'll just crush the life out of him.'

They laid her down on the stone. Blood soaked through the back of her shirt as the priests gripped her wrists and ankles, bending her backwards.

There was a priest with a knife. He felt the texture of blue and black paint on his face, and the coarseness of the stone blade in his palm. The knife had a little face of its own, a toothy mouth and a beady white eye that looked up at him.

One of the feathers from the banner tore itself loose and whirled away on the hot wind.

He said something to her in the language like rain, something important, and snapped awake, the answer to the riddle flying away with the feathers, falling over the waters of the lake.

He was sitting at the writing desk in his hotel room. Benny was standing behind him. She had come into the room without waking him up. That was disturbing. So was her question.

'How long have you known?'

His eyes tracked down to his own face in the mirror. He startled, just for an instant, as though . . . it were someone else.

He turned away from the mirror to face her. 'How long have *you* known?' he said.

'Normally,' she said, 'you're like a cat. Cats are completely relaxed all the time, except when they have

135

something to do. Then they're all purpose. They can snap from complete relaxation to complete tension.' She put her head on one side, considering his face. 'Even now, you're trying to look as though you're at ease. But you're taut as a violin string. When you walk, you march. It's someone else's body language, not yours.'

'What does Ace think?'

'I haven't mentioned it to her. I'm not sure I trust her right now.'

'Please,' he said, 'don't say anything.'

'If there's something wrong,' said Benny, 'I want to bloody know.'

The Doctor opened his mouth and shut it again.

'You told me you'd never play games with me,' said Benny. 'If this is a game, I'm walking out. I'll go and study the hippies.' She turned on her heel.

'Don't leave me,' he said.

She turned back. To her not inconsiderable surprise, he broke into a grin. 'A game,' he said. 'Yes, it's a sort of game. But not the sort you're thinking of.'

She sat down on the edge of the writing desk, hugging herself. 'Well?' she said.

'The hummingbird,' said the Doctor, 'is an extraordinary creature. Its wings beat as often as eighty times per second. The smaller species must eat more than their own body weight every day, just to stay alive. A human being with a metabolism that fast would simply burst into flames.'

Benny wasn't interested. 'Why did your eyes bleed when you looked at that piece of paper?'

'It was charged with psychic energy. Like an enormous battery. The words were dancing on the page, almost ready to rip free.'

'Another booby trap?'

'Of a kind. A very specific kind. The amount of energy contained in the entire book must have been phenomenal. And, if I'm right, all that power was meant to be released in one go. In response to a particular stimulus.'

'I see,' said Bernice. 'You're asking me to believe in magic spells.'

'There's nothing magic about psi,' said the Doctor irritably. 'It follows the laws of physics, the same as any other force. But since it affects consciousness, it can seem inconsistent. Incomprehensible. Better understood using symbols and pictures.'

'The Aztecs thought of the universe as a painted book,' said Benny, 'and the gods were the scribes who wrote in it.'

'Change the writing, erase the picture, and you change reality. That was what the book was for.'

'And Huitzilopochtli came to destroy it. Because it could have destroyed him. And instead, he destroyed Cristián.'

The Doctor closed his eyes. 'He just happened to be holding the page.'

'But the page,' said Bernice. 'When you tried to read it, the page attacked you.'

'Yes.'

'It mistook you for Huitzilopochtli.'

'Yes,' said the Doctor, looking at her.

They stayed there for a moment. She was intensely remembering her first journey in the TARDIS, the wrenching moment when she'd understood that everything was going wrong. She remembered wondering if this alien she suddenly realized she knew nothing about were turning into a monster.

'Your nest's been invaded by a cuckoo,' she said.

The Doctor swung around again, putting his feet up on the writing table. Still trying to seem relaxed. 'Looking for changes in yourself is like trying to look at your own eyes. You can't see them directly, you have to use a mirror.' He nodded at her. 'You're my mirror, Benny.'

'Why don't you want me to tell Ace?'

'I don't think she trusts me. I'm not sure what she might decide to do about that.'

'All right,' said Benny, 'I won't tell her – if you tell me everything. And don't lie, or I'll know.'

He folded his arms behind his head, elaborately. 'After the sacrifice,' he said slowly, 'I thought everything else had changed. I went on thinking that, because it was so much better than the alternative.' He waved his foot idly, as though looking for the words. 'I was partly right. Something fundamental in the fabric of the universe was altered. Like a colossal watchmaker adjusting a cog.'

'If mass murder was all it took, every war would warp reality. But you already knew that someone or something has been playing with your past.'

The Doctor didn't look at her. 'Yes, but it's not the fact of the change that we have to understand, but its nature. What changed. What marked the difference between the old and the new.'

'The difference was that you were there.'

He didn't say anything. Just waved his foot from side to side, as though accompanying some unheard tune. She stared intently at his face, determined not to let that alien expression scare her off. He was not going to shut her out.

Slowly, the foot stopped its movement. He sat stock-still.

'It wasn't only the world which had changed,' he grated. 'It was me.'

Benny closed her eyes. 'What are we going to do?'

'*La mort ne surprend point le sage; Il est toujours prêt à partir,*' said the Doctor. 'A change of place, a change of face . . . To you it's always been the Doctor and Benny, but to me it's been the Doctor and Ace, and the Doctor and Dodo, and the Doctor and Leela . . . Change is the only thing that doesn't change.'

'But that, that thing – '

'It's not a cuckoo that's invaded my nest,' he said. 'It's a hummingbird.' The look he gave her was sharper than the edge of a knife. 'He wants the very core of me, the only part that remains the same. He wants my heart, Bernice. And he can't have it.'

He came in through the basement window. It was round the side of the dilapidated Georgian terrace, at street level, an inch of snow piled up against the dirty glass. Macbeth crouched against the fence, carefully scooped the snow away, and swung the window outwards.

The window was not especially wide, and his descent into the basement was less than dignified. Fortunately

138

Molly had thought to pile up some black cloths on the floor under the window.

MacB picked himself up and dusted himself off. His gloves were wet with snow.

The basement was small, the walls glaring white; the inevitable naked lightbulb hung from the low ceiling on a dubious bit of cord. The marijuana odour of the main flat had not penetrated down here. It smelt of damp concrete, old rags and fresh paint.

MacB closed his eyes and waited until they adjusted to the strange light.

When he opened them again, he saw three things in this order:

A huge Aztec calendar, hand-drawn on a massive square of plywood, hanging over:

A bed, with:

A pair of handcuffs attached to the bedpost.

No wonder they'd thrown him out. There was stuff here they just wouldn't want people to know about.

MacB picked up the handcuffs, puzzled. Hippies had a reputation for weird ideas about sex – mostly invented by the tabloids, he suspected. No, that was the obvious guess, too obvious.

He fished under the bed, and discovered more hand-made stuff, all with an Aztec look: little wooden statues, some candles and incense. A couple of overdue library books on Mesoamerican civilizations. He flipped through one, and it fell open at a picture of a particularly grisly human sacrifice.

It was a shrine. Or a prison . . . the room had been pre-pared, made ready for something. The bed's single sheet was crisp and new, smelling of starch.

God only knew what they had in mind, with the solstice coming up. He needed to know more. If the hippies wouldn't talk to him, what about their strange visitor of yesterday?

It wasn't scary, thought Molly, that she might get it wrong.

What was frightening was the thought that she might succeed.

The plan was a simple one. It had taken all her bread, but everything was going just fine so far. She tapped her foot on the floor of the lift, impatient to get on with it. It was like speeding; once you'd made up your mind to do something, you just went out and did it.

The uniform was too tight, made for a boy and not a girl. At least the bellhop was about her height. She hoped he enjoyed his night off and didn't get too uptight about what happened in the hotel while he was away.

The lift slowed and bumped, making the plates on the trolley rattle. Molly gripped the handle tightly and slid the trolley out onto the faded carpet.

The carpet was alive with crawling orange colours; she felt them slither under her hair, under the bellhop's cap. But she felt cold and blue, the colour at the middle of an iceberg.

Okay. She had it all together. He'd only ordered a salad and some hot chocolate. She'd added the steak, taking it from someone else's trolley, giving her an excuse to bring the knife.

It was a pretty clumsy weapon, but right at the moment, she felt like she could do anyone. Do anything. She could throw the chocolate at his eyes first, and then, oh yeah, then, what could be simpler?

. What next? What do you do for an encore? Maybe she'd turn herself in. She couldn't decide. God was watching everything she did, over her shoulder, saying, *you'd better do the right thing by Me*. Well, she was doing the right thing, only no one would understand. Maybe she'd wait and see how she felt afterwards.

Really simple. She was wearing thick gloves, because it was winter anyway, and she wouldn't leave any finger-prints. She'd knock on the door and say 'Room service'. She'd push the trolley into the room, and give him a big smile when he said he hadn't ordered the steak. And then she'd throw the chocolate at his eyes, and when he was distracted with that, she'd stick the steak knife into him.

She had it all planned out in her mind, even the look of surprise on his face, just the right amount of surprise, so he'd still know why she was doing it. So he'd understand. All mapped out like a telly programme that she'd already seen.

She came to the right door and knocked. No answer.

She knocked again. Oh shit, what if he didn't answer?

He'd answer. He'd answer. The chocolate. Throw the chocolate at his eyes. This was going to be easy.

She manoeuvred the trolley aside and tried the door-knob. The door wasn't locked. The room inside was dark. She pushed the trolley in.

Someone snatched her hand away from the handle. She gasped, failing to scream as he grabbed both her wrists and wrenched her forward until they were face to face. 'You idiot,' he hissed. 'Didn't you realize I'd know you were coming?'

A single bad vibe stabbed down Molly's back like a dinosaur tooth. She tried to pull away, furious with herself for starting to cry. 'Oh shit,' she said. 'Let me go, I didn't do anything – '

'Why?' he hissed. She couldn't see his face. With a sharp movement of his foot, he kicked the trolley, so that it slid across the carpet and pushed the door closed with a crash.

'It's true,' she said. The darkness pulsed with flowery colours. In one of the adjacent rooms, a TV set was play-ing, just audibly. 'The healer has become the warrior.'

'What?'

'That's what they said, Lizzie and John. Oh man, let me go.'

He dropped her wrists. She wished he would turn on the light. If only she could see his face. 'Sit down,' he said.

She managed to get into the chair without dying or freaking out. He stood by the door, eyeing the trolley. He picked up the chocolate, thought better of it, and put it carefully back in its place. It was weird, but all the time, it was as though he were looking right at her. She didn't dare move a muscle.

'What do Lizzie and John do?' he said.

141

She panicked and told him.

'I see,' he said. 'So they sent you along with this.' She saw something glitter in the reflected light from the window. Her hands gripped the seat of the chair.

'Oh no, man,' she said. He was moving the knife about, as though testing it, wondering what it would be like as a weapon.

'I'm no one's sacrifice,' he said. 'No one's.'

The glittering movement stopped. Was he still holding the steak knife? The darkness was alive with searing colour, obscuring him.

'The same patterns,' he said. 'Happening over and over. Why did you come here, Molly?'

She imagined she could see his eyes watching her in the blackness, the hot blue of a gas flame. 'I didn't come to sacrifice you. Lizzie and John are into that occult scene. I'm a Christian.'

He didn't say anything, and Molly felt the sudden need to fill up the silence. 'I thought it was all rubbish, what they were doing. Black magic. It was just something to keep from being bored between trips. But they're really serious. I think they want to summon up the Devil.'

'Do you believe that?'

'I saw you in my dream.'

She wished she hadn't said it. 'What dream?' he said sharply, coming towards her. Did he still have the knife? Where was it? 'Molly, what dream did you have?'

The torrent of words stayed trapped in her throat. She quivered in the chair, the muscles of her hands cramping against the wood.

All of a sudden he was shaking her by the shoulders, violently, so that her head was snapping back and forth. 'Tell me!' he roared, and she squealed, her hands trying to come up between them to push him away. 'Tell me!'

Just as suddenly he had let her go, and in the pale light from outside Molly caught a glimpse of his face, lined with anger and something else. It was the expression her father had worn whenever he had hit her mother. Surprise and bitterness.

'It was you. It was you. I dreamed the colour of your shirt and I dreamed your face. I saw you looking at me. That's why, when you brought Cristián back, I just, I just freaked. I already knew you, I already knew who you were. You were in my dream. And. You turned into a monster,' she said. 'And that was jingle-jangle.'

'Jingle-jangle?' His voice was a disembodied insistence, prowling about the room. 'How did I turn into a monster?'

'There was you and the feather thing,' she said, groping for a description. 'And then there wasn't. It was like, there were two of you and then there was one. Like you were really the same person.'

'The feather thing,' said the Doctor. 'Can you describe it?'

'Like a man,' said Molly, 'but with feathers. And a big smile, an advertising smile. He was eating people's hearts, eating them, like he was selling hamburgers.'

'And that's why you came for me with the knife,' concluded the Doctor. 'To stop me turning into the monster.'

'Aren't you the Devil?'

He went to the window. The venetian blinds made weird slits of light across his face, as though he were half there and half invisible. 'No, Molly. I'm not the Devil.'

'How come you were in my dream, then?'

'Who does Cristián think I am?'

Molly got out of the chair. The Doctor didn't turn around; he was watching something in the street. 'Cristián doesn't think much of anything these days,' she said. 'His head's sort of screwed up. He has all these bad trips. At first he was interested in Lizzie's books and stuff, but then he just started dropping acid all the time, like he would have trips that went for three days.'

Suddenly he shouted at her, a sound that exploded in her head and made her ears ring. It took her several seconds to realize the room had been silent, that the yell was entirely between her ears. 'Mmm,' said the Doctor. 'It attracts psychics like moths to the flame.'

She inched across the floor, like an animal trying not to catch the attention of a predator. 'I don't understand any

143

of this,' she said. 'It's like you've all got some deal going, some big trip which I can't grok. I don't know what to do.'

'That's your lieutenant's car out the front. Come to save you from yourself, I expect.'

'So what is going on? Are you really turning into a monster?'

'Yes, Molly,' he said, without turning around. 'I rather think I am.'

He reached up to his head. With a sudden movement, he pulled something out of his hair and let it fall to the floor.

Molly stared at what was lying on the slash of moonlit carpet. It was a handful of feathers.

Like speeding. You decide what to do, and then you just go out and do it.

She picked up the knife off the trolley and came at him with it held over her head.

He turned at the last moment. His face was a zebra crossing, alternate stripes of black and white, his eyes appraising her without emotion.

The door slammed open behind her. Someone shot her.

There was no sound, just a muffled whoosh. The air vibrated and was still. Molly dropped the knife, spinning with the impact of the bullet. She did not see who had shot her. She followed the blade to the floor, mouth gaping in surprise.

'I'm sorry,' she told the Doctor, who was suddenly kneeling beside her. 'I'm sorry. I'm really sorry.' He brushed his finger lightly across her forehead, and all the pain sluiced out of her, leaving only the cold blueness.

'It's all right,' he whispered. 'I understand.'

'No. I mean now. Now you'll have to. Now you'll have to do it yourself.'

Chapter 10

The Cat in the Hat Comes Back

'I shot her,' said Macbeth.

The Doctor just stayed next to the body, sitting cross-legged on the floor, his forehead resting in his hands.

Macbeth stumbled over to the wooden chair and sat down in it gracelessly, almost falling off. He clutched the gun, warm metal pressing against his palm in painful detail. 'Well, don't say thanks or anything.'

The Doctor looked up, ready to deliver a withering word and an even more withering look. But all he saw was a young man who desperately needed to be told he'd done the right thing.

'You did the right thing,' he said shortly, got up and pushed the door closed.

Macbeth waved his gun hand. 'Why?' he said.

'She wanted to save me from a fate worse than death,' shrugged the Doctor.

'No,' said the young man. 'Why did I shoot her?'

The Time Lord came over to the unexpected visitor. They were the same height, now that Macbeth was sitting down. With difficulty, the Doctor prised the weapon out of the man's paralyzed fingers, engaged the safety and put it down on the desk.

He reached into Macbeth's coat pocket and extracted his wallet, flipping it open. He read the UNIT card with surprise. Lieutenant Hamlet Macbeth, Paranormal Division. A soldier who had never fired a gun before.

Macbeth saw the Doctor reading the card and said weakly, 'My parents hated me.'

The Doctor pressed his wallet back into his hand. 'Lieutenant,' he said, 'tell me about the Paranormal Division.'

'Especially my mother,' said Macbeth.

'Attention!' snapped the Doctor. 'Answer the question!'

'There are four of us,' Macbeth gulped. 'The UNIT personnel. Plus the students. And the wildly talented. Shit, I shouldn't be telling you this.'

'Tell me,' said the Doctor, 'about the wildly talented.'

'Three GESPers, a PK chap who can shuffle cards without using his hands, and – I was going to take Molly in for some tests.' He looked at the body on the floor. 'She must have been crazier than I thought.'

The Brigadier had never mentioned a Paranormal Division. Had he kept it a secret? Perhaps poor Clegg's death had put him off the idea . . . but the man's powers had been convincing, even to the bamboozled Brig. No, the Division must have been short-lived. The Doctor wondered why.

'For goodness' sake, Ace,' he said aloud, 'come into the room.'

The door opened. 'Everything cool?'

'Perfectly. Don't trip over the corpse.'

Ace stepped over Molly's mortal remains and tucked her gun into the back of her jeans. 'Busy night,' she observed.

'Yes. Don't tell Bernice. Will you help me hide the body?'

They could sleep anywhere, these two: Ace had slept on a burning spaceship and on a stinking battlefield, shells bursting in the distance. Benny had slept on grass and leaves and rocks. After a while she no longer woke up when the tiny insects skittered over her hands.

So they'd slept, dreaming restless dreams, and now they were eating croissants in the hotel's wood-panelled restaurant, and the Doctor was late for breakfast.

Despite the *do not disturb* sign, Benny had knocked on

his door. No answer. He was off somewhere in the London morning.

She tore apart a croissant and dipped it despondently in her cocoa. Not one little bit did she like this game of keep-it-from-Ace. Unless . . . the Doctor believed that Ace was also somehow affected? How would they tell? For that matter, what about herself?

She put down the soggy chunk of pastry. Whom gods destroy, she thought, they first make paranoid. All she could do was to trust the Doctor until she knew more about what was going on. And try to trust Ace.

Ace was watching Benny over the rim of her mug. She'd followed the Doctor's instructions: the archaeologist didn't know about the uninvited guest in his bathtub. She didn't think it was fair to leave Bernice out of the full picture.

When he was this reticent, it was usually because an enemy was listening. Was something the matter with Bernice? Was she still under the influence of whatever had made her smash in that curator's head? Ace didn't know what was safe to say and what wasn't. So she said nothing.

It was Benny who broke the silence. 'Amongst all this weird weirdness,' she said, 'Cristián is the weirdest. Little Cris. It's like looking at old hologram albums . . . what are we going to say to him?'

Ace put down her cocoa. ' "Hey kid, don't make any long-term investments"?'

Benny gagged on her croissant. 'That's disgusting.'

'Sorry. It's weird for me too. My mother is twenty-three years old, and sometime in the next couple of years she's going to get pregnant with me. I wonder if I should visit her and gran.'

'Time travel,' said Bernice, 'is like banging your head on a brick wall. Only someone keeps moving the bricks.'

'At the moment I'm in Crook Meersham having a lousy Christmas. I feel like a paper doll – dozens of copies of me cut out and scattered about.'

'Perhaps we should pop over to Woodstock,' suggested the Doctor. 'There must be at least two of me there already.'

Both of them started. He was standing next to the table, peering myopically at *The Times*.

'We're a bit early for Woodstock,' said Bernice.

'Oh? I've got my dates a bit mixed up.' He grinned cheerfully and sat down. 'I see Apollo 8 is ready for blast-off.'

'Early spaceflight, Woodstock, hippies,' said Bernice. 'It's like a sightseeing holiday.'

'Perhaps we should pop over to Viet Nam,' said the Doctor darkly. 'You'll have the chance to talk to the restless natives this evening.'

'So we're going to the Christmas party?' asked Ace.

'These particular hippies,' said Bernice, 'worry me greatly. One minute they don't want us in their house, the next minute they're all smiles and hospitality. What are they up to?'

'Ah, they're out of their heads,' said Ace.

'Think yourself back to 1994,' the Doctor said. 'Or forwards. I'm convinced that this is the "Happening" Cristián told us about.'

'You mean the Happening he didn't tell us about. I find myself confused. What happens if we run a mile and let the Happening take care of itself? In the future, Cristián told us that we were there. Now, does that mean he actually would have told us that we weren't there, but then we wouldn't have had a warning, so we would have gone anyway . . .'

'Good grief, don't start that.'

Ace began to systematically shred her napkin. 'The enemy's setting snares for us all over the place. This has to be another one.'

'The only way to avoid all the snares,' said the Time Lord, 'is to abandon walking. No. Running a mile won't tell us what's up. And besides, Cristián needs help.'

'He blew his mind,' said Ace. 'Like Achtli eating those little mushrooms.'

Benny sighed. 'It doesn't seem fair on the hippies,' she said. 'They just want to be free, they shouldn't be caught up in this. I can't think of two groups of people who are more different than Aztecs and hippies.'

'Both of them use mind-affecting substances to alter their states of consciousness. The hippies use marijuana, amphetamines, lysergide . . . the Aztecs did it with peyote, morning glory seeds, magic mushrooms. And those who had psychic powers could tune in to the Blue when they were turned on.'

Ace shot the Doctor a glance that said *Molly*? He returned it with a quiet stare that said *Yes*.

'But drugs were an integral part of Aztec culture, with rules and traditions governing their use,' said Bernice. 'The hippies are deliberately stepping outside the bounds of their own society.'

'So the game is not the same.' Shred, shred, went Ace's napkin. 'Cris is going to keep dropping acid until he leaves his groceries at the supermarket.'

'Which may be why he ended up in a mental hospital.'

'We need to know what he's sensing,' said Bernice. 'Before his brain melts under the onslaught.'

The Doctor nodded.

'So we have to go to the Happening.'

The Doctor nodded.

'Oh, goody gumdrops.'

Cris was lying on the floor between the window and the bed, a blanket wrapped around him. Looking at the sky outside the window and thinking. He was wearing two sets of socks.

The floor bumped rhythmically against his back as *Birthday* started blaring out of John's old mono speakers. But, thought Cris, whose birthday was it?

Inevitably someone was going to want to use the bed, but for now the spare bedroom was empty and relatively peaceful. He'd retreated up here when he'd heard them laughing and saying, *hey, the cat in the hat came back*.

Cris' recollection of the previous day was somewhat confused. He remembered turning on in the morning; after that it was all nightmare, all disconnected images. He still hadn't found his shoes.

He did remember that moment in the snow on Primrose Hill, awareness stretched painfully to its limits, the face leaning down over him while the sky wheeled overhead.

At first he'd seen something out of his *Nahuatl* childhood, listening to stories at his grandmother's knee. She had a Masters degree in Mesoamerican culture as well as her medical qualifications. On her rounds as the community's midwife, she administered herbs as often as standard medicine, raising a wrinkly finger to her lips as she shared the secrets with Cristián Xochitl. Her little flower.

If you thought about it logically, that had been the source of the vision; one of grandmother's fireside tales, about the god of sun and war and his hideous face, blue and black. About how when the Spanish came and discovered the Aztecs worshipping this flesh-eating horror, they'd burned down the temples and slaughtered the people.

And then she'd laugh, and tell him about Moteuczomah Xocoyotl and Cuauhtemoc and the others, all the heroes of the final battle, fighting off the Spaniards' lust for gold. And she'd describe the idols the surviving Aztecs had made, hidden in the stones of the Christian churches, facing down into the dirt where no one would discover them.

Cristián remembered those pictures, the despairing face of an empty-chested victim, lying tangled on the stairs of the temple. The twisted face and body of the god, laughing overhead.

That was what he had seen yesterday, just for a moment. Then the acid image had melted and resolved itself into that little man in his hat. Only the eyes had remained the same. Burning Blue.

I'm going insane.

'Cristián Alvarez,' said a voice from above him, 'you are not going insane.'

Cris scrambled into a sitting position, gripping the blan-

150

ket. The cat in the hat was sitting on the bed, cross-legged, looking down at him.

'Who put all those things in your hair?' he said breathlessly.

'I want a word,' said the little man. He held his fedora in his lap, and Cristián found himself fascinated by the tiny, perfectly formed feathers peppered through his hair. 'In fact, I want several words. But one will do to begin with. There's a word you want to say, Cristián. What's the word?'

Cris thought of half a dozen swear words, Spanish and English, his heart thumping and his mind a tumbling jumble. But one word suddenly came ringing out, shaking itself loose from grandmother's stories, from memories of being a child, from memories older than that. It rang like a bell through him, louder and louder, and he felt himself sliding into the flashback.

'*Ixiptla*,' he whimpered.

'Oh,' sighed the Doctor. 'I was rather hoping you wouldn't say that.'

'Time,' said John, 'is not as simple as people make it out to be.'

'No,' said Benny, chewing on a samosa. She had bought a cheesecloth caftan and had dug up a pair of blue jeans. Camouflage, she thought, wondering if she were convincing anyone.

There were four of them sitting about in what was obviously someone's bedroom. A couple, identified as Eleanor and Eleanor's old man, clutched one another on a mattress lying on the floor, beneath a *Yellow Submarine* film poster bright with primary colours. Bernice eyed a grinning blue monster.

'Everybody lives by this clock, the day divided up into twelve slices, and on one slice you go to work and on another you go home again. Why not thirteen slices, or a hundred?'

Eleanor and her old man were watching *Nightshade* on TV, intermittently agreeing with John with a 'yeah' or

151

'right on'. 'Clocks are just one more thing in the way, one more barrier between people and reality. You can't slice up time, it flows on like a river . . .'

Benny had the urge to take notes. On-the-spot archaeology. *Never mind*, she thought, *just put it in your diary tonight*. 'Is that an idea from Eastern religion?'

'A lot of what we believe is. I'm more into Tarot and things. Lizzie's reading Watts and the *Dhammapada*, doing the whole mysticism bit, but I don't think she'd really know what Zen was if Nansen came up and hit her with half a cat.' He laughed.

'You sound as if you know a bit about it.'

'I have half of a theology degree. Maybe I'll go back and get the other half eventually . . .' He jumped up. 'You want something to eat?'

They found Ace downstairs, sitting on a beaten-up sofa, a bowl of noodles carefully balanced in her lap. Steam rose, fogging her sunglasses. Behind her was a huge sign done in crayon on butcher's paper, each letter a great swirl of colour. MERRY XMAS. Streamers hung down from the ceiling like an inverted field of seaweed, swaying as people's hair brushed past.

There were a dozen hippies in the room, some lying down with their heads next to the speakers, listening to John Lennon mournfully belting out *Yer Blues*. A couple were quietly smoking. Someone plucked at the strings of a guitar, their fitful music swamped by the blare from the record player.

Benny sat down next to Ace, who was wearing a leather jacket over her usual jeans and T-shirt. The younger woman did not look at her, expertly snatching noodles out of the bowl with a pair of chopsticks. To any of the others in the room she must seem absorbed in the meal, relaxed. Benny could see the tension in her shoulders.

It suddenly occurred to her that if these people constituted a real threat, Ace would kill them.

Benny glanced around. They seemed harmless, almost childlike. Cheerful clothing and smiles, and genuine friendliness, wanting to get to know you as much as tell you

152

about themselves. Casual conversation was tricky when you came from the twenty-fifth century, so Benny spent her time asking questions, fascinated. It was a movement that had blossomed and faded within a few short years, and yet the social upheaval it had accompanied made permanent changes in Western culture. She realized she was thinking like a journal article. The hippies were here, and now, breathing and alive, and Ace probably had a nuclear missile hidden under her jacket.

It struck Benny that she felt more at home with the hippies than she did with Ace.

'You want some noodles?' John proffered a bowl.

Benny took it from him. 'Tell me more about time,' she said.

'Telepathy has traditionally been confused with mysticism,' the Doctor was saying. 'It's difficult to scientifically study something that affects the mind of the observer. And those very rare cases of genuine psychic talent fuel the millions of hopefuls who believe they have a handful of psi . . .'

Cris listened from inside his blanket. He had pulled it over his head, so that he formed a peculiar tartan lump on the floor. It wasn't working: he could still hear the Doctor clearly.

'I know the sorts of things you've been sensing,' said the stranger. 'But they're not messages from God or the Devil. You've had a profound psychic experience. It's like being the one-eyed man in the kingdom of the blind.'

Cris peeped out from the blanket. There were weird vibes coming from the little man, ripples in the air, an invisible pressure. He seemed calm, and rational, and yet there was some sort of distortion hovering around him . . . *ixiptla*. The god in human form. Cris shuddered and went back inside the blanket.

'Different places have a different feel,' the Doctor was saying. 'A different time has a different *Zeitgeist*. You can sense that, I know. It attracted you to this place. These people, at this time. Now, why do you think that was?'

Cris said, 'The rent was cheap.'

'Ah,' said the Doctor, 'but you didn't have psychic experiences while you were in Mexico.'

'I'm not psychic,' protested the Indian from inside the blanket. 'It's just the acid. I came to London because I've finished university and I want to see the world, you know, get some experience. Maybe make the East, if I get together enough bread.'

'There were bad vibes before the lysergide,' said the Doctor.

'Look,' said Cris, putting his head out of the blanket. 'If I could read people's minds, I'd go and work on the stock market and make a fortune.'

'Your psychic ability is largely dormant. Just the tip of the iceberg is showing. Molly, on the other hand . . .'

'She's split,' said Cris. 'Maybe gone back to her parents' place in Birmingham.'

'Mmm.' The Doctor lay down on the bed with his arms folded behind his head. 'Why are you taking so much LSD?'

'To expand my mind, man. Lizzie says it's a skilful means, a way to get closer to enlightenment.'

'No. That's why the others are taking it.' There was a curious tension in the man's voice, as though he were forcing himself to be patient. 'Why are you taking it?'

'You couldn't understand. What've you got in common with us?'

'I have no home,' said the Doctor. 'I wander from place to place.'

'Yeah?' Cris smiled. 'You made the East?'

'Repeatedly. I dropped out a long, long time ago, Cris. Now I'm looking for answers.'

'Yeah, aren't we all.'

'I need the answers to a very specific set of questions. I think you have those answers.'

Cris rubbed his forehead with his thumbs, agitatedly. 'I see better when I'm tripping,' he said. 'I've got to find out what this thing in the back of my head is. There's some-

154

body out there, trying to get through to me, trying to tell me something. I thought – '

'Yes?'

'I thought it might be you.' Cris turned his face up to the stranger, his eyes hopeful and afraid.

'It's part of growing up,' said Lizzie. 'You grow away from your parents. You grow away from your home.' There was a mellow bitterness in her voice, the sound of pain that should long since have passed. 'For us, well, it was different. We grew away from everything.'

The black woman wore an amazing fluorescent purple T-shirt and a long gypsy skirt, sitting cross-legged on the floor next to the sofa. She'd got the clothes from the Apple Boutique when it closed down, giving away the stock to anyone who wandered in the shop. One of the Beatles' less successful projects.

Ace listened to her impatiently, wondering whether it was time to go and find the Doctor. He'd been gone for thirteen minutes, disappearing almost as soon as they'd arrived at the Happening.

'So,' she said, trying to make conversation, 'what are you planning to do?'

'How do you mean?'

'You know, what's your next step from here? What'll you be doing in ten years' time?'

Lizzie shrugged. 'You should really live one day at a time, keep your head in the here and now. You know? I'm trying to live just one day at a time. Just trying to forget the past and not worry about the future.' That bitterness was there again.

Ace suddenly felt old, so much older than the woman at her feet. It had something to do with travelling the universe and fighting Daleks and having the stuffing knocked out of you emotionally and physically until you felt you might be hollow.

Or it might be the longing in Lizzie's voice. She'd heard that timbre in the speech of soldiers who had ended up getting killed doing reckless things. The suicidal types, the

155

ones who had become soldiers because they thought they'd screwed up their lives.

Screwed up their lives. What was she going to be doing, ten years from now?

The Doctor came down the stairs, trailing Cris, who looked befuddled. Ace smiled to herself. No wonder, if the Time Lord had been talking to him.

She was here to protect the Doctor, because he needed someone to watch his back. The promise still held: she wasn't going to let him die alone. But after they'd sorted out this monster, there'd be another one, and another one ... the TARDIS was a roller-coaster, plunging from one battle, one adventure, to the next. Not much different to being a starship trooper, though you did get more variety. But eventually they'd come up against a monster which would either kill her or do something worse. Or the Doctor would snafu and get himself killed. Who knew, this might be that time.

He'd never give up the crusade. But this might be the time to leave him to it, when he at least had Bernice. Ace could be like these hippies, be like she had been when the time storm had torn her away from Earth, throwing everything away and starting again.

She wanted to say something understanding to Lizzie, but the black woman was staring up at the Doctor, her eyes totally fixed on him.

'Smile,' shouted somebody.

Ace looked up just in time to be dazzled as Cris took a snapshot of the Doctor and Bernice, arm in arm with their backs to her.

Oh, yeah, she thought.

Half a dozen of them had gathered in the kitchen, sitting on the floor around a camp stove. The weak blue flame sputtered and spat, filling the kitchen with the sharp odour of methylated spirits. A kettle perched on top of the stove, centred precisely over the flame. The sink was full of unwashed dishes, but there were beautiful bits of pottery

156

on the window-sill, cupping tiny flowers in their clay mouths.

John was given the honour of passing out the tea cups. The Doctor took two, solemnly, and handed one to Bernice. They sat side by side on the floor, feeling the contrast between the coldness coming up from the basement and the thin warmth of the stove. The hippies had been chatting, but now they fell silent, listening to the river-noises of the water inside the kettle.

The whistle seemed to come out of nowhere, making Bernice jump. She looked at the Doctor, hoping for some sort of reassurance, but he was staring blankly into the blue flame.

Lizzie was fussing with something on the kitchen counter. Now she carried a small bowl of sugar cubes to where the group was sitting, and put them carefully down next to the stove.

John lifted the singing kettle from the flame. He left the stove on while he added level teaspoonfuls of Earl Grey to each cup, and carefully added water from the kettle, stirring it with a wooden spoon. The hippies stared into the flame or watched as their cups were filled.

Lizzie picked up a cube in the sugar-tongs and asked, 'One lump or two?'

The hippie to her right, a woman with long straight hair who was wearing a green turtle-neck sweater, said, 'Just the one.' She swayed slightly as the cube was carefully dropped into her cup, without a splash.

'Two,' said the next member of the circle, a moustached black flashing a grin at Lizzie as she topped up his cup.

'One,' Eleanor said, and her old man had two, stirring the tea with his finger before sipping it.

And so it went, until it came to Bernice. She opened her mouth, and suddenly caught a glimpse out of the corner of her eye. The Doctor was shaking his head, ever so imperceptibly.

'None for me, thanks,' she said, trying not to sound bewildered. There was more to these sugarcubes than just

157

sugar, evidently. She rummaged in her mind for the piece of twentieth-century trivia that would explain.

Lizzie shrugged. 'What about you, Doctor?' She and John were watching him like a pair of vultures.

The Doctor smiled sweetly.

'Three,' he said.

Ace was asleep on the battered beanbag, snoring gently. Her sunglasses had tilted off her nose and landed on the litter of peanut shells on the wooden floor.

A handful of hair hung down over her face, its anger softened into curves, almost like a little girl's face. The Doctor gently brushed it back, his fingers discovering a collection of tiny scars above her right temple, hidden in the hair. Tiny pieces of flak had carved their signature into her scalp. Probably from an exploding Dalek.

She had been drugged, of course. She'd drunk only a little alcohol, but in combination with the contents of one or two tranquillizer capsules . . . He checked her pulse for a full minute, listened to the gentle sound of her breathing, shutting out the heavy thumping of the music.

His own pulses were up just noticeably, his blood pressure increasing with them, and his core temperature was up almost a quarter of a degree. Normally, his system metabolized poisons very rapidly. But when he had taken the psilocybin in Tenochtitlan, he had slowed down key pathways to prevent its being broken down too quickly to have any effect.

Those pathways were still blocked, keeping the lysergide in circulation. It cut into the dance of his neurotransmitters, made tiny changes to the chemistry of his mind. Gallifreyan biochemistry was not too wildly different to Earth's, which was why he could breathe the air, eat the food. But the drugs, ah, he had to be careful there. One good dose of aspirin would be enough to kill him.

'Hey,' said Lizzie. He glanced up at her, and blinked rapidly, the livid purple of her T-shirt setting off flashbulbs behind his eyes. 'Come on now. You look like you should lie down.'

'Unhand me, madam,' he muttered, as she hauled him to his feet.

'She'll be fine there.' Lizzie ran an eye over Ace, who shrugged in her sleep, a hand batting at the squeaky surface of the beanbag. The Doctor imagined he could hear every single bead rolling around inside it. 'It's jingle-jangle morning now. You come on now and lie down.'

He let her lead him along by the hand. Best to let her continue to believe that this was her idea. Around the flat, people were talking in quiet voices or lying in languid circles, passing a joint from hand to hand in the time-honoured ritual. In the front room, two women swayed slowly in front of the booming speakers, their skinny arms swinging back and forth to a beat which had nothing to do with the music.

And now the music was flying away, pounding silently at the air, a giant mouth opening and closing. The message was too loud to be audible. It was embedded in the wood of the walls and the floor. It pumped in the blood of the men and women scattered through the house. It danced between the molecules of the cold and smoky air, filling up that microscopic vacuum, until the air was as thick as treacle, every space filled with the hidden message. Waiting to be heard. Waiting to be understood. Waiting to be released.

She led him to a red door, its paint peeling in excruciating detail. Behind the door was darkness and bitter cold, concrete steps leading down. She sat him down on the bed and took away his hat and tie, carried away his jacket over her arm like some mystical maitre d'.

The bed had no blankets, only a single sheet smelling of laundries and ironing. He lay down on his back. Brilliant patterns overlaid the dark ceiling, kaleidoscoping pleasantly. He closed his eyes, and could still see the patterns.

Almost reverently, Lizzie took his left hand and lifted it behind his head. There was a snapping sound and the press of cold metal against his wrist.

She still thought she was in control.

He shrugged, trying to get more comfortable. Once you

159

took your seat on the mystery tour, there was no way of getting off the ride.

And the message went on booming in his ears, just beyond the range of his hearing.

The bathroom door was propped open with half a brick. Bernice stepped in, feet sliding on the wet tiles. There was a Hendrix poster taped over the mirror, the paper rippled and puckered with moisture. A mouldy curtain hid the bathtub.

A freezing wind was blowing in through the window; a handful of snow had built up on the window-sill. With an effort, she pulled it closed, the snow wetting her wrist.

Earth was frozen and hostile. And she was alone. It always came back to that; you meet people, you exchange a few words, a few ideas, maybe a little love. And then they move on. The hippies had made her feel homesick for the Travellers, a time she could never go back to, a dream that became diseased and withered away.

She hated evil and she'd seen a lot of it, and she felt as though she'd been fighting it forever, just going on and on . . . was she really cut out for the Doctor's big celestial game? It had been fun, a really good laugh, but now it was going sour.

Benny closed her eyes and blew out a white breath into the air, trying to think. It had seemed so natural for her and the Doctor and Ace to work separately, confronting the Garvond with their different sets of skills. There had been no discussion; no arguing or games; no chance for arguing or games.

Now they were trying to work together. Something was wrong with the Doctor, and Ace was withdrawing further and further into herself, leaving behind only the warrior facade. Benny felt as though she had to try to protect them both, to save them from themselves. Someone had to do something.

Three, he had said. Three lumps of LSD-spiked sugar.

Ace was half-comatose on a beanbag in one of the bedrooms; even slapping her hadn't brought her round. And now the Doctor was simply missing. She didn't think he had left, but he was somewhere here, doing – what? Or having what done to him? The friendly hippies didn't seem so friendly any more.

There was a muffled moan from behind the shower curtain. Bernice spun, shoes slipping, one hand ripping aside the curtain as she scrabbled for balance.

Cristián was in the bathtub. He had taken off his T-shirt and was wringing it between his hands, a shapeless mass of cloth. The strap of his camera was twisted around his ankle.

Benny knelt down on the cold tiles. 'Cris?' she said.

He looked bleakly at her. His pupils were swollen, his eyes solid marbles of black. His face was a child's face, so far from home, looking for answers in the big bad world. Why here, of all places? How had he become entangled in the catastrophe?

Cristián grinned at nothing, mirthlessly, hallucination dancing in his eyes. 'Will you weep for me one last time? Will you feel sad for me?' he asked.

'Cris,' said Benny urgently, 'it's happening again, isn't it?'

His eyes changed colour, startling blue in his copper-coloured face.

'*Otiquihiyohuih*,' he said.

Benny bolted.

Lizzie came down the stairs into the basement, carrying a single candle in a chipped cup. London light pushed through the black curtains. She waited a few moments while her eyes adjusted to the flickering darkness.

'How do you feel?' she asked the man on the bed.

'Bored,' he said.

'No, seriously,' said Lizzie. She squatted on the chilly floor, carefully positioning her candle. It sent a dim circle of light up over the edge of the Doctor's expressionless face, onto the complex scrawl of the Aztec calendar behind him. She could see his eyelashes in peculiar detail as he blinked. 'I don't want you to get sick or anything.'

'Sympathomimetic effects,' he muttered. 'Fever, some tremor.' He raised his right hand; it was shaking. 'Moderate synaesthesia.'

Lizzie looked up at a sound. John came into the cellar, carefully shutting the door behind him. He was carrying a bowl of water and a reasonably clean tea-towel. 'Everyone's either stoned or asleep,' he announced quietly, 'so we'll have some privacy for a while. Anything yet?'

'Nothing,' said the Doctor. John looked at him sharply, as though surprised he could speak. 'What is it you're expecting to happen?'

John sat down on the bed, wetted the tea-towel, and carefully wiped the sweat from the Doctor's forehead. 'To tell you God's honest truth,' he said, 'I'm not sure. This is a sort of experiment.'

'Wonderful,' said the Doctor.

'Cris and Molly both have the sixth sense,' said John patiently. 'Molly won't drop acid any more because she was freaking out too much, and because she thinks Jesus wouldn't like it. But it's too late. She still dreams about Aztecs. I think she's picking it up from Cris. Like radio interference.'

'When Cris turns on,' Lizzie continued, 'he gets visions. He knew you were coming. That's why we got all of this ready. We wanted to know what visions you might have. We know who you are, you see.'

'Oh, yes?'

'*Ixiptla*,' said Lizzie.

'*Ixiptla*,' said John.

'The image becoming the god,' said the Doctor. 'The god becoming the image. The same patterns happening again and again.'

'That's what the psychics are tuned into. The reality behind the appearance, the Void.'

Lizzie said, 'People are always asking "who am I?", but the question doesn't mean anything – you're somebody now, but in a year's time you'll be somebody different. "Who am I?" is just an outer skin. That's what acid's for. Peeling back the skin.'

'This – ' John tapped the Doctor on the chest ' – is the image. So we'll wait for the real thing. For jingle-jangle.' He smiled, wringing out the tea-towel. 'Imagine trying to explain that to some cat in a suit. The straights are so locked into their clock they've forgotten about the big spirals of time. They don't even know it's the sun god's birthday. December 21.'

'The winter solstice?' The Doctor wiped his free hand across his brow. John washed his face again with the tea-towel. 'I think you're getting your mythologies muddled.'

'Not everyone has forgotten the old religions,' said John. 'The sun god is reborn every year on this day. That's why we organized the Happening for tonight, the longest night of the year. When Cris brought you here yesterday, we knew we were right. This was all meant to happen.'

'It's time-permeable,' said the Doctor suddenly. 'That's how it knew who I was in 1487, after we'd met in 1994. That's how it was able to arrange this.' He tried to sit up, but the handcuffs pulled his arm backwards. 'Past and future are the same to it, because it – it – '

He snapped into a convulsive arch, mouth and eyes opening as an excruciating flower tried to blossom inside his chest. The bowl of water fell off the bed with a crash. With a gunshot noise, the window broke, a crazy set of lines etching themselves across the surface. The room filled with the smell of ozone, as though something electrical was burning.

Lizzie squealed. An awful grin split John's face.

The Doctor suddenly relaxed, gulping air, blood gushing from his nose. His free hand spasmed, clutching at the wall, flakes of paint coming off under his fingernails.

'Jingle-jangle,' said Lizzie, hysterically.

John got up, pushed the Doctor's shoulders down against the bed. 'If you keep pulling on that cuff, you're only going to hurt yourself.'

The Doctor's face twisted as another wave hit him, those petals pushing against his hearts, those thorns tearing at the inside of his skin. Cris had never been like this in his worst moments. John grabbed the man's arms and held

163

him still as he thrashed, panicking, the handcuff clanging against the metal leg of the bed. Metal sounded on metal in a desperate rhythm as he wrenched at the bond.

'I can hear it – ' the Doctor gasped. His eyes glittered. 'I can hear, I can hear it, this is what happened before, in Tenochtitlan, *oh I remember now* – ' The next paroxysm threw John backwards, yelping, his hands seared where they had been touching the Doctor.

And there was a breeze blowing now, a cold wind gushing out of nowhere, smelling of roses and bleeding, carrying the sound of clattering bells. Lizzie's cup tipped over as the candle flared and died. The air around the bed boiled and ululated with energy. Both hippies sprang backwards, raising their arms against the outflow of power, Blue light, Blue sound.

In the maelstrom, the Doctor howled, *burning*, being *erased*, being *unmade*, until until

'Unbind me,' said Huitzilin.

John fell to his knees. Lizzie's mouth opened and closed, tears streaming down her cheeks.

Where the Doctor had been, there was a tall man, naked except for a loincloth and a pair of sandals. A rainbow of feathers cascaded down over his face, mixed with the milky colour of his hair. He glowed like snow in moonlight.

The room was silent.

Third Slice

An infallible method of conciliating a tiger is to allow oneself to be devoured.

Konrad Adenaur

Chapter 11

Jingle-Jangle Morning

i remember now

It was not unusual to see the police in St John's Wood, not since the hippies had begun to move in. They were objects of special interest, with their conspicuousness, their vagabond lifestyles, their buying and selling of drugs.

This bright December morning more than just the police had come to the Wood. The locals peeped out of their windows, through the letter slots in their doors. How much pot did you have to have, they were wondering, before the whole army turned out?

The street was cordoned off. Armed men stood beside the road barricades. Thin streams of smoke rose from cigarettes in the dawn light. More soldiers waited inside jeeps, or stood leaning on the vehicles, boots crunching in the Christmas snow.

All was silent. Except for a blazing argument going on outside number twenty eight.

'Holy cruk!' exploded Bernice, waving her arms exasperatedly at the accumulated firepower. 'I expected you to come, plus maybe a couple of police. Not half the crukking marines.'

'They're not marines,' said Macbeth, rolling something between his fingers. 'They're UNIT. This sort of thing is their job.' He sealed the paper and popped the first smoke of the morning into his mouth. 'No sense in taking any chances.'

'All you have to do is walk in and retrieve the Doctor. You haven't even done that.'

'You were the one talking about unknown psychic forces.' He gestured at the house. 'At the moment, everything seems very quiet.'

From high up in number twenty eight, a dreadful scream resounded, lingering in the cold air. The soldiers shuffled and muttered. Bernice blanched. Macbeth's mouth fell open, and his cigarette fell down and burned a hole in his shoe.

Without a word, Benny ran for the front door. Macbeth waited a dignified moment and signalled his men.

oh i remember now

His mother had named him Hummingbird because when he grew up, he would be a warrior. Little Huitzilin studied his namesakes as they swarmed around the long flowers, their iridescent feathers glistening like sunshine on water. One would pick out a bit of territory, some bush rich in nectar, and then it would defend it.

He had spent hours watching them. They were not afraid of him, the little Aztec boy with the shrivelled foot. Sometimes a hummer would fly right up to his face and hover an inch away, as though studying him, its wings an invisible singing blur.

And they would fight. He'd watched a tiny hummer fend off a hawk that must have been fifty, a hundred times larger than itself. And they'd fight one another for a flower or a branch. There'd be a clacking of beaks, longer than the bodies of the birds themselves, as though they held swords in their mouths. They would break apart and collide, smashing together, losing feathers. Sometimes one would fall to the grass and lie still. Huitzilin was always careful to collect the little corpses. Sometimes they would still be alive. He would sacrifice them to the gods, smashing the tiny bodies with a rock.

Once he came so close to a hummer it almost attacked him, hovering agitatedly near the long, tubular yellow blossom it was planning to feed on. It finally decided he was just a bit of scenery, and thrust its long sword into the flower, drinking deep.

Little Hummingbird watched and watched as the tiny creature drained every last drop out of the yielding flower. When it was gone he plucked one of the blossoms and squeezed its base against his tongue. Tasting the sweetness.

Huitzilin did not know the man's name, or his rank, or his tribe. He only knew that he was a foreigner, and that one of them would kill the other.

The swamp dragged at their feet. They snapped fat branches from the trees to hit one another with. They fished rocks out of the mud to throw at one another's heads. No one knew they were here.

At last they ran out of weapons, tumbling over and over in the water as they wrestled, slapping and punching. There was no thought of capture, no thought of sacrifice; only the need to kill, to break up the opposing mass of flesh. Only in rape and in combat can you do whatever you want to the other person's body.

Huitzilin screamed in rage as he clawed at his opponent's eyes. The other was bigger than him, with two working feet; and yet he could see the uncertainty on the foreigner's face. The scout had not been expecting to find anyone in the swamp, much less some witch with blue eyes and feathers. It was Huitzilin's only advantage, and he pressed it, howling like the spirit of a dead mother returning to claim her children.

The bigger man tore Huitzilin's hands away from his face and flung him bodily into the water, jumping on his chest to try and press him down into the mud. Huitzilin shrieked, trying to gather air into his lungs as the scout pushed all his weight against the Aztec's ribcage. He scrabbled in the ooze for stones, for something solid to mark the other's face and send him falling into the water. But there was nothing.

Death stuck its skinless hand in through Huitzilin's face.

He reached inside his opponent and opened the burning

169

Blue flower in his heart. A shock travelled through him, touching every part of his body, like the wave of sensations that accompany the first kiss.

He held the tiny, gorgeous blossom in the palm of his mind, tasting it.

The warrior screamed in rage and horror, clawing at the skin of his chest.

Little Hummingbird drove his lethal beak deep inside him and drew out the nectar.

Later, when the singing in his head had stopped and he had dragged himself out of the mud, he saw that he was alone in the swamp. And he laughed and laughed until the swamp birds flew away and the frogs hopped clumsily into the next puddle.

The soldiers kicked down doors, discovered terrified hippies cowering in the kitchen and under the stairs. They rounded them up in the living room, counted heads. The stash had long since been flushed down the toilet, but it wasn't the drugs they were after.

In the upstairs bathroom, they found Cristián Alvarez, huddled in the bathtub. He had torn the shower curtain loose from the rings and was half-twisted in it, a mouldy plastic shroud. His pupils were huge. When they tried to move him, he screamed again, the sound echoing off the tiles.

Bernice found Ace where she had left her, snoring gently on the beanbag. Whatever it was had been in the noodles, of course; Benny had put hers down, absorbed in her conversation with John, and when she'd come back to them they'd been cold.

A medic and two soldiers came in and started fussing over Ace. They got her onto a stretcher, snoring peacefully all the while. Bernice left them to it. Where was the Doctor?

'Huitzilin! We will not attack Tula!'

Coyolxauhqui threw down her weapons, angrily. She

stood at the head of a large group of Aztecs, men, women, and children.

'Do you speak for all of them?' Huitzilin limped to a rock and pulled himself up onto it to get a better view of them. The clearing was littered with campfires, equipment, dogs and mewling babies. The priests were saying the morning prayers beside the magic idol in its litter, pretending to ignore the argument. 'Or is it just your cowardice speaking?'

'By the gods, little brother,' growled Coyolxauhqui. 'Are words your food? They're in your mouth all the time. There's nothing cowardly about avoiding a hopeless battle.'

'The Toltecs are toothless and decadent,' said Huitzilin, his voice ringing out through the clearing. 'We can take their city easily. Or are you happy to go on wandering, without any piece of land to call your own?'

'Listen to me!' Coyolxauhqui shouted. The Aztecs were silent, her followers brandishing their weapons nervously. 'Wasn't it me who kept you alive all these years, bringing the game animals to us? Who's going to call the deer and the birds for you?'

Huitzilin jumped down off his rock, surprisingly fast and agile given his club-foot, and grabbed her by the blouse. 'You might have the same sorcerous blood as I, sister,' he spat, blue eyes looking into blue eyes. 'But we can survive without your magic. *Ia?* We don't need you.'

'What're you going to do, little brother?' she said mockingly, putting her face close to his. '*Ia?* Are you going to drink me up like a blossom, little Hummingbird? Eat me up in front of everyone?'

Huitzilin snarled and let go of her. He let loose a wordless cry of rage at the crowd. 'With courage, we can take Tula!' he yelled. 'With weapons, we can take Tula!'

'With greed and with death,' sneered Coyolxauhqui. 'What corpse can bring back treasure from the ruined city? What lifeless body can possess the Toltecs' land?'

'It's sweet to die in battle. It pleases the gods.'

'Does it really?'

'Oh yes, sister,' said Huitzilin. 'It pleases them very much.' He raised his voice again. 'If you're too afraid to fight, then stay here with the women and spin. Look after the babies, if that's all you're good for.'

The women warriors shouted their anger, clashing their swords against their shields. 'We're staying here,' hissed Coyolxauhqui.

Huitzilin peered at the weapon, turned it around in his hands. It was pale greenish-blue, a short handle becoming a curve that looped back on itself. It looked like a snake, a turquoise serpent.

The weapon had been an heirloom of Huitzilin's family for as many generations as they'd had the sorcerous blood. No one knew precisely what it was, or how you were supposed to use it; he wasn't even sure how they knew it was a weapon. It was light, and there was no force to its swing, no balance.

But it felt like a weapon. Standing on the hillside, holding the turquoise serpent, he felt as though he could overthrow the world.

'Your sister's armies are coming closer,' said Quauilticac. Huitzilin nodded at him, staring out over the valley. He imagined he could hear them, half a thousand pairs of feet trampling the earth as they marched towards his camp.

Uncle Quauilticac had made a good spy. Without his information, they might well have been taken by surprise by that bitch Coyolxauhqui's army. When Huitzilin ruled the Aztecs, by the gods, there'd be no more women generals. Let them make cloth and children, and keep their mouths closed.

On the other hand, Huitzilin was sure Quauilticac was also giving intelligence to Coyolxauhqui. He did like to prattle, and who knew what he might have told his favourite niece, especially if she'd plied him with cactus wine.

He spat in the dirt, gripping the *Xiuhcoatl*. It didn't matter. His troops held the high ground; within a day they'd have wiped Coyolxauhqui's rebels from the face of the earth.

With a great cry the army came swarming out of the forest, out of bushes and thickets, hurdling streams. Their shouts and yells echoed back from the hillside, an arrhythmic clatter of rage.

Huitzilin's soldiers held their ground, waiting for their general to give the order. They watched him, expectant and nervous. Idly he noticed that some of them had added feathers to their head-dresses, in imitation of the plumes that grew from his scalp. Someone shouted as they picked out the brightly coloured shield of Coyolxauhqui herself, held high like a banner, leading her warriors on.

And still Huitzilin didn't move, just stood there with his eyes half-closed against the glare of the noon sun, as if listening to a voice none of them could hear.

Abruptly he raised the *Xiuhcoatl*, as though it were the most natural thing in the world to do.

And now there was no forest, no stream. Where the army had been was charred earth and a great billowing cloud of steam that raced up the hillside and exploded into the sky, stinking of lightning and seared rock.

Huitzilin's warriors raised their arms against the scorching cloud, screaming. They'd never seen anything like this before.

Huitzilin looked at the little device in his hand, and smiled. It was so simple, easier to use than a toy!

He looked out over the devastation he'd created. The plain, boiled down to the rock, was shimmering with lifeless heat. The vegetation at the base of the mountain was scorched and shrivelled, and here and there he could see parboiled corpses littered amongst the cooked trees.

He spotted the multicoloured shield part way up the mountain, and went jumping and running down the slope. Everything was covered in warm dew, and the air was like a steam house. But it felt *good*.

He found Coyolxauhqui face down in the dirt, her back and legs seared by the steam. He pulled her to her feet. She tried to scream, but her throat was burnt, and her scorched eyes were full of madness.

'You see, little girl!' he spat in her face. 'Everything

you've built I'm tearing down. Everything you've done I'm wiping out. All the stories they're going to tell, they'll tell about me, not you, and then they'll tell them the way I want them told.'

Laughing, he devoured her, the air trembling with the power of his hunger.

He screamed at his men, 'I'm not going to fight with witchcraft. I'm going to fight with weapons. My orders will be obeyed in every land from the east coast to the west. I'll protect every border of our land. I'll make sure we live in luxury. I'll make our nation glorious, I'll lift us up to the sky!'

They watched him from the bushes, from behind rocks, shuddering. 'Our conquests will get us gems and gold and feathers and emeralds and coral and amethysts and animal skins and cotton,' he said giddily. 'I'll have it all.'

He'd never have to use the weapon again. When they saw what he had done, the Toltecs weren't going to put up much resistance. And from now on, every warrior would be called *hummingbird*.

'Sir,' someone said to Macbeth. The paranormalist sauntered over, surveying the basement door.

'It's locked,' said the soldier.

'Well, kick it in, then,' said MacB.

'Yes, sir.'

He kicked the door once, lightly, and it tore loose from its lower hinge, hanging like a stiff red flag over the stairs. The soldier carefully pushed it to one side. MacB went first, Benny hovering at his shoulder.

They said that the Tezcatlipocas spoke to the emperor in a tongue no one else could understand, a language with the sound of flutes. Tlacaelel heard it, and he understood it better than anyone. Including the emperor.

Advice for the king's adviser, laughed the voice, waking young Tlacaelel out of his sleep. He rolled over on the mat, smiling in the darkness of his house. 'What is it?'

Tlacaelel, said the voice, *you're the emperor's nephew*

174

and his trusted general. I've given you more secrets than anyone before.

'And I'm grateful. And we have an empire now, to protect and to drain. And to enlarge.'

It's a very simple pattern, Tlacaelel. The more wars, the more cities we rule. The more cities we rule the more tribute we receive. We can build the empire on food, and jaguar skins, and precious stones.

'What if we stop fighting?'

The reputation of power is power. You can never stop fighting. Should any town rebel, slaughter every man, woman and child, and no one will dare rebel. But grow peaceful and fat and the empire will slip through your fingers like sand.

'And if the Aztecs won't fight?' asked Tlacaelel.

The sun needs sacrifice to stay alive. As he sacrificed himself in the fire when the world began. You know the tale: the gods bled for humanity. Now humanity must bleed for the gods.

Tlacaelel nodded in the darkness. 'The warriors who are killed in battle die happy, feeding the sun.'

The warriors who aren't killed in battle die happy, feeding the sun.

'And when our enemies see a thousand men die on the altars they'll think twice before rebelling, withholding tribute.'

Precisely.

'As the empire expands,' said Tlacaelel, 'we will need more wars.'

Yes.

'And more sacrifices.'

Yes.

'Death will spread out from us in ripples, growing ever wider. The empire will grow unstable as it grows outwards.'

Glory is as brief as the flash of sunlight on water, said the whisper. *And I need more deaths.*

'Yes.'

Tell the king. And I'll make you my general, Tlacaelel,

175

and you'll rule this empire from behind the emperor for the rest of your life.

'Yes.'

There was one person in the basement.

The bed was overturned, the metal of the legs and springs twisted and scored subtly in patterns that disturbed the mind. The huge Aztec calendar behind it, with the hideous face of the sun pouting out from the centre, had great lines burned into it in meaningless patterns, as though someone had run a searing finger over its surface.

Bernice hesitated at the top of the stairs, feeling a familiar awfulness creeping into her stomach, a bitter tang that reminded her, reminded her ... screaming in a Mexican hospital. Of Macbeth, an older Macbeth with grey in his red hair and a broken nose, exploding into fragments of light. The Blue had been here. The air was still poisonous with it.

There was a pile of ashes and glass on the floor under the shattered window, mixed with charred scraps of black cloth. MacB pressed a hand against the peeling paint on the wall. 'It's warm,' he said.

The Doctor lay in a small pile in the corner of the basement. There was snow on him; flakes were still drifting in through the window. His face was hidden. There was a small puddle of blood around his head. Benny stood stockstill for a moment. Then she was walking towards him, fingers twitching, wondering what she was going to see.

She gently turned him over, supporting his head, listening hard for the sound of breathing. Nothing. His face was white, not the colour of death, thank God, but pale, so pale ... blood had exploded from his ears and nose and mouth, drying in horrible black streaks across his face and hardening in his hair. A mangled pair of handcuffs clung to his left wrist.

'Jesus,' said Macbeth, standing behind her. He had taken the pillow from the bed. Benny carefully laid the Doctor's head on it, straightened out the tangle of his limbs. She pushed her face close to his, listening, concentrating absolutely. Still nothing.

So suddenly that she almost screamed, he drew a ragged breath and grabbed the back of her shirt, fingers digging into her skin. His eyes did not open. It was like being clutched by a corpse.

She untangled herself from his grip. His hands were as white as his face, the skin frighteningly cold. His left wrist was badly lacerated. 'I'll get a medic down here,' Macbeth was saying.

'No,' said Bernice. 'Your medic's no good, because –' She bit down on the words.

'Look, lady, he needs to get to a hospital.'

'A twentieth-century hospital,' said Benny, a little hysterically, 'on twentieth-century Earth. I suppose you're still sewing people up with thread.'

She could feel MacB's gaze boring into her back as she pressed an ear to the Doctor's chest, left side . . . right side. His hearts were beating sluggishly, but they were beating. He had survived. He was alive. And now this military idiot wanted to drag him off to the tender embrace of primitive medicine.

'Wait outside, will you?' she heard Macbeth telling the soldier. Sound of footsteps on stone. Silence for a moment or two. 'Why can't he go to hospital?'

'Because he's from outer crukking space,' spat Bernice. 'A crukking twentieth-century hospital would probably do a crukking brilliant job of killing him!'

More silence. A small sound: MacB flicking ash from his cigarette.

'No hospital, then,' he sighed. 'We'll have to think of something else.'

Benny put her head in her hand and said, 'What the cruk happened last night?'

He was suddenly alive again.

'Unbind me,' said Huitzilin.

Someone took the handcuff off his wrist. He sat up on

177

the bed, stretching, stretching, filling his lungs. He hadn't breathed for centuries, not for centuries.

It was cold. He felt the tiny hairs on his skin standing up. He held his hands out in front of him, examining his fingers.

There were two people kneeling before him. They took his hands, clutching them in adoration.

'You'll tell me, won't you?' said John. 'You'll tell me what I want to know?'

'Oh yes,' sobbed Lizzie. 'You'll make everything all right. You'll wipe it all away.'

He devoured both of them. Then he stood up and stretched, passing through the tingling air where they had been, feeling that ecstatic tremor on his skin, all through him. Alive.

He couldn't stay for long. Just long enough to remember the sensation of breathing, feel his stomach rise and fall and the cool air aching in his lungs.

It was better than nothing. And there'd be more later. So much more.

Interlude 1

Three weeks passed.

Chapter 12

You've Got Him Just Where He Wants You

Bernice slowed the rented Renault as she drove past the house, taking in the details. It looked no different to any of dozens of houses they'd passed; big garden and driveway, big walls to keep out the noise of the motorway. Ivy scraggling all over the stone. No sign of human beings.

Benny waited until the motorway was quiet. She drove the car across the gravel edge and between a pair of trees. The wheels left a conspicuous trail in the snow, but it couldn't be helped. Besides, Ace wouldn't be long.

'Okay?' she asked Ace.

'All right. Be cool.'

'I'll leave the heater off,' joked Benny feebly, turning off the engine with a violent twist of the keys. She was angry about having to stay behind, of course. Despite her connections, Ace had only been able to swing a pass for herself. And that wasn't all there was to be angry about.

The mercenary climbed out of the car, boots crunching in the gravel as she made her way down to the house. It was dead quiet, not even any birds singing. They were smack in the middle of nowhere. It had taken Ace two weeks to get the address of the place, let alone official permission to visit. Then again, her business wasn't entirely official. As Lieutenant Macbeth was going to discover, to his regret.

The iron gate was high and locked. She pressed the buzzer a few times and then waited, hands in the pockets of her anorak. After a while a uniformed soldier appeared, UNIT badge clipped to his beret. She handed him the pass through the bars.

She could see his little booth inside the gate, a cup of cocoa steaming on the table next to the phone. If he called for advice she might be in trouble, but he didn't. There was a motor hum and the gate slid slowly aside. 'Just knock at the front door, ma'am,' he said, pointing across the gravel driveway to the house. She smiled and took the pass back.

She'd spent whole days on the phone, trying to get that little bit of paper. Lethbridge-Stewart was always away somewhere, and besides, they hadn't yet met; no one had heard of her. Even the Doctor was a new and little-known entity as far as UNIT was concerned.

She'd changed tactics, called the RAF. Air Commodore Gilmore had retired. She spent another day with the phone book, trying to track him down. At least he remembered her – gave him a good fright, when he'd recognized her voice. He had no official standing, of course, but could he put her in touch with the Brigadier?

She pulled back the great brass loop of the knocker and let it fall against the door. It opened instantly. 'Ma'am,' said another soldier. He led her in through the wire frame of a metal detector and into the foyer. It smelled of must and wood polish.

'I'm here to speak to Lieutenant Macbeth.' She proffered the pass. The soldier glanced at it and handed it back. Like magic, Alistair, like magic.

'Right you are. Up the stairs, first door on the left. There's a sign.'

'Cheers.'

Easy so far. Her heart pounded, a healthy pounding, ready for action.

She resisted the urge to kick in Macbeth's door.

She knocked, counted to three, and went inside, shutting the door behind her.

He was at his desk, staring into space, a copy of *Monsters from Outer Space* clutched in one hand. When he looked

181

up and saw her, he double-took, dropped the paperback and started to open his mouth to shout.

Ace whipped the pistol out of her pocket. It was livid purple, with a series of red coils at the front and a single green fin on top. It looked lethal. 'You know I'm from the future, right? So if you don't want to be reduced to your constituent quarks, just shut up.'

Macbeth closed his mouth.

'Got some news for you,' she said. 'Brigadier Lethbridge-Stewart is on his way back from Switzerland to inspect this place. I'm here to collect the Doctor.'

The redhead's eyes were fixed on the Flash Gordon pistol. 'Does the Brigadier know about this?'

'No. I really, really hate red tape. So I'm going to put the weapon back in my pocket, and I'm going to keep it aimed at you while we go see the Doctor.'

'There's no need for this, eh, is there?' protested the Scot. 'The Doctor's in our care, and you're welcome to visit.'

'A bit tricky for visitors if you don't tell anyone where you actually are. If you've done anything to him that I don't like – '

'No, no.' Macbeth raised his hand. 'He's just fine.'

In a mental hospital in London, Cristián Alvarez turned in his sleep, disturbed. Nurses went back and forth in the cool darkness, glad of the quiet, no matter how brief.

The room must once have been a large dining hall. They had converted it into some sort of laboratory, complete with those old computers with the chunky coloured lights and big tape DASDs spinning around for all they were worth.

There were scientists with clipboards, someone trying to guess cards from behind a screen, a young girl with electrodes attached to her forehead while she watched a strobing light. The white-coats smiled or nodded at Macbeth as he moved through them, glanced at the short woman in the anorak. He did his very best not to look terrified.

182

No sign of the Doctor. He'd be kept separately, of course, Macbeth's prize project.

A small corridor led off the main room, to a smaller room, perhaps an old bedroom. Macbeth unlocked the door and took Ace inside.

The room was small, cold, no window. A second door led into a tiled *en suite* bathroom. Another hospital bed, another EEG, this one recording meaningless squiggles as it tried to process alien input. 'Close the door,' Ace told Macbeth quietly.

The floor was concrete, the walls white plaster, bare and featureless as the inside of a ping-pong ball. Incongruously, there was an Escher poster on the wall over the bed, two hands drawing one another in a loop that went on forever.

Ace felt something change inside her when she saw the Doctor in the bed, his head propped up by a pile of pillows, the covers pulled up to his shoulders. She realized she'd been expecting a corpse, a dissecting room. If she'd found the Time Lord in jars and sponges she'd have whacked Macbeth like a bug. Now she felt the killing tension go out of her: there was other business to take care of.

The Doctor was the colour of the plastered walls, eyes closed. Wires ran from white discs on his temple and neck to an old-fashioned EEG machine, its needle scratching noisily over a slow-moving reel of paper. Not showing a lot of activity. Was he going grey, grey at the temples? It didn't seem possible.

She wrenched down the covers. He was wearing hospital pyjamas. His wrists and ankles were handcuffed.

'Get those off him,' said Ace. Rage climbed up her spine in lumps. 'What the frag have you been doing to him?'

'Nothing,' said Macbeth, taking a step back. 'Nothing. Really. Just observing him. Trying to look after him.' He carefully produced the key from his pocket, making no sudden moves, and undid the cuffs. 'We had to restrain him. I would have preferred something a lot less crude than this. But we couldn't tranquillize him.'

The Doctor opened his eyes. 'I'm not asleep,' he said, very quietly.

Ace shoved Macbeth to one side and leaned over the Time Lord. 'Hey,' she said. 'Sorry we took so long.'

He seemed to be having trouble focusing on her. 'Ace,' he said, at length. His eyelids flickered again, and the pen of the electroencephalogram went *scritch scritch*, dancing roughly over the paper.

In the hospital, Cristián sat bolt upright, his eyes electric.

'Here we go again,' sighed one of the nurses.

Scritch scritch scritch.

Ace looked from the Doctor to Macbeth to the machine and back again. 'What's this?' She kept the weapon aimed at the paranormalist.

'I don't know,' said Macbeth, peering at the EEG. 'We still haven't been able to determine the significance of these readings.'

'You mean this has happened before?'

The Doctor was sitting up, one hand clutching at the side of the bed, breathing in gulps. Ace started to move towards him, but he waved her back. She actually saw beads of sweat start out of his forehead.

'The blood tests we did – the ones that worked – showed there's still lysergide in his system.' Macbeth traced a finger along the EEG scrawl. 'I think he's having a flashback.'

Cristián screamed.

A wind was blowing. It came out of nowhere, chilling the heated room. 'Oh shit,' said Ace. Macbeth started for the door, but Ace grabbed his sleeve. 'How often?' she shouted, over the rising sound of the storm.

'Once every four to six hours,' he yelled.

The Doctor's eyes were open wide, the pupils shrunk to points. He was seeing something else, not the room, not them, something else.

And then there was an explosion, inaudible and unseen. Ace felt it ripple through her, sickeningly, pushing her back as she tried to get to the Time Lord. Macbeth was thrown against the EEG machine, knocking it off its table.

The Doctor convulsed and fell halfway off the bed, tangled in the sheets. His back arched against the floor.

Ace forced her way through the tempest, shouting, her voice carried away. She knelt beside him, reaching for his hand.

Her fingers passed right through him.

'Sing for me,' said Huitzilin.

The Doctor screamed.

The storm stopped, suddenly, the wind falling away into nothing, leaving only the cry.

Ace got a grip on his fingers as he solidified, grabbing her hand for support. And then he started laughing. It was a weak sound, but triumphant.

Every four to six hours. Jesus.

She tried to imagine the long days in the room, researchers coming and going with clipboards and needles and little trays of food, the long silences, and the screaming in between.

'I'm taking him out of here,' she told Macbeth, who was sitting next to the shattered EEG machine, looking dazed.

'You can't,' said the lieutenant. 'Do you think you can handle that any better than we can? Do you realize what happened the first time he tripped? People died. We still haven't found those hippies. A rabbi in Birmingham went out of his mind and started talking in tongues. In Lancaster, the lunatics burnt down the asylum. One of my psychics miscarried, for Chrissake – '

Ace hauled the Doctor to his feet. He was exhausted, barely able to stand up. 'What's the date?' he muttered.

Ace slid the coloured plastic gun into her sleeve. 'Come on,' she snarled at Macbeth.

'It must be, what,' the Doctor was saying hoarsely, 'January the tenth?'

'Yeah, you missed Christmas. Take it easy, Doctor. Everything's going to be fine.'

* * *

A hundred miles away, in London, Cristián Alvarez was sobbing for his mother, his grandmother. Anyone. The nurse said soothing words and tucked him back into bed.

Bernice's mouth and jaw went hard when she saw the Doctor. The Renault's engine started with a roar as Ace bundled him into the back seat. 'It all went all right?'

'Smooth as milk,' said Ace. She wrapped a couple of blankets around the Doctor. He wasn't taking any notice of the cold, or anything at all for that matter. 'Nobody gave us any bother.'

Macbeth fidgeted outside the car, glancing back at the house. 'Is he going to be all right?' There was serious concern in his voice, and something else, something pleading. Like a child who didn't want his favourite toy taken away.

Ace sighted along the barrel of her pistol at him. 'Maybe we should take you away in our UFO,' she said. 'Do experiments on you. What d'you think, Bernice?'

'What, keep someone locked up, cut off from their friends?' grated the archaeologist. 'Perform experiments on them without their consent? I'd call that torture. What would you call it, Lieutenant?'

Ace slammed the door. Macbeth was virtually hopping from foot to foot. 'Please,' he said, 'I only want to know – '

But the Renault was already backing out onto the road, the melting snow squelching under its tyres. Macbeth gaped at it.

Suddenly the car stopped. The door opened, and Ace got out, striding towards him across the snow. Benny's face appeared at the window, watching with a worried expression.

'Nearly forgot something,' said Ace.

'Yes?' said Macbeth, hope trembling in his lungs. 'Yes?'

Ace smiled, and broke his nose.

They changed cars at Tunbridge Wells, swapping the Renault for a Mini. Ace dived into a pub, emerging with sandwiches and crisps. The sky was overcast, a single metallic colour from horizon to horizon.

Bernice climbed into the back with the Doctor. The Time Lord was leaning on the window, covered in blankets, his eyes half-open. He'd barely noticed when they'd moved him into the new car. Now Bernice nudged him gently, stroking his hair. 'Lunchtime,' she said with tinny cheerfulness. She peered more closely at the grey in his hair. Mixed in with the dark strands were tiny white feathers.

She met Ace's eyes in the rear-view mirror. Ace was thinking about the time he'd dislocated his arm (which had been her fault), the sudden startling realization that he was made out of flesh and blood, that he could be *damaged*. Usually finding the Doctor was a good sign that things were going to be all right. Not this time, then.

Ace pulled out onto the road, steering with one hand while she ate crisps with the other. 'Cunning,' she said. 'Fool your enemy into thinking they've got the upper hand by letting them kick the shit out of you.'

'Oh yes?' said the Doctor from the back seat. 'Is that what you think?'

Ace swore. The car skidded as she straightened it.

'Conference,' said the Doctor.

They conferenced in the kitchen in Allen Road. The house seemed quiet, muffled by snow; the jungle of the garden was silent and dead-looking. Inside the kitchen even the air seemed to be hovering, waiting for something.

The Doctor drank tea, pouring milk out of the bottle Ace had bought. His face had a strange look; he was ill, but it made him powerful, like some sort of tribal healer high on funny leaves. His eyes burned, the pupils tiny in rings of bright blue.

'The enemy's name is Huitzilin,' he said.

'Huitzilopochtli?' asked Bernice.

'Just Huitzilin. Once upon a time, he was an Aztec chief. Long before they were *Mexica*, when they were still nomads, wandering in the wilderness. They were sheltering

187

in a cave when they found something the Exxilons had left behind.'

'Aliens interfering in human development,' said Ace.

'In this case, just an accident. They left behind a bit of radioactive rubbish. The result would have been mostly poisoning, cancer. But in one set of chromosomes . . .'

'Huitzilin was a mutant?'

The Doctor nodded. 'He was – he is one of the most powerful psychics ever to exist on Earth. When the time came to die, Huitzilin used his power to . . . not to stop his physical death, which he had already postponed. To survive.'

He stirred his third cup of tea thoughtfully. Ace had bandaged his wrist, where the UNIT handcuffs had chafed the lacerations. 'Think of it this way. A living person is real. A dead person stops being real, and becomes imaginary, existing only in the memory and the imagination of other people. Huitzilin survived as an imaginary person.'

'Like a ghost?' said Ace.

'Like a Jungian archetype?' asked Bernice. 'Present in the collective unconscious?'

'Either of those analogies will do. But he survived. His was the ghost voice that led the Aztecs. And being non-corporeal, he needed a new kind of food.'

'The sacrifices,' said Bernice.

'When a person dies,' said the Doctor, 'they give up their reality. Or they produce a certain amount of psychic energy . . . it's not that different to the mundane food chain. The eagle eats sunlight energy stored in the form of a rabbit.'

'Macbeth said the police are still looking for John and Lizzie,' said Ace.

'They won't find them,' said the Doctor. He pushed his tea away.

Bernice was rubbing her thumb across her forehead, agitated. 'Where'd all this information come from?'

'The door swings both ways,' said the Doctor.

'Oh my God,' said Bernice. 'You're his *ixiptla*.' She stood up suddenly, hands gripping the back of the chair. The penny had finally dropped. 'His *ixiptla*.'

'We're one and the same person,' said the Doctor. He smiled whitely. 'Twice now he's tried to open the gate between us. The second time, he succeeded. For six minutes and twenty seconds, I didn't exist.'

'At the Happening,' said Bernice. The panic she'd felt in the basement came crawling back up her spine. 'And he ate Lizzie and John. He ate them.'

'The whole thing was premature of him,' said the Doctor. 'Even with that energy, he couldn't make the switch permanent. We haven't grown close enough together for that. It will take some time . . . and whenever the two of us blur together, I get to see into his vicious little mind. Know thine enemy. I know who he is, and who he was, and what he wants. And I know how to kill him. *C'est double plaisir de tromper un troumpeur*.'

Ace had not moved a muscle. 'So,' she said. 'What do we do now?'

The Doctor grinned ferociously.

'We win.'

Soldiers were all around him.

He sat in the foyer, catching flashes of green and olive out of the corner of his eye. They were carrying furniture, phones and things, computers in huge cardboard boxes. A stout sergeant went past, clutching a vase of flowers.

The nurses helped the subjects out, some still dressed in their pyjamas, swaddled in two or three dressing-gowns against the cold. Researchers carried clipboards and pieces of electrical equipment, the wires trailing down.

Everything must go, Macbeth thought blankly.

The whole place had been closed down. Orders from the very top, the very, very top. There would be a huge investigation. He would probably get court-martialled or something.

But I'm not a soldier, he thought. Blankly.

The extraterrestrial was gone. He had never had a chance to ask the questions he wanted answers to, needed answers to. He had dipped his toes in a far ocean and he would never be allowed to swim there. Never. UNIT would take away the money and the research and he'd never be able to work there again. It was gone, all gone, all wiped clean. Blank.

Blank.

And deep inside him, something Blue was itching –

In the attic, Ace was sitting cross-legged on the end of the big brass bed, like a guard dog. She had her anorak on; it was freezing cold. The Doctor was wearing thick flannel pyjamas and a dressing-gown with a little embroidered cat on the pocket, and the quilt was pulled up to his middle.

He lay on his side, fingers digging into the pillow, mouth open as he dragged in ragged lungfuls of the chilly air. His eyes were squeezed shut, the smile lines standing out sharply against the pallor of his skin. He was back in that hippie cellar. Ace didn't want to know what he was seeing.

Even when the flashback finished he did not completely relax, but lay still, just concentrating on breathing. A bead of sweat ran down his face and onto the feather-stuffed pillow.

Ace looked at her watch and said, 'It's been nine hours.'

'Mmm,' said the Doctor weakly. 'Getting fewer and further between. He's got something else to concentrate on.'

'You should try to get some kip.'

'I don't think I dare,' said the Doctor.

'Hey?'

'What if he should take me in my dreams?'

Ace said, 'Lie on your stomach.'

The Doctor rolled over. The bed rocked as Ace sat down next to him, gripping his shoulders. 'What're you going to do?' he asked, muffledly.

She pushed her fingers through the material of the dressing-gown and started to massage his shoulders. This close she could see the feathers in his hair, some of them fine and downy like a baby bird's, some of them longer and fully formed. She'd watched them sprouting as he'd struggled with Huitzilin. 'Better?' she asked, shoving her thumbs into his shoulder-blades.

'Argh,' he said.

'How long're we going to stay for?' she asked. 'We're not safe, not even here. Not from a ghost. Especially a portable one.'

'Mmm. Not long. Lots to do. Won't be so bad while his attention is elsewhere.'

'Close your eyes. Close your eyes and relax.'

The Doctor's eyelids half-lowered. 'I've been possessed more times than I can remember. Usually it's like being inside a fist. Something comes from outside and grabs you.'

'Mmmm.'

'This is different. It comes from inside. The way a head-ache does, or an idea.'

'And in the meantime,' said Ace, 'you can read the monster's mind.'

'Yes.'

'So,' she asked, 'what are we going to do if the monster takes you over first?'

'Well,' said the Doctor, 'if that does happen, there's something I'd like you to do for me.'

She took her hands away from his shoulders and got up off the bed. Slowly the Doctor rolled onto his back and looked up at her.

'Think of it as damage control,' he said.

'No.'

'Or triage. Anyone you can't save you have to leave to die. You know that.'

'No crukking way.'

'Benny can't do it. You have to.'

She reached up and pushed a stray bit of hair out of her face. 'All right,' she said. 'Why waste any more time?' She reached into the anorak and brought out her Flash Gordon gun. She did something to it, manipulating controls embedded in the plastic. She pointed it right between his eyes.

He focused past it, to her face. His pupils snapped open, black overtaking the blue. He was surprised. Beautiful.

'That's a child's toy,' he said.

'Nope,' said Ace. 'It's a lightweight flechette thrower.'

More surprise.

'You took this thing on board,' she said. 'You're the door it can use to get into our world.' The Doctor lay very still, watching her. Was she supposed to do this? *Who cares?* 'It's screwed around with everybody's heads and it's killed a lot of people. It's too bloody dangerous to let out.' She spoke steadily, keeping the gun aimed at his face. 'And now you're telling me you can't control it? You're ready to give up? Ready to die? Are you ready to die? Are you?'

She pulled the trigger.

The Doctor flinched.

The gun went *click*.

He *flinched*.

'Nah,' said Ace. 'Didn't think so.' She stowed the flechette pistol away and walked out.

Beautiful.

Interlude 2

The old women stroked his face with their leathery hands, soft as kid gloves, cool fingertips brushing back the hair from his temples. It was just another hallucination, another of the diminishing flashbacks, but he could feel the texture of their ragged fingernails as they smoothed out the tension in his face and shoulders, calling him baby, baby.

I'm no one's sacrifice. No one's.

There was a laugh like a bell jingling.

His head was full of gibberish, like a cupboard that had been pulled open, all the junk tumbling out onto some hapless cartoon character.

Peter Pan ripped loose his shadow. The shadow danced over the walls, reaching out black and sticky hands to smother little Peter, not so immortal as he thought he was. Wendy was off-stage, screaming something, but Peter's mouth was full of shadow, tasting of dust and gunpowder, blood and cactus wine.

The old women cooed to him like a newborn, cradling his tired body, their voices dripping like raindrops into his head. Go to sleep, little midwife, go to sleep, melt into the shadows.

Who was he the midwife for? What would be born?

What do you want me for?

A grin in the dark. *Lunch.*

What, you've never heard of pizza?

Wonder what the Brigadier makes of all this? Didn't happen the first time round. Must ask him next I see him.

Wonder if he noticed the change, noticed his past shifting . . . someone playing around with time . . . somebody playing . . .

Don't like this pawn side-stepping me, the pawns should move in a straight line, not hop about unexpectedly. Another *en passant* from Ace? Just in passing? Once upon a time, a man was travelling across a field. Suddenly, he was set upon by a tiger. He ran from the tiger, and found himself at the edge of a cliff.

Don't like not knowing the enemy.

Jangling laughter.

The real enemy, the shadow behind the shadow. Behind every great monster stands a great megalomaniac. Why do they want me? Who's the enemy? Who is it? Who? S/he's trying one experiment after another. This one's a butterfly effect: tiny change in time, tumbling down the years, blowing out into a storm. Doesn't care about the damage done. If Huitzilin gets out –

Don't like having to play Mina *and* Van Helsing.

Taste of blood and cactus wine. The old women feeding him a courage potion, washing the dregs from the sacrificial knife into the liquid, pouring it onto his tongue. He choked and spat out the foul stuff, and they touched his face and hair, soothing, soothing.

The man caught hold of a vine growing at the edge of the cliff, and, in desperation, swung himself over the edge. The tiger looked down at him, roaring hungrily. Another roar came from below, and the man looked down to see a second tiger at the bottom of the cliff.

Molly bringing him a steak, a stake, ha ha. Tlotoxl and his stone knife, hovering by the altar, ready to slay the *ixiptla*. Benny screaming on the altar, howling out her horror. Ace with an obsidian knife. Ace with a knife. Ace. *En passant.*

A white mouse and a black mouse began to nibble at the vine.

The old women held him in their arms and crooned to him, baby, baby, until the darkness got into his face and he was back in the bed, the cool air brushing the back of his neck, bright drops of sweat running onto the sheet from his face.

No more psilocybin, no more lysergide. Only Huitzilin's voice coming out of the Blue, singing, singing, *sing for me*. Dead man dancing in his hearts. Just a little bit longer, if he could hold on for just a little bit longer, another day, another hour, another heartsbeat, if he could stand it for just a little longer –

The enemy wanted him, wanted him, they would crush universes to have him. Make *him* crush universes, snapping the bright mainspring of their existence, leaving them to run down, down into the darkness. Thousands and thousands of lives snuffing out, sobbing as their candle burned at both ends and was gone. Doesn't care about the damage done. You reprobate, you abomination, you demon, how could you make me do that? How could you?

Dead man dancing in his hearts. Soft laughter behind his eyes. *The healer becomes the warrior.*

Keeping hold of the vine with one hand, the man reached out and picked a strawberry that was growing from the cliff face. Oh, how sweet it tasted –

Chapter 13

Because He Doesn't Know the Words

London, January 30, 1969

Too much time.

They had spent altogether too much time in hospitals during this jolly jaunt. Hospitals, thought Bernice, were not hospitable. They were the last place you wanted to find yourself – and probably the last place you would find yourself.

She stood in the snowy hospital gardens, hands stuffed deep into the pockets of her duffle-coat. The asylum was a great angular brick, dozens of windows reflecting the pale, searing sky. She imagined the story behind each pane, tales of illness, of aloneness. She imagined the horrors of twentieth-century medical treatment and didn't want to know.

The building didn't seem to be any warmer on the inside. Or was it an illusion of the cool grey walls? The nurses went about in dazzling uniforms, their faces as pale as their white stockings in the fluorescent light. Their bare arms looked frozen, inhuman. This was what she'd come to rescue Cristián from. But how would she find him?

She didn't have to. He was waiting for her in the foyer. 'I knew you'd be coming,' he said mournfully.

Cristián the eighteen year old, skinny and miserable inside his oversized pyjamas, a name-tag looped around his wrist to mark him as the hospital's property. Cristián the fifty year old, dissolving in a shower of sparkles. Past and future, collapsing together into a cosmic pudding. Benny closed her eyes, suddenly convinced of the unreality of it all.

'Are you all right?'

'Sorry,' she said. 'Just having an existential moment.' She sat down.

Cristián had changed a lot in three weeks. His long hair had been shorn into respectability by some zealous nurse, but that wasn't it. There was something different, something about his face. He didn't look eighteen any more. He looked old.

'How are you?' she ventured.

'Better,' he said. 'The fits have stopped, and I – I guess I'll be going home in a couple of weeks.'

'Back to Mexico?'

'Yes.'

'How did you know I was coming?'

Cristián scratched the back of his neck slowly, as though it required a lot of attention. 'Those army people have been asking me a lot of questions. About your UFO, and coming from the future.' He said it blankly, as though it just wasn't interesting. 'When the Blue was grabbing at the Doctor, my head would just open out, you know? I understood a lot of things I don't understand now.'

'Grabbing at him?'

'Yeah, trying to get him. Over and over.' He looked at her dully. 'Why'd you leave me there?'

'We didn't have any choice. Macbeth split us all up.' At least the lieutenant hadn't squirrelled Cris away somewhere, sticking wires in his head to find out what was different about his brain. Or had the hospital been doing that? 'We've been trying to find you for weeks, to help you. To rescue you.'

'I shouldn't have to be rescued. The trap wasn't set for me.' He pushed his fists against his eyes and bent over in the chair, looking like a broken doll. 'I don't want to be rescued. Just leave me alone. Please.'

Benny stood up. There was nothing she could do to help

him. Time would just tick on for Cristián, flavourless years following one another to the final catastrophe. Even his last moment of heroism wouldn't matter, as Huitzilin reached out to kill him as casually as swatting a fly.

The anger grabbed hold of her feet and she strode across the echoing floor and out into the snow. If he looked up in surprise, watching her go, she didn't see.

No more victims. No more victims!

'No more victims!' she shouted, kicking a beer can into the gutter. 'Enough of this!'

Hyde Park was crammed with people. Ace's taxi slid past the demonstration, faces reflected in the windows for a moment, gone again. The sound of bagpipes and drums rose over the noise of the crowd.

The taxi driver had been muttering under his breath all the way from St John's Wood. Apparently London was on strike today – no phones, no post, no banks. Of course, taxi drivers had to keep on working, despite the demonstrators choking the streets as though they thought it was some sort of holiday. A bunch of anarchists, the lot of them.

A day of chaos, thought Ace. Appropriate.

She'd spent ages trying to hide a weapon under the minidress. In desperation she'd eventually stowed a gun in her handbag. When she reached for her purse to pay the driver, she discovered that the gun had been replaced by a large potato. Now that, she thought, was just downright unfair of the Doctor.

Savile Row was singing to itself. Ace watched the taxi go, waiting for the sound to resolve: guitars being tuned, microphones being tested. The noise seemed to come from all around. People in the street were craning their necks, trying to make out the source of the sounds. Men in ties and women in flowered blouses leaned out of windows.

Ace smiled. She remembered the time U2 had started performing on top of a building in LA, until the police had come – it had made a good video, anyway.

'Okay,' said John Lennon, his voice booming out over

the street, and the sounds further clarified themselves into the beginning of a song.

Ace crossed the street and went into the building opposite Apple Corp. There was a lift. She took the stairs.

On the third floor she passed a typing pool crowded around a window, and paused to peer over their shoulders, unnoticed. Across the street, Apple's roof was covered in wires and amplifiers. Paul was singing in that neat and tidy voice of his, long hair blowing in the wind. Ace spotted Yoko sitting to one side of the group, a small bundle of dark hair and clothes looking rather miserable in the cold.

And there was the man himself: long hair, sideburns, those trademark glasses, a fox fur coat. Like a photograph in 3D. She could see his fingers moving over the neck of the guitar, dancing from chord to chord.

The secretaries were saying what a surprise it was, how lucky they were to be there at just the right place and the right time to catch this little moment in history: the Beatles' last concert. Ace left them behind, found another set of stairs.

How much had the Beatles thought about the dangers of taking to their roof? Probably they'd just bundled their equipment upstairs and gone for broke. After all, an assassin would have to be pretty quick off the mark to take advantage of something this impromptu. Unless, of course, they knew it was coming.

Top of the stairs. She kicked open the cleaners' store-room door.

It required one second to take in the random detail of the room, sink and shelves and boxes and buckets, another second to make out the shape of her quarry against the grimy window.

The cleaner turned, a portly woman in a housecoat. Winter glared in through the dusty glass, making her a rounded, faceless silhouette, the long shape of a rifle clutched in her podgy hands. She was already bringing it up when Ace strode in, knocked it neatly out of her grasp and applied a nerve pinch to the base of her neck that sent her to the floor like a deflated balloon. 'Ooh, Mrs Knicker-bocker's exploded,' said Ace, picking up the gun.

The Doctor had been wrong about the precise make of rifle, but otherwise, everything was as he'd described it, down to the ashtray on the window-sill. At last she was beginning to understand what the Time Lord was up to: his psychic connection with Huitzilin was a two-way street. What harm could the Aztec do when the Doctor knew everything he thought?

She stubbed out the charlady's cigarette. She'd been having a quiet smoke, waiting for the concert to get under way. Huitzilin wanted people to see this; their horror would be the sauce on his meal. Ripples of rage and despair would have spread out from this one act. Rippling out –

She felt a violent lurch between her lungs, just like the time in the lift. She grabbed the window-sill, trying to keep a grip on the rifle, but it wasn't an attack, it was just an overwhelming sense of presence. His presence.

He pushed a question into her head: why was she fighting him?

Because he was a monster, she answered, and she fought monsters.

But he was the god of war, and she was a warrior. She could always just open the window and do what she'd been trained to do. Do what she was good at.

Ace reeled to the sink, the gun clattering out of her hands. She gripped the rusty sides and threw up. She wrenched open the tap and flushed out her mouth, splashed her face and hands. She was filthy, she was contaminated –

It's because you've been with him too long, said Huitzilin. *You might have been a waitress, you might have been a chemist, you might have been a mother if not for him –*

I'll stick with the Doctor! she protested.

Little girl, said Huitzilin, *he and I are the same person.*

Ace threw up again.

Outside, the guitars paused. There was a smattering of applause, and John's voice again, ringing out across the street. 'I'd like to say thank you on behalf of the group and ourselves, and I hope we passed the audition.'

* * *

200

The TARDIS stood in the shade of the trees growing alongside Abbey Road. It was still in its police box guise – certainly made it easier to find, as long as you didn't make an idiot of yourself trying to walk into a real police box.

Benny and Ace walked side by side down the street. They passed the groupies outside the studio and Paul's house across the road. The hippies took no notice of the time travellers, hanging out for a glimpse or a wave.

'How'd it go?' asked Benny.

'Fine,' said Ace. 'No problems. How about you?'

'Oh, fine.'

They kept walking.

Benny glanced up and down the street as they went into the TARDIS. It probably didn't matter if anyone saw them dematerialize. After all, what would they do? Tell the police one of their boxes had been pinched?

The doors closed behind them and the rotor began its smooth pumping motion. Slides and controls operated themselves in a ghostly dance. Ace ran her eyes over the console, irritated. The Doctor wouldn't let her fly the machine, but he couldn't even be bothered to pilot the TARDIS himself.

From somewhere in the maze of corridors, there was an irregular clattering noise. They followed the sound until they came to a huge, empty room. The Doctor ignored them, his eyes fixed on an archery target perhaps a hundred feet away. The tall bamboo bow was drawn back as far as it would go, the long arrow protruding by a foot or more. He stood utterly still, shoulders and face completely relaxed despite the tension in the string.

Abruptly he let the arrow fly. It shot past the target and made a drum roll sound as it struck the back wall.

The Doctor sat down on the floor, holding the bow across his lap. 'Not one hit,' he said, running his hands through his dishevelled hair.

Benny sat cross-legged on the floor, a little distance from him. 'Can't you concentrate?' she said gently.

'I can't stop concentrating.' He was glowing with fever. 'Tell me about Cristián.'

'They're letting him go home.'

The Doctor nodded slowly. 'Best thing for him. He's been through rather too much. And he won't be able to remember it clearly.'

Ace was leaning on the wall, arms folded. 'That's your doing?'

'Our minds were slammed together,' said the Doctor. 'Everything melted together.' He put a hand to his forehead. 'Far too much for Cristián to cope with. Perhaps it's for the best that he doesn't remember.'

'There are some things that man was not meant to know,' said Benny.

'Don't joke,' said Ace. 'You don't ever want to be inside his head.'

The Doctor didn't appear to be listening to them. 'We still need Cristián's help. He's one of the few clues we have, the few links with the Blue.'

Benny said, 'New York. We know when he was there. All we have to do is find him in a city of fifteen million.'

Ace scuffed the floor with her shoe. 'Haven't we put him through enough yet?' The Doctor looked up at her sharply, and she concentrated on tracing a complex pattern on the floor with her toe. 'Why don't you just track down Huitzilin yourself?'

'Not yet. I don't want to get any closer.' He plucked the bowstring, and it gave off a deep, disconsolate note. 'Supposed to scare off evil spirits,' he said.

Ace said, 'You said something had changed. When we were in Tenochtitlan.' It seemed like centuries ago.

'Huitzilin couldn't have gone on as a ghost. The amount of power required to maintain that state would have increased exponentially. Like Xanxia,' he said thoughtfully. 'The crisis point was the dedication of the Great Temple.' The Doctor stood up, nocking another of the long arrows. 'Huitzilin was desperate; he thought that if he could exceed a critical amount of energy, he'd stabilize. He was wrong. He should simply have dissipated, like a handful of smoke. But someone dipped into the stream of time and made a tiny change.'

'Someone who?' said Ace. 'Huitzilin himself?'

'No,' said the Doctor. 'Huitzilin was the effect, not the cause.'

'If they've manipulated the time lines,' said Benny, 'why don't we just manipulate them right back again?'

The Doctor blew out a long, slow breath. 'Do you know why so few species develop time travel?'

'Why?'

'They keep wiping themselves out of existence. They always insist on tinkering with their history. Perhaps thousands of worlds are developing temporal technology every day, and simply erasing themselves. A tidy self-regulating mechanism.'

'We might create something worse,' said Benny. 'Like – like the Silurians' world.'

Ace said, 'But we're stopping him making changes to the time line. We've done it twice.'

The Doctor sighted along the arrow at the target. 'He's not going to let us spoil his fun like this,' he said. 'He's already found someone who wants to bring about the end of the world.'

'The cold war is still on, isn't it?' said Benny, alarmed. 'He's not going to push any red buttons, is he?'

'He wouldn't wipe out his food stock. He wants something vicious, something that will emotionally entangle people. A handful of gruesome murders will be adequate. These days an atrocity can travel around the world by satellite in a day.'

'But he didn't get to kill John Lennon,' said Ace.

'Oh grief,' said Benny. 'Helter Skelter.'

'*Bozhe moi*,' said Ace, pressing her palm against her forehead. 'Charles Manson. Fix one leak and another one opens up.'

'The Beatles,' said Benny. 'Manson said he knew the end of the world was coming from listening to the Beatles. And he murdered all those people to start it happening.'

'Huitzilin just wants to make sure we don't miss the point.' The Doctor pulled back the string.

'Enough of this,' said Ace. 'Let's trash the bastard.'

203

'But if we destroy Huitzilin,' said Benny, 'what happens to –'

'*KYA!*' shouted Ace.

The Doctor, startled, let the arrow fly. It struck the target dead centre.

New York City, December 8, 1980

The receiver had been torn clear off the wire. A thick tube of electric skin hung down from the phone, trailing the ragged ends of copper wires. 'No problem,' said the Doctor, and went to work.

Benny and Ace stood in front of the phone booth, obscuring it. New York was big and dirty and packed wall to wall with people. There was a seemingly permanent traffic jam, bikes and motorbikes winding their way through the stalled mass of cars. Fumes hung in the cold air.

Benny was watching the people. In ten minutes, she had seen punks in silk shirts and slit sunglasses, a pair of tall blacks in African costumes, a troupe of street mimes, a tour group, a book-laden scholar in a *chador*, a small crowd of prostitutes in coloured wigs, several blank-faced police, and twelve cockroaches as big as her thumb.

A bag lady trundled along the pavement with a supermarket trolley of unidentifiable objects. Benny remembered Zamina calling them *catfood monsters*, remembered Ocelot's tin with the cat on the label. *Grief*, said a little voice in her head, *these people eat pet food to stay alive*. People moved around the homeless woman in smooth twin streams. No one looked at her, she looked at no one. Benny realized she was just part of the garbage that littered the streets, part of the long chain that began with junk food and ended with junk people.

The Doctor had soldered the loose ends of the phone cord to a bundle of optical fibres and was trying to plug the improvised mess into the back of his palmtop computer. Figures started flashing across its liquid crystal screen. He typed used a ball-point pen, leaving smudged black dots on the miniature keys.

Somewhere out there in the gathering evening was a lone assassin with a Charter Arms Undercover .38 revolver.

Much as she was fascinated by the twentieth century, it was difficult to keep a scientific perspective on it when you were hip-deep in New Yorkers. Benny hugged her arms to herself, watching them pass by, eyes carefully averted from one another. It was the opposite of Mexico City; the *chilangos* were so curious about everyone else's business that muggers didn't have a chance. In the Big Apple, schoolchildren were taught how to hide under their desks from automatic gunfire.

All the homeless and all the victims. Five centuries on, and they were still practising human sacrifice.

'Hail a taxi,' said the Doctor.

Ace didn't move. Bernice went to the roadside, where the traffic was beginning to trickle more quickly. She waved at a passing cab, a huge, rounded yellow contraption like a particularly large cockroach. The doorhandles were worn loops of rope. The driver wound down three-quarters of an inch of window and said 'Where to?'

The Doctor passed a strip of computer print-out through the gap.

The taxi ride was brief and quiet. Ace sat on Benny's left and stared out the window. The Doctor sat on Benny's right and stared out the window. She was watching the feathers in his hair grow. At first she thought it was an illusion of the irregular light – the feathers couldn't really be moving, be moving around in his hair, could they?

They were getting longer. And some of the white ones were becoming coloured, taking on pastel shades as they lengthened, lemon and rose and metallic green. It wasn't quite the most horrible thing she had ever seen, but it made her stomach lurch as the taxi turned a corner. On the other hand, in New York, who was going to notice?

Cristián opened his door, yelled involuntarily and slammed it closed again.

Benny knocked again, slowly.

The door pulled reluctantly open again. Cris looked at her. He was grown up, not yet going grey.

'How did you find me?' he said dully.

'The Doctor used the hotel reservations computer,' she explained. 'Do you think we can come in?'

Cris clung onto the door. After a moment, he let it swing open.

There were enough contemporary jokes about New York hotel rooms to compose a thesis on the subject. Benny was pleased to see that the room was not entirely awful. Yes, it had been painted a lurid shade of green; yes, there were rusty bars on the inside of the window; yes, there were loose wires hanging from the ceiling of the bathroom; but there was enough room to cram four people inside, and there weren't any roaches.

Cris sat down on the bed, next to a dresser, keeping the Gideon's Bible between them. The Doctor went to a chair next to the window and peered out through the bars. Ace leaned on the wall next to the door, as though she were expecting someone to break in.

'Long time no see,' said Cris sourly. 'Why now?'

Benny looked at the Doctor. The Time Lord just stared out the window. Cristián looked at his hair and whispered, 'Jesus.'

'We need your help,' she said gently.

'Help,' Cris laughed. 'Help. I've had nothing but help. Pills and tests and therapy, and all of it useless. I've had more help than I know what to do with – '

He tugged open the dresser drawer and extracted a pistol. Bernice felt Ace's sudden attention between her shoulder-blades, the change from disinterested slouch to combat-ready tension. Was she armed? 'In North America, everyone has to have a gun, for protection, because everyone else has a gun.'

Suddenly he was pointing the thing at the Doctor. He was holding it all wrong, but it didn't take expertise, not at a range of two feet. 'I bought this to scare off the big bad monster,' said Cris hysterically. 'Do you think it'll frighten him? Hey? Do you think it'll stop him in his tracks?'

'Ace,' said the Doctor, 'disarm him.'

There was motion too quick for Benny to follow. When it resolved itself, Cris was lying on the floor behind the bed, looking terrified. Ace was holding his pistol. Bernice found that she had put herself between Cris and the Doctor.

The Time Lord was still staring out the window. 'Don't kill him,' he added, almost as an afterthought.

Ace tossed the pistol back into the drawer and shut it. She sat down on top of the dresser, crossing her legs.

Cris started crying. It looked pathetic. 'I came here to get away from it,' he sobbed. 'But it followed me. It's coming to get me. What's it want? What's it here for?'

'Perhaps you're following it,' said the Doctor. 'You followed it to London.'

Cristián shook his head. 'I don't understand,' he said. 'It's not fair.'

'Handkerchief,' Benny told the Doctor. He didn't respond. She pulled it out of his pocket and gave it to Cris. He blew his nose loudly.

'I'm going for a walk,' said the Doctor.

'Oh,' said Benny. 'Anywhere in particular?'

The reply was a moment in coming, as though they were communicating by satellite. 'I'm just going to wander the streets aimlessly.'

He handed Ace something and went out the door. 'Oh fine,' said Benny. 'And why not? It's not as though we have anything important to do.'

Cris said, 'It's all going to happen again, isn't it?'

Ace handed Benny the palmtop computer. 'Stay here.'

Ace couldn't make herself believe that the Doctor didn't know she was following him. So she knew that he knew. Did he know that she knew that he knew? Smeg!

She stayed perhaps a block behind him. He did not turn to look at her, but she couldn't shake the feeling that he was watching her.

His path through New York was erratic, elaborately purposeless. He stopped at a hot dog stand and had a long chat with the vendor. He went up one street, changed his mind, and walked back down it against the flow of the crowd.

He stopped on a corner and hovered as if lost, then abruptly went into a sidewalk café thick with jazz music and cigarette smoke.

He sat with a bag lady on the steps of a tenement house, watching two boys graffiti-ing the wall and the street signs, while the starlight tried to push its way through the pollution. Ace watched them from the shadows, two odd figures in a pool of yellow light.

What was he looking for? What was he trying to find? Or was he trying to get away from something?

Professor Summerfield sat at the writing desk with the complimentary pen clamped between her teeth. The Doctor's palmtop was attached by electric spaghetti to the phone, which beeped occasionally, as though irritated by the intrusion. The LCD flickered rapidly as the palmtop searched for a short file of keywords.

Cris sat on the bed and watched her, clutching the pillow to his chest. 'Any luck yet?' he asked.

'Mmmm,' she said. 'No, not really. It's slow work. Not many of the big computers are talking to one another. We're really ten years too early for this.'

Cris nodded distractedly. The Blue was curling up his spine in sticky ripples. All these years he had been hiding away from it, buried in the crowds in Mexico. And now they'd followed him here. How'd they known he'd be here? What was significant about this particular day?

'I came up here for a holiday,' he said. 'They said I ought to have a holiday. I've been stuck in this room ever since I got here.'

Benny turned away from her computer. 'Agoraphobia,' she said.

'I can't go to work any more,' he said. 'I can't even go shopping. I don't know what I'm going to do.' His eyes watered over again. 'Look at me, I'm just a *bambino*.'

Maybe they'd come here because today was the day he died.

Professor Summerfield was watching him, doing her best to look sympathetic. Suddenly there was a tremendous knot in his chest. 'I'm just going to get a glass of water,' he said.

The Doctor's wanderings had reached their inevitable destination. He stood at the mouth of an alley, almost invisible in the shadows. Ace was perhaps fifty feet away from him, watching him watching.

When she was a little girl she had seen a charity thing at the shops, a great plastic parabolic dish with a container under it. You let a coin go at the rim of the dish and it rolled all over the place in repeated curving patterns. But no matter where it started from, the coin always ended up in the centre, falling through the little hole into the container.

The limo pulled up outside the apartment building. Ace looked at her watch. Dead on time.

The passengers were silhouettes, anonymous in the warm night. She got out first. He followed, carrying something. Groceries, maybe.

The Doctor was going to try and stop it. That's why he was here, that's what had drawn him here. He was going to try and get in the way. She'd have to run – tackle him, get him down –

Just as they were going through the gate, a voice said, 'Mr Lennon?' John turned at the sound of his name.

The Doctor did not move.

There were five shots and a scream.

A great wave of Blue crashed down over everything, blowing away from the sound of the gunfire. The walls of the alley channelled it like a firestorm, pushing the Time Lord back as though it were something physical. Ace felt it rip through her, nauseating, boiling cold.

She was in time to catch the Doctor as he fell. She felt ice inside her flesh as his fingers slid through her shoulders, desperate for a grip on reality. The feathers in his hair curled and blossomed, and he sizzled with energy, neon

209

lines tracing the movements of his limbs, Huitzilin's power spiralling outward from the human sacrifice.

It hadn't been the Doctor's idea to come here after all. Huitzilin had dragged him here, dragged him here to the human sacrifice.

'No,' said Ace. 'Don't you dare!'

She slapped the Doctor's face, as hard as she could. He twisted his head round to look at her, and she felt Huitzilin's gaze squirming in her guts. She cried out, 'You're not him, you're not him!'

Was this it? She didn't have a weapon, what would she do?

'Sing for me,' said Huitzilin.

'I will not!' shouted the Doctor.

She raised her hand to strike him once more, but the silent storm was beginning to calm. The crackling light faded into a nimbus and finally back into darkness. Streaks and spots danced in front of her eyes.

There were sirens, now, no louder than the sound of poor Yoko screaming and screaming. Jesus. What was the point of saving Lennon in sixty-nine when this was going to happen to him?

'Consider,' said the Doctor hoarsely, 'the ice-cream cone.'

He leaned his head on her shoulder, his hair soaked through with sweat. She wrapped her arms around him, listening, not sure if she were taking in the words.

'The ice-cream cone is immensely clever. No matter how much of it you eat, you always have a cone, until it finally diminishes to a point and is gone.'

'What's your favourite flavour?' she asked, frightened by the note of hysteria in her voice. She found herself rocking back and forth, gently, as though comforting a child.

'Boysenberry ripple,' said the Doctor, after a moment. 'The perfect counterbalance of textures and colours. And the flavours – the intense sweetness of the syrup, the civilized blandness of the vanilla ... You mustn't let him through the door, Ace.'

'No.'

There were lights and shouts now, but no one could see them, no one took any notice. 'He was born five centuries ago and hasn't ever eaten an ice-cream cone. He doesn't understand the important things in life. Life's short but it's sweet, and he wants it to go on and on . . . No matter what, Ace, you mustn't let him in.'

'I promise you,' she said. 'He won't be coming through.'

The sky explodes inside Cristián's head. The glass of water hits the floor of the bathroom. It shatters, like a grenade, like a rose dipped in nitrogen. Pieces of glass spray in all directions, making screeching music as they skid across the tiles.

He follows the glass to the floor, his cheek slapping the cold tiles. Bits of glass embed themselves in the side of his face. His mouth is open, but no sound is coming out. The scream is too big to fit through it.

'Do you know what you've just done?' shouted the doorman.

'I just shot John Lennon,' said Mark.

Morning.

Outside the apartment building on 72nd Street, a crowd has formed overnight, like dew. The people in the crowd are young and old, many without coats, some in evening dress. They have come out of their homes, out of bars and restaurants. They hold candles, or flowers, or one another, speaking in hushed voices.

A hot dog seller saunters up the street, his cart slowing as he nears the margin of the crowd. 'Hey. What's goin' on?'

'John Lennon is dead,' someone breathes.

'Naw,' says the hot dog seller. 'Y'mean it? Naw.'

But there's blood and chalk on the steps, and the building's gate is decorated with roses and Christmas wreaths, bits of tinsel blowing in the winter wind. Boomboxes play Beatles music, or the same news report, over and over.

211

After a while the hot dog seller closes up his cart and joins the crowd, listening.

Benny woke up with a start. The dawn light was squeezing in through the bars on the window, making her squint. Her mouth tasted terrible and she was cramped all over from sleeping sitting up, leaning against the window-sill. She stretched gingerly, listening to her joints crack. *Getting too old for this*, she thought.

Body count: Ace asleep on the floor, stretched out like an enormous cat. Cris in his bed, looking awful. The Doctor at the writing-desk, examining the print-outs Benny had made the night before. He held them close to his face, peering at the tiny computer print.

'I thought it was particularly appropriate,' said Benny softly.

The Doctor glanced at her. 'Yes?'

'The location of the last recorded copy.'

'Mmmm.'

'How are you?'

He waved the question away. 'I imagine Huitzilin succeeded in having most copies destroyed during the Christian purge of Aztec religious books. Like Tlacaelel's rewriting of Aztec history – Huitzilin covering his trail. That's why the Institute only had one page.'

Benny picked up one of the print-outs. 'According to this, the *Nahuatl* text was never written down. All that exists are the painted pictograms. Unless we have an Aztec priest who can translate for us, we won't have the full text.'

'Given the power in that one page, I imagine the Codex Atlaca is capable of doing its job without a translator,' said the Doctor. He tapped a pencil against the print-out. 'We just go there, get it, and get on with it, Bernice. We can't waste any more time.'

'What abut Cristián?'

The Doctor turned. The Mexican was watching them quietly from his bed, hands clasped together.

'That's very much up to him,' said the Time Lord.

212

Interlude 3

I don't think I actually want to write this down. But it's therapeutic (?) & besides, I can always change it later if I feel like it.

It's so difficult making these diary entries when I don't know what day it is. There's no time inside a time machine. Night follows day, of course; at the moment the TARDIS has decided it's night, & all the lights are down.

I suppose that's why I thought I was dreaming.

I was asleep in one of the libraries. (There are dozens, scattered about the place; at first I thought the books kept changing, but then I realized it was the rooms. The TARDIS likes to play musical rooms when she's bored.) The libraries are lined with books, scrolls, datacubes, you name it, floor to ceiling, wall to wall. They have that gorgeous musty smell of old paper; one or two even have cobwebs, but I'm sure they're merely for effect. There's a big comfy chair & a table to put the books on & I know, I know, get to the point.

I woke up, having dropped off in the chair. *Bronze Age Burials in Gloucestershire* had fallen on the floor. I wandered out in that heavy dazed state one normally achieves at three in the morning when trying to find the bathroom. I hadn't been drinking. I didn't dare. Something might happen.

The lights were very dim. I couldn't see clearly at first. There was a rustling sound.

I'd forgotten about the cupboard monster. But now I

have a very clear recollection: Mother switching on the light, and the menacing shape in the bedroom turning out to be some pyjamas thrown over the back of a chair. I must be three, four. I remember her saying that she couldn't sleep with the cupboard open either, closing the door. I remember her laughing.

The cupboard monster was coming towards me, very slowly, keeping against the wall as though finding its way in the dark. Little shape moving almost without sound, without apparent purpose.

It was a few seconds before I said 'Lights on.'

I was dazzled, the light hitting the back of my eyes like a handful of nails. I was still fuzzy in the head. Stupid dream to be having.

The Doctor was coming towards me, perhaps 3 metres away. He was as white as the wall he was clinging to. His eyes were closed & I saw that he was leaving a line on the wall, a long red line that oozed softly down the white stuff like freshly applied graffiti.

I *still* thought it was a dream.

My eyes – I remember it felt like they were moving on their own, without me – my eyes followed the line back along the wall. Back to Ace.

She was wearing her combat suit. I'd almost got used to her wearing normal clothes. I thought how hard she'd tried to stick to at least that part of her agreement with the Doctor, & what a shame it was. What a shame.

She was holding a knife.

The Doctor said, 'B – ' & fell down.

The line of red curved down, suddenly, & I was still just standing there. I saw his hands go to the awful spot of red on his shirt, I saw the blood squeeze out between his fingers.

Ace came towards us.

I could tell at once it wasn't her. She doesn't walk like that & her eyes were Blue.

I couldn't believe any of it. I remember thinking, please don't make me fight you, please don't make me hurt you. But I felt calm, safe: I was waiting to wake up.

The Doctor's hands went limp, & I saw the lines of pain on his face smooth out like an equation approaching zero. He breathed out, almost a sigh. Then there was a sort of rattling noise as he tried to take another breath & didn't.

Ace's eyes rolled back into her head to show the whites. She collapsed like a pile of dustbins, the knife clattering away across the floor.

Cristián, wearing a set of ridiculous blue & white striped pyjamas, came out of a side corridor & said, 'Ace has stabbed the Doctor.'

& then I woke up.

Later. Just checked on the Doctor in the infirmary. He looks determined, but very weary. This was nearly the last straw. I think I prefer him when he's in control of everything – he's more frightening, but he also makes you feel more confident (& glad he's on *your* side).

Cris had a proper panic, which was good, because it forced me to think straight and take charge. I sent him running to the sick-bay for the kit.

In the meantime I turned the Doctor over and unbuttoned his shirt. Blood was getting on my fingers (it's darker than human, with a hint of orange in the red). There was a wet stab wound right over where a human's heart would be. It looked like a slice in a piece of fresh meat. (I was *really* glad I hadn't been drinking, because I felt very much like throwing up.) You never get used to it happening to people you know.

Cris bolted back with the Feinbergers and I pulled out the vital stats scanner – I don't know the technology, but it looks like a pocket calculator and is as easy to use. Oh ho, we had some green lights: the Doctor was alive.

He confirmed this diagnosis by suddenly coming to, making the scanner bleep and bloop in confusion. He took a deep breath, and it obviously hurt. 'Hold still,' I told him.

'Ace,' he said, and the silly idiot tried to sit up. At least there was no blood coming out of his mouth or nose. 'Is she?'

'Is she what?' I said, peeling the back off a derm.

215

'Is she breathing?'

At that point, dear Diary, I didn't care whether she were breathing or not. But Cristián had already hopped over to her, and he nodded at me. 'Get the knife,' I said.

I eased the derm in place just under the wound. 'He had a go at her,' muttered the Doctor. He was already relaxing; the stuff would stop the pain and the worst of the blood loss. Time to try the tissue scanner. 'Is she breathing?' he asked again.

'She's fine. She can wait.' Cris handed me the knife. It was made of obsidian – she must have been carrying it since the trip to Tenochtitlan. The blade was broken off, which confirmed what the scanner was telling me.

'The knife snapped off on a rib,' I told the Doctor. 'She got clumsy or you got lucky.'

'Lucky,' he breathed.

'I'm going to have to take the broken piece out,' I said. 'Señor Alvarez, come here and hold onto him.'

Cris didn't quite know what to do, but he ended up holding the Doctor's hand while I eased the fragment out with a pair of padded tweezers. He kept shuddering, making me have to stop. I never want to have to do that again. I never want to have to reach inside some-body again.

It was better once I'd got the piece out. I put a strip of stuff over the wound to close it – by this time he was giving me instructions – and attached a little doohickey which would monitor and speed up the healing.

'Why did she try to kill you?' Cristián wanted to know. 'He needs to keep you alive. Doesn't he?'

'Just trying to even up the odds.' Cris had brought a stretcher, and now we slid the Doctor onto it. This time he had the sense to hold still and let us look after him. 'There's one last confrontation left. He's coming with us, Bernice, he'll be there.'

I looked around, I remember – it must have looked brilliant, as though I were expecting H to pop out of the wall and jump us.

We put the Doctor to bed and then we got around to

doing something about Ace. I still hadn't grasped the fact that it wasn't her fault. It just seemed like all that tension had inevitably blossomed into something horribly physical.

Not fair, is it? I can remember trying to shoot the Doctor's head off, for some terribly good, some very logical reason.

She was feverish and breathing raggedly. He'd just used her and dumped her – like the cleaner. Another bloody human sacrifice. Cris helped me carry her to her room. It took me forever to work out how to get the suit off. I don't know if she's going to be all right.

What scares me the most is remembering the Doctor's face when he 'died'. He says he faked it so that H would let Ace go – otherwise she would have burnt up the way Macbeth did. I think he *let* her stab him.

He looked peaceful. I'm having trouble remembering the last time he looked peaceful. And now we've got this 'last confrontation' to look forward to. I just hope he's not planning to get out of this the easy way.

Chapter 14

Futility

Let's pause the videotape for a moment.

Cristián Xochitl Alvarez is caught before the mirror in mid-struggle, his bow-tie half-twisted into an elaborate knot. He's never worn clothes like these before. His reflection is caught in the full-length mirror of the TARD-IS's changing room. The Doctor explained that it was called the changing room because it was always changing – the clothes in it were never the same from day to day, and the room itself moved around, as though looking for customers. It had been behind the first door Cristián had tried.

His expression is blank, eyes half-closed, as he runs through the breathing exercises the Doctor has taught him. Panic, explained the Time Lord, is fear of fear. Control the body's fear reaction and you control the fear itself.

He is about to do the most dangerous thing he has ever done, go to the most dangerous place he will ever visit. This is not the imagined danger that makes his heart beat too quickly in the subway or an elevator, it is not the ethereal ambush that felled him in New York. It is a peril as genuine as walking out in front of a truck.

There's only one comfort: there is nothing else he can possibly do. It's like going through with an operation. You'll be terrified, but you must let it happen.

His grandmother had run from the soldiers once, when the whole village was surrounded by government troops looking for the Zapatistas. She had climbed into a crevice in the hillside, down into a gorge, clutching his father and a string bag of tortillas, with bullets whizzing around them and the soldiers shouting and breaking windows in the village. She hadn't had any choice but to keep going, and to whisper to her tiny son, don't cry, don't cry or they'll hear us and they'll kill us, pull yourself together!

Breathe this way, the Doctor said, *and just let it happen. Let it all wash over you.*

Ace's eyes are half-open, and her breathing is shallow and irregular, her pulse fast and weak: shock, and more than shock. Sometimes when she draws breath she shudders, as though her lungs reject the outside world's intrusion.

Professor Bernice Summerfield sits beside her bed, in a wicker chair with a peeling arm. She is frozen in the moment of soaking a tea-towel in a bowl of ice water, her fingers just breaking the surface tension of the liquid. A single drop of water is running down her arm under the woollen pullover.

She might be a painting hanging in a gallery, one of those studies of water and women and domestic life captured in thick coloured strokes. Her young brow is wrinkled, just slightly. She is trying to look after three people at once. It's like a juggling act.

The medical instruments they have are useless; a selection lie on the bedside table, abandoned. They record Ace's heartbeat and breathing, show the activity of her brain and body. They do not show what Bernice needs to know. Either Ace's mind is there or it isn't, and until she either wakes up or dies there's no way of knowing.

Cristián is so afraid he can hardly put a sentence together. And the Doctor ... the Doctor is taking less and less care of himself the longer this awful dance goes on. This will be the third time he has offered himself up as bait, holding out his hands to the god in the hope of dragging him to earth.

Just once Bernice has seen him push his fingers through a wall, tentatively, as though testing whether such a thing is

219

possible. He is unravelling. If this last plan of his fails, he'll be gone like a drop of water dissolving into the ocean. And Bernice must stay behind, must let him go. Let them both go. Because someone has to stay behind to look after Ace.

The swimming pool is paused in mid-ripple. Cold circles spread out from the point of impact. An inch above the water, a dragonfly is suspended in time, a single drop of water clinging to its undercarriage as it lifts away.

The ripples have passed half-way through the reflection of the Doctor, obscuring his face. He can see the bottom of the pool through the reflection, a single bright light overhead burning like a white sun. The jungle of pot-plants that surrounded the pool are in darkness, leaves hissing silently as they breathe.

Perhaps, the Doctor is thinking, he is really the reflection. A two-dimensional image, thin as a scrap of paper bobbing on the breeze.

He sits on the end of the diving board, cross-legged. He is wearing a red velvet dressing-gown. The deep wound in his chest is almost healed, though there will be a scar in the bone where the knife-point turned. A scar over the heart. His face is like paper, the colour of his eyes standing out sharply. Blue energy sizzles in his fingertips.

It isn't even death he's facing. Her features he knows from a hundred, a thousand encounters. He's felt her sleeve brush past him again and again. He remembers the morning he woke up and realized he had lost count of how many people he had seen die. He had promised himself he would not forget them, not one.

He knows what it's like to lie back in her cold arms and let her hands come up over your face, touching your mouth . . .

But this, not even to die, to be erased. Ashes to nothing, dust to nothing. Live fast, die young, and leave a beautiful empty space where you used to be.

Time to unpause the tape. Take your seats for the final act!

Ladies and gentlemen, welcome aboard the Royal Mail Ship *Titanic*!

Sunday, April 14, 1912
7.30 pm
Second Wireless Operator Harold Bride scribbled rapidly on a piece of paper, listening intently to the pattern of dots and dashes that thumped in his weary ears. The irregular rhythm resolved itself into letters, into words, a pithy message, a series of numbers.

'Jack,' he said, 'it's another ice warning. It's the *Californian* – she's spotted three bergs.'

Jack Phillips grunted a response without pausing in the message he was sending. 'Better take it up to the Captain.'

'At this rate, we'll never be finished,' muttered Bride. He stuffed the message into his pocket and headed for the bridge.

The First Wireless Operator sighed, looking despondently at the pile of paper in front of him. The passengers thought it was a jolly game, sending all these telegrams, as though the wireless radio were some sort of toy. He and Bride were desperately trying to catch up with the backlog of frivolous personal messages. It wouldn't be until they were in touch with Cape Race in Newfoundland that they could relay the bulk of them.

Bride was right. If they kept being interrupted like this, they'd never get any sleep.

8.33 pm
Cristián's stomach lurched, and he closed his eyes, putting a hand against the wall to support himself. He felt ill.

The boat was steady as a rock, except for the inaudible thrumming of the engines he could feel through his feet and fingertips. The room they were in smelled of metal and rust, and distantly of cold air and sea-water.

Cristián felt ill because he was terrified. He couldn't get his mind off it for a moment. He tried to remember the pattern of breathing.

He was startled as the Doctor switched on a torch,

waving it at random about the room. After a moment the Time Lord got out his pocket watch and pointed the torch's circle of white light at its face.

'It's not here,' said the Time Lord.

'Where are we?'

'Cargo room. Right at the front of the boat.' The Doctor shone his torch on crates, trunks, a vintage car. The TARDIS had obligingly turned itself into a large featureless box, the better to blend in. 'I'd wanted to arrive on the Wednesday, while she was still in the Channel. No such luck. We've got about three hours before the Titanic has its close encounter.'

Cristián closed his eyes again. 'How do you know the codex isn't here?'

'The same way that you do.'

The Doctor was right. He would know if he came anywhere near such a large knot of Blue. 'What happens when the iceberg hits?' he asked. 'Does the ship blow up?'

There was amusement in the Time Lord's voice. 'The *Titanic* brushes against the berg, and it dents the starboard bow side, pushing in the metal plating and popping the rivets. The ship takes nearly two hours to sink.'

'Oh. That gives us a bit of extra time.'

The torch beam danced across Cristián's closed eyes. 'I told Bernice to wait for us. But I've set the TARDIS to automatically leave shortly before the ship sinks. She doesn't know that. This is your last chance to turn back, Cristián.'

The Indian pushed his forehead against the palms of his hands. One strand of greying hair fell between his fingers. 'I keep thinking,' he said, and his voice wobbled. 'I keep thinking, if only you would give me a pill, something to stop me from being afraid.'

The Doctor listened silently. 'And then I think of all the pills I've been given, all the therapy. The doctors and nurses have helped me as much as they can, and it's not enough.' Cristián looked up at the Time Lord. 'We both need an exorcism.'

'What I need,' said the Doctor gravely, 'is a haircut.'

* * *

222

Anna saw the Mexican gentleman before he saw her. He was standing at the railing, looking out over the ocean. The stars blazed incredibly over the Atlantic, billions of them. It was so different to London's featureless night sky. Anna imagined she could read just by the light of those stars.

She did not see the man's face until she was almost upon him. She recognized his features at once; her father did a great deal of business with South American Indians of one breed or another. It seemed a curious contrast, the primitive face and the dinner dress.

She had not seen the Mexican before, and yet he was clearly a first class passenger. And now here he was, staring out at the glassy ocean all alone. He could only be aboard for one purpose. Anna wondered if she could slip past without his noticing, go and tell her father at once.

Then she changed her mind. No Indian, no matter how well-heeled, would push her or her father around. Better to confront him at once and get to the bottom of the matter.

So she gathered her shawl about her, strode up to the Indian and put on her sternest voice. 'I know why you're on board,' she said sharply.

He started so badly that for a moment she thought he would fall overboard. 'You do?' he said, astonishment written all over his dark face.

Aha, I have scored a point already, thought Anna. 'There's no use lurking about here like some sort of spy. You should speak to father immediately, and we can clear it all up before we reach New York.'

'Yes?'

He seemed to be having trouble with his English. She wondered if she should address him in Spanish. 'We've dealt with your sort before, you see,' she said boldly, 'and we've always been able to come to an amenable arrangement all round.' She lowered her voice a little. 'You may come and see the things tonight, and then we can sort you out.'

'The things.'

223

'The ar-tee-facts,' said Anna, as though speaking to a backward child.

'Yes? Yes? The artefacts. Brilliant. Excellent.' The Indian suddenly broke into a tremendous grin. It looked peculiar in his dusky face. 'Mexican artefacts, right?'

'Right,' said Anna. 'So, you come along to my cabin at about ten.' She told him the number and walked off without looking back.

'Yes, ma'am!' said the Indian to no one in particular.

9.07 pm

'Best to keep still if you value your ears, sir,' joked the barber dourly.

The Doctor rearranged himself and settled into the chair, putting his feet up on the stool. It had taken a little effort to arrange a haircut this late in the evening, but the first class passengers were accustomed to getting what they wanted when they wanted it.

The barber paused, scissors hovering above the Doctor's head. 'There are feathers growing out of your scalp, sir.'

'No there aren't.'

'Oh. Sorry, sir, you're right. There aren't.'

The Doctor let himself drift, just let it all go, feeling the easy rhythm of the boat underneath him. There was nothing on earth quite so relaxing as having one's hair cut.

But he was still as tense as a crushed spring. He could sense the Blue, and the colour itched at the back of his neck, surging and sparking at random moments. The Codex Atlaca, somewhere on board. And something else, elusive Blue fingers tickling up and down his spine, something he hadn't encountered before.

The barber clucked his tongue as the Doctor moved again. But the Time Lord was drifting, thinking over the details of the plan. It was a good plan, tidy and conclusive, with three possible outcomes, all of which were reasonably acceptable. He didn't mind which way the game went. He just wanted it to finish.

Yes, it was a good plan, guaranteed. Unsinkable. As the iceberg said to the *Titanic*.

He was getting nostalgic now, as though his whole life were limping past his eyes. He remembered assuring Borusa that he'd had nothing to do with the liner's sinking. Wasn't worth going back and telling him about this, of course. He'd only get a stony stare.

Yes, unsinkable, no matter what surprises the wily old Aztec tried to pull. They were trapped together now, like two actors stuck on the stage, following the script to the inevitable conclusion. Trapped together on a doomed speck of metal in the middle of an infinite waste of water.

Suitable, thought the Doctor, *appropriate*.

Huitzilin agreed.

9.21 pm

Cristián was still waiting on B deck, watching the ocean, as though keeping an eye out for the iceberg. What would they see, he wondered? How large would it be? For all he knew a wall of ice might be invisible against the new-moon ocean.

Below, couples walked arm in arm, taking the air after their dinners. He fought down the urge to scream out a warning, plead with them that they were heading for disaster, they must turn back.

'They wouldn't believe you,' murmured the Doctor, coming up beside him. 'This ship couldn't possibly be sunk by a little piece of ice.'

They stood side by side for a few moments. Cristián wondered if one of the glittering stars was the Doctor's home. So far away . . . he was suddenly sad for his grandmother, dying all alone in her little mountain hut. He'd never had a chance to say goodbye to her.

So many people.

'Two thousand, two hundred, and twenty-four,' the Doctor was saying, 'of whom one thousand, five hundred and two will drown. There are thirteen honeymoon couples, from which four people will survive. Fifty-three children drown, all of them from third class.'

Cristián twitched. 'How can we just stand here and not help them, not warn them?'

'It's history. We can't just play with it. You're the one who was frightened of stepping on butterflies.'

The Indian peered at the Doctor, whose face was hidden by the darkness. When had he mentioned butterflies? In his future – his hidden future? What had they discussed? 'You're happy to play with my history,' he protested.

'The sinking of the *Titanic* is part of the web of time.' The Doctor paused, as though looking for human words to explain what he meant. 'Prevent the disaster and you may cause another.'

'How can saving fifty-three children be a disaster?'

'The *Titanic* sank – will sink – because of tremendous carelessness,' said the Doctor. 'The ice warnings were lost, ignored. They didn't see the berg until the last moment, and even then they didn't turn quickly enough. There were lifeboats for only about half the people on board, and some of those were half-empty when they were launched. When a ship ten miles away saw her flares, it didn't do a thing. And their radio operator had gone to bed.'

Cristián put his hand on the Doctor's arm. It was an aborted slap. Anything to get him to stop. 'Are you saying it won't happen again?'

'From now on, ships will have round-the-clock radio surveillance, and lifeboats for everyone. The International Ice Patrol will be formed. Save the *Titanic* and you'll be condemning future passengers.'

'No,' said Cristián, 'it won't do. It's not good enough. Why can't we save this boat *and* the future ones?'

'Make one change, and you may have to make another, and another. Do you have the skill to arbitrate history?'

'But you must have changed history. Doesn't my life count? Haven't you changed history, just by landing your time machine in New York?' Cristián blew out a frustrated sigh. 'So many people must have asked you these questions.'

'The very first was a teacher who wanted to change the Aztecs. Stop the sacrifices.'

'I wish she had.'

'Mmm.'

226

'I have a message for you.'

9.40 pm

Jack Phillips blew out a tense sigh of relief. At last they were in range of Cape Race.

He finished writing down the ice warning from the *Mesaba*. That made, what, six in one day? It was as though they were were floating around in an enormous cocktail.

Ah, well, that was the bridge's problem. He'd take it up to them when he got a free moment. He put it to one side, under a paperweight, and went on hammering out the passengers' messages.

9.50 pm

Sir Charles is in his stateroom. Despite the cold, he has opened a porthole, and the sea breeze pushes slowly in. Sir Charles likes the smell of the sea.

Sir Charles opens his writing desk, lifts away the *Titanic* stationery inside. Everything appears to be in order. Under his bed is a small metal box, and in his clothes trunks are a number of small packages, carefully wrapped, like a pile of belated Christmas presents.

He lifts his head for a moment, taking a deep breath of that salty air. The backs of his hands are tingling; there is a sense of anticipation tonight, of something about to happen. The most important event of his life is about to take place. He will not appreciate this until it happens.

He and Anna have travelled a great deal in the last few months. In order to sell what they have acquired, they have been to Paris and to Prague, negotiated with a Turkish holy man and with an Irish museum director.

But it has not been a particularly successful expedition, not compared to past endeavours. Sir Charles knows it is bad luck to hang on to an item for too long, for the very practical reason that the more ports one passes, the more likely it is that one's luggage will be searched. Still, all this travel is broadening for Anna's mind, and his daughter is becoming as astute at negotiations as he is.

There's another smell in the air now, an extra tang mixed

227

with the salt. Storm coming, says one part of Sir Charles'
mind, while another part is mapping out their American
itinerary. If New York isn't interested in the remaining
items, there's the west coast – he's never been to California
– and there is always the Mexican government. It would be
ironic to sell them back their own artefacts, but there you
have it.

On the other hand, if what Anna told him is correct,
they might be able to unload those particular items before
they even reached New York.

Sir Charles goes into the bathroom to comb his hair and
straighten his tie. He is short and stubby, with a broad nose
and thinning mouse-coloured hair. You would not notice
him in a crowd. Despite the mild thrills of smuggling, he
considers his life to be a bit of a grind, a bit dull. Even
travel becomes wearing when one is only revisiting places
one has seen before.

From all over the ship, from behind space and between
space, from the air and the walls, from the freezing water
and the steam in the engines, oozing out of nothing, Huitzilin comes.

There is a soundless sound, like a colossal cymbal being
struck in reverse. Sir Charles' cabin is suddenly full of the
smell of ozone.

He comes out of the bathroom, wondering if there is an
electrical fire.

The air itself is on fire with Blue light. Great black
slashes appear in the wallpaper, as if something is clawing
at the solid matter. On the writing table, a glass of port
wobbles in circles and shatters, spattering the desk with
purple.

Perhaps Sir Charles screams. The noise and the brilliance wash through the cabin in a tidal wave of energy.

Huitzilin pulls himself together.

In the TARDIS, Ace hears the backward cymbal sound.
Her eyes snap open. The great fist around her heart lets go.

The Doctor is examining the clock on the grand staircase.

He's seen photographs of it: a pair of angels with a laurel wreath on either side of the clock-face. Honour and Glory crowning time. Cristián sits on the top step, his bow-tie undone, loosening his collar.

He feels the sudden build-up of energy as a sizzling at the back of his neck, the tiny hair standing up. Panic explodes through him. Desperate, he turns to the Doctor.

The Time Lord's mouth is open, his eyes are closed, his head is tilted back slightly. A great flurry of electric blue sparkles swirl around him, cascading up in a spiral from his shoes to his hair. There is an expression on his face which is not pain, which is something beyond pain, some intolerable awareness.

Cris has not seen this before. But he knows what it is. A great hand reaches for the Doctor, like a mother snatching at a wayward child.

The sound comes together in a sudden crash – and then silence.

The Doctor opens his eyes. Cristián moves backwards, too frightened to know what to think, what to do. The Blue is coming from the Doctor. From the *Doctor*. He's shining with it, it's like trying to look into the sun, into the *sun* –

All at once the little man sways and falls forwards. Cristián has caught him before he knows what he's doing.

The Doctor's hands catch at him, searching for support. Cristián flinches, frantic to get away from that Blue. Fingers dig into his arm, try to hold him, but they're insubstantial as a bubble on the breeze. *What happened*, he doesn't ask, because he doesn't want to know.

'We killed someone,' the Doctor gasps, and he's solid again, gripping Cristián's jacket. 'Huitzilin killed someone.' He starts to laugh. 'Oh we killed someone.'

A final coruscation of sparks explodes around the Doctor, matching his laughter. Cristián drops him and backs off.

'You see?' says Cristián furiously. 'You see what I mean? This isn't just between you and him. Everyone here is involved! Everyone!'

'Don't leave me.'

229

'I can't stay with you. I can't.'

'Please.'

Cristián hears his internal voice shouting *do it without thinking, don't think about it*! He grabs the Doctor and hauls him to his feet, all the while thinking about his grandmother, the talcum smell of her make-up and clothes. The Time Lord is shaking all over. Mother of God, thinks Cristián, this could be happening to him. And he would have drowned in that first wave of Blue, never could have lasted this long. Only the Doctor could trap Huitzilin like this, trap him on board a doomed ship, trap him inside his own flesh and blood.

A young gentleman and his lady friend stroll into the foyer. 'I say,' he calls out. 'What's the matter with your friend?'

'He's seasick,' says Cristián.

'Seasick? On the *Titanic*?' The couple walk on, laughing.

Behind them, the clock begins to strike ten. 'We have to get to Sir Charles's cabin,' says the Doctor.

'The meeting,' says Cristián.

'No,' says the Doctor. 'That's who we killed.'

10.00 pm

Bernice brought Ace breakfast on a silver tray. The younger woman was sitting up in bed, looking as though she'd rather be anywhere else.

'Take it easy,' said Benny, parking the tray in Ace's lap. 'You nearly died. Just get your breath back.'

'Where is he?' said Ace. 'What's he doing?'

Benny put a hand on her forehead. 'You're going to love this,' she said. 'He's on board the *Titanic*. We're parked in a cargo hold while he and Cristián look for the codex.'

Ace did a soldier thing, which was to keep on eating while the bombs came down around her ears. 'What happened?' she said.

'Oh,' said Bernice lightly, 'Huitzilin had a go at you. But you're all right now. Once we've got that book, everything will be fine.'

Ace looked at her strangely, but it was clear that she

230

didn't remember anything. Probably for the best, thought Benny. No. Definitely for the best. 'How do you feel?'

'He's gone,' said Ace. 'He was here and now he's gone. I guess he had something better to do.'

'Huitzilin?'

'Yeah.' Ace picked up a slice of bacon between her fingers and chewed it thoughtfully. 'The *Titanic*. I guess it was inevitable we got here eventually . . .' They looked at one another.

Benny said, 'I keep thinking back to the good old days when we all got on so well.'

'We never got on so well,' said Ace.

'No,' said Benny. 'I guess you can't stuff three personalities this strong into a phone booth and not have some conflict. I've been thinking . . . perhaps two's company.'

Ace looked surprised, and then she thought about it, munching on her bacon. 'Maybe,' she said eventually. 'I always felt sort of connected to the Doctor. Even when I went away I came back again. Sometimes I wonder whether that was really my call or not.'

Bernice frowned. 'He doesn't play games with me. He wouldn't dare.'

'So,' said Ace, 'you going off on your own?'

'I don't know if I should,' Bernice crossed her arms. 'Who's going to keep an eye on you two if I go?'

Ace threw the bacon rind at her.

The wind was blowing through the rigging, whistling its meaningless tune. It felt like being struck by a snowball, outlining cheekbones and ears in sharp pangs of cold. The sky was a black apron filthy with specks of paint.

Frederick Fleet and Reginald Lee climbed into the crow's-nest and took their first glance at the Atlantic. 'The bridge says to keep an eye out for icebergs,' said the men they were relieving.

Fleet tucked his hands under his armpits, warming his fingers. The sea was so smooth it might be a single sheet of ice. They were steaming at full speed or something like it. Like rolling a marble across a table.

They could see the whole ship spread out beneath them, a sixth of a mile long, her lights blazing like a challenge to the stars. Perhaps they felt small, just a tiny part of the flock of humanity on board the ship, itself a tiny speck in the endless blackness of the ocean and the sky. They were safe inside God's pocket.

10.30 pm
Cristián knocked on the door of Anna's cabin. The Doctor leaned on the wooden wall behind him, pale yellow in the electric light.

No answer.

Cristián knocked again. 'Anyone home?' he called out.

There was a sound from inside, a human sound, without any words. The Indian gently pushed the door. It swung open.

Anna sat on the end of her bed in disarray, a far cry from the self-assured figure who had accosted Cristián on deck. Her shawl fell down around her shoulders and tangled in her hands as she wrung the lace. The sound of her hysterical sobbing filled the cabin.

Cristián sat down on the bed beside her as the Doctor fumbled for the light switch. He hesitated, and then put an arm around her trembling shoulders. 'What is it?' he said, though the sinking feeling in his chest told him he already knew.

Anna just went on sobbing, as though she hadn't noticed they were there. The Doctor sat cross-legged in front of her and caught her eye. Suddenly she calmed, her gulping breathing slowing down. 'It's Daddy,' she said miserably. 'My poor Daddy.'

The Doctor sat back, folding his arms tightly across his chest. 'You'd better stay with her.'

'Hey,' said Cristián, 'we shouldn't split up. I don't think we should split up, I think that's a really bad idea – '

'No one else dies,' said the Doctor. 'Enough. Enough of this.'

* * *

The door to Sir Charles's cabin was ajar, allowing a flat line of light to leak into the dim hallway. The door was jammed open by one of Anna's shoes. She'd dropped it as she fled, like Cinderella leaving the ball, all her fantasies turning into pumpkins and rats.

The Doctor picked up the shoe, holding it in his hand for a moment. Then with a sudden motion he kicked the door open.

Huitzilin was not inside.

The Doctor went into the cabin and closed the door.

The cabin was another piece of *Titanic* opulence, with its plush carpet and wood panelling and antique furniture. Sir Charles's mortal remains lay at the foot of the bed. The Doctor sat down on the floor with his back to the door, took a piece of paper out of his pocket and carefully unfolded it. It was a typewritten list of seven hundred and twenty-two names in alphabetical order.

Anna and Sir Charles were not among them.

He put the paper away and knelt next to Sir Charles.

There was something wrong with the corpse. It wasn't the look of horror on the man's face, the random tangle of his limbs. He had been taken by surprise, and by more than surprise. There was no worse way to die. And more than die. Erased.

He had seen it before. There were worlds whose improbable ecologies were like a serpent swallowing its own tail, life draining life in a chain of vampirism until only a single creature was left, licking hungrily at the sky. He had been touched by more than one psychevore, hovered on the edge of falling into their well of interminable thirst.

And for those six minutes in London, it had actually happened. He'd been virtual, fictional, someone's dream.

He could see the pattern of the carpet through Sir Charles's body. The design was becoming clearer as the thief's mortal remains faded away into nothing. This was what Anna had found: perhaps she'd tried to touch him, to check for a pulse, and her fingers had slid through him as though he were made of ectoplasm.

The Doctor clung to the foot of the bed, like a drowning man clinging to a bit of wood. The Blue was singing to him, singing rest and peace, singing that it didn't matter. Singing the Blues.

Blue. It was here.

He jerked open the top drawer of the writing desk, pulled out the complimentary stationery, hurled it onto the carpet in a sudden shower of white wings. Until he saw the first sheet of fragile, yellow paper.

Codex Atlaca, said the writing scrawled on the cover.

He slammed the drawer shut, leaning on the desk until the spike of pain in his head subsided.

He went to the *en suite* bathroom, rinsed the blood out of his eyes, the red tears from his face. He drank from his cupped hands, splashed the water on the back of his neck.

He took a towel from the bathroom and went back to the writing desk. Gingerly he extracted the codex and wrapped it in the towel, feeling the caustic touch of the paper when it accidentally brushed his skin. Once a blue spark crackled agonizingly around his hand, and it was all he could do not to drop the book.

This will hurt you more than it hurts me, said the flute in his head.

'What's the difference?' asked the Doctor, clutching the lethal package to his chest.

Don't you care about being hurt?

'I meant, what's the difference between you and I?'

Soon, said the flute, *nothing at all*.

'I'm ready when you are.'

Ready. Like a good captain. Ready to go down with the ship.

The voice was gone, and with it a pressure inside the Doctor's head. He felt his nose start to bleed again, fumbled for a handkerchief.

Under the bed, something made a noise.

The Doctor stood still, gripping the book, like a vampire hunter clutching his supply of crucifixes. There it was again. He turned his head slowly, wondering what trap might have been left for him. There was a new sensation

234

pressing at his brain, tantalizing, just at the edge of consciousness, elusive but powerful.

He put down the book and reached under the bed. There was a metal box. He pulled it out.

The box clanked and jumped on the carpet. The lid sprang open. White light washed into the room, floating from the object in the box. He leaned over it, squinting into the sudden tide of power.

It was a stem and a loop, the thickness of his wrist, a rod that curved back on itself. Markings danced up its sides in an alien language, geometrical symbols like Mayan writing.

He touched it, just a brush of his little finger against the stem of the object.

10.55 pm

'WE'RE STOPPED AND SURROUNDED BY ICE!'

Phillips yelled and ripped off his headphones. The other boat was so close that the message had nearly burst his eardrums.

'Keep out, shut up!' he keyed angrily. 'You're jamming my signal. I'm working Cape Race.'

11.27 pm

Anna slept fitfully, curled up on top of the bedclothes with a corner of the blanket wrapped around her.

Something woke her up. She wasn't sure what it was. Some noise in the night? She sat up, sniffling, rubbing her red eyes. Cristián was gone, probably to tell the ship's surgeon about her father.

Oh God, her father . . . shock, that's all it had been. An illusion of the grieving mind. Only to be expected.

There was a sound in the air, just loud enough to be heard. It sounded like the wheel of some great engine starting up, an electric sound that sent a chill down her spine. Whatever was it?

She sat perfectly still, listening with all her might.

Oh, dear God – there was someone in her cabin –

She reached backwards, her hand banging loudly against

235

the dresser beside her bed. She wrenched open the drawer and rummaged frantically amongst her stockings.

Her fingers closed around something metallic. Her brother's present. You'll need a gun in America, he had said, jokingly.

'Who's there?' she said tremulously, holding the gun out in front of her.

He stepped out of the shadows, literally out of the shadows, as though he were made from the same stuff as the air.

He was six feet tall. He had long white hair, tied up in a sort of crest decorated with a rainbow of feathers. His face was painted half black and half blue. He was naked – no, he was wearing a loincloth, and some sort of cloak. Gold glinted at his ears and on his lower lip. His teeth were white. His eyes were Blue.

Anna screamed and fired the gun. It kicked against her hand twice before she dropped it, her mind melting under the gaze of those inhuman eyes.

The bullets went straight through Huitzilin, and he threw his head back and laughed and laughed.

Cristián did not bother to knock.

'Doctor?' The cabin was brightly lit, making him squint after the dimness of the hallway.

The Time Lord was sitting on the floor with his back to the writing desk. There was a metal box lying next to the bed, the lid open, a faint radiance coming from inside. Cristián's scalp and stomach tightened. The air was awash with Blue.

The Doctor was looking at the box as though it were a poisonous snake, as though he didn't dare move in case he attracted its attention.

'What is it?' whispered Cristián.

'Won't you please close the lid of the box,' said the Doctor.

'But – '

'*Close it!*'

Cristián slammed the metal lid shut, cutting off the light

from inside. He caught a glimpse of the object it contained, a meaningless shape. It could have been anything. It could only be one thing.

'The *Xiuhcoatl*,' he said.

'Yes,' breathed the Doctor.

'What is it?'

'You can use it to fuse two molecules of hydrogen or you can turn a puddle into a nuclear bomb. You could hollow out a planet with it. You could write your name on a tree with it.'

'I don't think I understand.'

'It's one of the most powerful and precise weapons I have ever seen.' He let out a long sigh. 'How fortunate for the universe that the Exxilons were eaten by their own technology.'

'This is what Huitzilin wants,' said Cristián. 'He wants the weapon.'

'He used it once,' said the Doctor. 'Just once. He vaporized a mile-wide stretch of forest. Four hundred people were hiding in the forest, soldiers coming to attack him. He never needed to use it again. The reputation was enough.'

'And now he can't use it,' said Cristián, 'because he's not tangible. He can't pick it up.'

Someone snapped their fingers inside Cristián's head. He put his hands over his ears. The Doctor twisted and howled, the howl turning into a terrible laugh as he slid down the desk to the floor. He giggled into the carpet.

Cristián sat down shakily on the bed. 'Anna,' he said. 'Oh God. God God God.'

'It's what he brought me here for,' muttered the Doctor into the carpet. 'What I brought him here for. I want the book. He wants the weapon. The only way to get them both is to come back here, to this disaster.'

'What are we going to do?'

'Can you carry that for me?'

Cristián looked at the towel on the bed next to him, lifted it to see the folded book.

'I'll carry you if I have to,' he said.

* * *

237

11.40 pm

Frederick Fleet looks out over the ocean.

Frederick Fleet sees something black. He thinks it is something small.

Frederick Fleet watches as the small black something grows larger and larger and larger.

Frederick Fleet rings the crow's-nest bell three times and picks up the bridge phone.

'What did you see?' the phone wants to know.

Frederick Fleet says, 'Iceberg right ahead.'

'Thank you,' says the phone.

Thirty-seven seconds pass.

'Did you feel that?' says the Doctor. He is leaning against the hallway wall, eyes closed.

Cristián, holding the book, shakes his head.

'We've got about two hours before she goes down.'

'That's it? We hit it? We did?' The Doctor nodded. 'Shouldn't there be an alarm or something?'

'Soon the stewards will be knocking on the first class doors,' said the Doctor. 'And the band will begin to play. And Huitzilin will go on eluding us.' He held out a hand, and Cristián could see the wall through it. 'He only needs to wait a little longer. Just a little longer.'

Ace came into the console room. She was freshly showered, wearing a frayed grey and blue dressing-gown, her hair hanging down over her shoulder in a single brown wave.

Bernice was standing next to the console, frowning. 'What is it?' asked Ace.

'I can't get the scanner to work,' replied the archaeologist. 'It was working before.'

'She's probably just sulking again,' said Ace lightly, running a finger along the console. She pulled the lever that opened the door.

Nothing happened.

Bernice said, 'Should that red light be flashing?'

'Crukcrukcruk*cruk*!' shouted Ace. She pounced on the console and glanced left, right, scrabbling at the controls.

238

'What? What?'

'This little light here,' Ace pointed, 'indicates that the automatic take-off controls have been set. He's set us up!'

Benny said bitterly, 'It's kill or cure. Either he finds the codex and destroys Huitzilin, or everyone ends up at the bottom of the sea. The idiot. How long have we got?'

'I can't tell.' Ace was already furiously tapping the keys of the Index File, trying to get the computer to give the information in English. 'But we're not going.'

Monday, April 15, 1912
12.00 midnight
Harold Bride yawned and opened the curtain that separated the sleeping area from the telegraph room.

'Oh, hullo,' said Phillips. 'You're early.'

'Oh, it's been a hell of a night,' said Bride. 'You might as well go to bed. How's it coming along?'

'I've just finished the last of the Cape Race messages. But you've been missing the excitement. Apparently we've hit something – maybe we'll have to go back to Belfast for repairs.'

Bridge laughed. 'And on the maiden voyage too. How embarrassing! Right, let me get presentable.'

Phillips waited by the telegraph while Bride pulled on his uniform. There was a loud noise coming from outside which he couldn't place, like some great machine being started up. He put his head outside the door, to see the *Titanic*'s boiler funnels jetting great plumes of steam like a trio of mammoth tea-kettles.

Bride re-emerged. 'Off you go, then.'

'They've shut down the engines.' Phillips yawned and went behind the green curtain. Bride sat himself down at the telegraph, sorting through the remaining bits of paper. *Engine trouble*, he thought. *I hope we don't end up adrift in the middle of the Atlantic. In this weather!*

A head appeared around the doorway. Bride was so startled that he forgot to salute.

'We've struck an iceberg,' said the captain. 'I'm having

239

an inspection made to see what it has done to us. Get ready to send out a call for assistance.'

'Yes, sir!' Bride pulled on his headphones.

'But don't send it until I tell you.'

'No, sir.'

The Captain disappeared again, his fading footsteps lost in the sound of the funnels.

Phillips re-emerged, half-undressed. 'What was that?'

'You won't believe this,' said Bride, 'but we've gone and hit one of those messages.'

12.10 am

Ace clung to the edge of the console.

Bernice said, 'There has to be a way to stop this thing.'

Ace said, 'Come on.'

Bernice said, 'Couldn't we break something – sabotage the circuit?'

Ace said, 'Come *on*.'

Bernice said, 'A code. There must be a locking code we have to decipher.'

Ace said, 'Come on, you bitch.'

Bernice stopped to look at her.

Deep within the console there was a curious noise.

12.15 am

The steward knocked on the door, waited politely. Knocked again.

'What's the matter?' said a figure, coming through the dark.

'Everyone is to put their lifebelts on, sir,' said the steward, whose hair was in disarray.

'I'll see to Miss Anna. You go on.' The figure opened the door a fraction.

'I'm sorry,' the steward said. 'This is first class space.'

The Doctor turned to see Cristián looking at the steward in confusion. 'He's my servant,' said the Time Lord.

'Oh. Right you are, sir.' The steward beetled off to rouse another of the first class passengers.

'Sorry about that,' murmured the Doctor.

'I don't think I can go in,' said Cristián.

The Blue here was thick as paint, filling up his mouth and nose, ringing in his head like a bell. He remembered the Hallowe'en Massacre and the Happening and it all came pouring into him like a great river of badness, bad feeling, bad. His skin crawled. His heart jumped and leapt. He was sure he would have a coronary or lose his mind.

But it was just another panic attack.

Just another one. It wasn't real. He had had so many panic attacks again and again, and it was just another one.

Pull yourself together, said the little voice in his head.

The Doctor had already gone into the cabin. Cristián pulled himself together and went in to confront the god of war.

'CQD MGY CQD MGY CQD MGY CQD MGY CQD MGY CQD MGY.'

Six times Phillips tapped out the signal, distress *Titanic*, distress *Titanic*.

Other ships heard the call, sent it out in ripples across the Atlantic, ripples that spread outwards from the sinking ship as though it were a stone tossed into a pond.

The cabin was quiet, perfectly quiet. Outside the room, doors were being knocked on, shouts were being voiced, the band was playing a cheerful ragtime tune. In the cabin the air was still, everything was calm.

Huitzilin faced the Doctor across the cabin. '*Otiquihi-yohuih*,' he said, and his voice rang in the air like a bell.

'Shut the door,' said the Doctor. Cristián shut the door. Neither of them took their eyes off Huitzilin.

He was tall and muscular. He glowed palely, blue-white, like a young star. He wore a loincloth and embroidered cape. There were geometric designs printed onto his cheeks. Golden pendants hung from his ears; a gold and jade plug was fitted into his lower lip. His left foot was distorted, malformed, feathers sprouting from the skin.

His hair was bleached white with time, mixed with long

241

feathers of a dozen colours. His eyes burned Blue like volcanic flame.

He was transparent, he was intangible, but he was real, just a fraction, but real.

'*Ixiptla*,' he said, and the word was full of affection.

The Doctor stood ramrod straight, Huitzilin's pale light reflecting off his white jacket and throwing strange shadows across his face. He reached up and tore a handful of feathers out of his hair, the quills trailing blood.

What was left of Anna lay on the carpet between them, already fading into oblivion. Cristián took a step towards her, his shoe bumping into something on the floor, but the Doctor restrained him with a gentle hand.

'Give me the book, Cristián,' said the Doctor quietly.

Cristián opened his mouth to say something, but Huitzilin turned his gaze on his descendant. 'Shut up, little flower,' he said. Cris's arms went slack, and he dropped the Codex Atlaca onto the floor.

'His part in this is finished,' said Huitzilin.

The Doctor carefully knelt, still keeping his eyes on the Aztec, and picked up the book. A flock of blue sparks exploded from inside the towels, wreathing his arms. He did not flinch.

'The priestess who tried to use that spell against me was vaporized,' said Huitzilin, smiling.

'Why?' said the Doctor. 'Why did she try to use it against you?'

Huitzilin tilted his head, not understanding.

'The Aztecs lived for war. They ate and drank war. Why try to kill the god of war?'

Huitzilin shrugged a graceful shrug. 'Perhaps that priestess did not want her sons to die. She carried my blood, she had the magic eye. She knew who I was.' He laughed nostalgically. 'Of all the peoples I have encountered over the last five centuries, my own people were the only ones who really understood war. We saw it in the street and in the marketplace. We saw the captured warriors and their fate, we saw our fathers and brothers and sons go into battle and not return.

'Did you know Ahuitzotl poisoned the emperor before him? Poor old Tizoc couldn't keep up the fighting, and the empire was coming apart at the seams. It was Tlacaelel's suggestion, of course. The old man lasted nearly as long as the empire did, handing out advice to the emperors. My advice.'

'It must have been a disappointment when the conquistadors came.'

'No,' said Huitzilin. 'Half the population were killed in the battles, and thousands of the survivors died of smallpox. It was a banquet. I didn't have to lift a finger. As usual.'

'You pushed the Aztecs into conquest.'

'We both know I didn't. Tlacaelel's suggestions were always politically expedient. The dedication of the Great Temple was attended by nearly every enemy leader in the region. They were terrified. Kept them cowed for years. The Aztecs were superb warriors. If I hadn't been there, they just wouldn't have been as efficient.'

'And you left with the Spaniards.'

'I've travelled the world. Going wherever the action is hottest. I've never had to sing for my supper. Disappearances in Chile. Famine in East Timor. China fighting Viet Nam. Rhodesia fighting itself. Terrorists in Brazil. A menu, a great menu spread out for me. I have caused nothing.'

'Nothing?'

'The rioters and the terrorists and the murderers need no prompting from me.' He laughed again, the flute becoming the beating of flamingo wings. 'Nothing.'

The Doctor glanced down at Cristián, who had slid to the floor, his eyes awash with Huitzilin's light. 'Nothing.'

'Oh, sometimes I've spiced things up a little,' said Huitzilin. 'But what's an extra death, a few thousand extra deaths when millions are dying? No one knows, no one cares.'

'No one.'

Huitzilin laughed again. 'You think you'll stop the killing by casting your magic spell. But the wars will go on and on and on.'

'Actually,' said the Doctor, 'that's not what I think at all.'

243

Huitzilin lifted a perfect white eyebrow.

'You're not supposed to be here,' said the little man. 'You died, Huitzilin, all those centuries ago. You faded away into nothing.'

The god was shaking his head, but the Doctor went on. 'Someone or something pulled a string of the cosmic web. You should have melted at the temple, but you didn't. Because I was there for you to cling to. And you went on existing, like a parasite licking up spilt blood.'

'It was by *my* will that I continued to exist!' snarled Huitzilin. 'My will and no one else's. I went beyond the boundary of death, and I'm still here. Why else do you think they called me a god?'

'Putting aside all the suffering that you have caused – to the thousands of corpses, to Cristián Xochitl Alvarez – '

'Who's he? He's no one.'

'No one is *no one!*' roared the Doctor. 'How can someone be no one! Except you, you vampire! You shouldn't be here at all, not as a man, not as a ghost. But if you become real, if I let you overtake me, you'll be able to use that weapon, that thing in the box, that *thing* – '

'My *Xiuhcoatl*,' sighed Huitzilin. 'My dear Turquoise Serpent. Oh, war will be very different from now on.' He grinned at the Doctor. 'Are words your food, world killer? All this talk, and still the healer is becoming the warrior. How many people have you seen die, killer of worlds?'

The Doctor grabbed the book in both hands and held it out in front of him. The towel fell to the floor. A shower of blue sparks exploded up his arms, dancing around his fingers. A hot smell filled the air.

'You can't use that,' said Huitzilin. 'We're too closely joined together.'

But the Doctor's eyes were losing their focus, his breath coming in shallow gulps. He did not need to open the book, read the writing that burned on its pages in deep blue ink. A word trembled ecstatically in his lungs, forced its way into his mouth.

'*Iaquetl*,' he said convulsively.

Huitzilin quivered in place, struck by the sound.

The Doctor's teeth were clenched involuntarily, but another word fought its way out. '*Ohuihuihuiya.*'

Blue light was coming out of him, as though he were a bit of cellophane that someone was shining a torch through. Light leaked out of his sleeves and from between his teeth. '*Anen nicuic tociquemitla, yia, ayia yia yio uyia!*'

Huitzilin shrieked. He tried to take a step forward, but something stopped him, as though a sheet of glass hung in the air between them. 'Stop it! Stop reading!'

The Doctor wasn't reading. He was swaying slightly, eyes closed, the words pouring out of him. Smoke was rising from his hair and hands.

Que ia noca oia tonaqui yiaia yia yio

'Stop it or I'll kill you!'

The door of the cabin opened and slammed shut. Objects picked themselves up and danced about the room; a comb, a shoe, an empty glass, tracing poltergeist waltzes in the sizzling air. The window exploded outwards, spraying the deck below with glass.

Tetzavitztli ia mixtecatlce i mocxi pichauaztecatl

Huitzilin clawed the air, screaming. The luminescent lines of his body bent and convulsed, as though he were being crushed.

Tlapo ma ia ova yieo ayia yie

It was working.

Smoke curled around the Doctor's fingers. He pushed them into the fragile book, fingernails tearing the paper. '*Ai,*' he gasped, '*tlaxotla t-t-t-tenamitl ihuitli m-m-macoc* – '

Huitzilin's face was drawn into a hideous mask of hate. 'You can't do it!' he howled.

'*Mopopoxotiuh,*' the Time Lord tried to catch his breath, '*I – Iautlato* – '

'Go on!' laughed the Aztec, through his pain. 'Go on! Say it!'

'*Noteouh – noteouh* – ' The Doctor's eyes opened; he was shaking violently, the energy exploding around him in brilliant patterns, striking the walls, the floor. '*Noteouh aia tepquizqui mitoa ia* – '

And then he dropped the book.

Chapter 15

Epiphany

Monday, April 15, 1912

12.19 am

And then he dropped the book.

The light and the sound vanished in an instant. In the sudden ringing silence there was a pitter-patter of tiny sounds as the airborne objects dropped onto the carpet. The Doctor crumpled to the floor as though someone had cut his strings and curled around his seared hands, making a single, tiny sound of pain. Wisps of smoke rose from him in graceful patterns.

The Codex Atlaca flared orange and exploded into flames. The carpet smouldered around it as it self-destructed. The raw fragrance of burning paper filled the cabin.

Huitzilin straightened, stretched luxuriously and came across the cabin like a jaguar.

The Time Lord gasped as the Aztec reached down and hauled him into the air by his collar. Huitzilin wrapped an arm around his throat, a ghostly and intangible arm, suddenly horribly real and strong. They were converging. It was happening.

The Doctor reached for the constricting arm, but Huitzilin grabbed his wrist and gripped it so tightly he thought it would break. He tried to kick backwards at the psychevore's shin, but he didn't have the strength.

'Now,' the flute said in the Doctor's ear, 'what do you have left to fight me with?'

'Cristián' – gasped the Time Lord, before Huitzilin pulled the arm tight across his throat.

'None of this is real to him,' whispered the god from behind. His voice was almost tender, gentle now he knew that he had won. He looked over the Doctor's shoulder at Cristián, sitting like a broken doll with his back against the wall. 'It's a dream. It isn't happening.'

Huitzilin smiled, and sank his teeth into the Doctor's neck.

12.21 am

The TARDIS juddered and thumped and was suddenly still.

'What was that?' cried Bernice. 'Have we gone?'

'No,' said Ace. 'No, we haven't.'

'She listened to you.' Benny ran tense fingers through her hair. 'She actually listened to you.'

'I don't think she did,' said Ace. She patted the console the way a rider might pat a familiar horse. 'She just didn't want to leave him.'

'Right,' said Bernice. 'Now all we have to do is save the day.'

12.22 am

For the first time in twenty-two years, Cristián was not afraid.

He remembered a childhood accident, three neat stitches above his eye. Pushing his thumbnail into the skin in fascination. The nurses had swabbed the bit of skin with cotton wool before they'd started sewing. And now the skin had no feeling at all. Cotton wool. He was wrapped in it, sounds and movement trickling into his mind.

He was looking at someone, as though watching them on a television screen. Someone. Or two someones? They blurred together, as though they were a double image.

One of them looked vaguely familiar.

The man's feet were an inch off the floor, one hand

247

grasping desperately at the naked arm around his throat, the other held by the tall man standing behind him. The tall man's – the tall – *Huitzilin's* face was buried in his victim's shoulder, gripping his neck firmly in his mouth. And how else, thought Cristián dully, would you eat, except through the mouth?

The Doctor.

Take away the cotton wool, and Cristián would be frightened again.

The Doctor was screaming.

It wasn't a human voice. It wasn't a human sound at all. It was a howl of anguish like metal being torn apart, high and alien. It was the sound of someone's soul being ripped out.

The floor lurched, and the scream continued. An explosion sounded in the distance, and the scream continued. People were shouting and running and still the awful cry went on and on. Cristián wanted it to stop.

Cristián's hand was resting against something on the floor.

The image in front of him was changing, melting. He could see through the Doctor. The Time Lord was becoming transparent as Huitzilin tore the reality out of him.

The scream was growing weaker as the Doctor faded, becoming a ghostly echo, going on and on, just an echo, a memory of pain. Cristián wanted it to stop. It had to stop, it had to *stop*, it *had* to STOP –

IT HAD TO STOP

Cristián snatched up Anna's gun from the floor and shot the scream.

The Doctor was a ghost. The bullets went right through him.

Huitzilin was thrown backwards, stumbling. He dropped his victim, tripping over a chair, tumbling backwards until he struck the wall of the cabin. He roared in pain.

Cristián watched, his eyes round as saucers. Huitzilin put a hand to his chest, where blood was sizzling.

'I always wondered,' he said, and died.

* * *

12.25 am

Benny fought her way along the deck. Panic was rippling through the crowd now, in waves of sobbing and frantic conversations. She passed a woman shrieking that she was too terrified to get into the lifeboat. Perhaps she was frightened of drowning.

Where were they, where were they?

The boat was a quarter of a klick long. She was looking for the proverbial needle. Her questions had met with blank stares, with offers to assist her to the boats, with questions she couldn't answer about the ship's captain and the flares that had shot dazzlingly into the night.

A man in a uniform grabbed her arm, and she shook herself free, angrily. 'You must get in the boat, miss,' he said, trying to steer her towards it.

She briefly contemplated kicking him in the shin, but he was only trying to save her life.

Oh my God.

She could get in the lifeboat and go.

She could leave it all behind – the squabbles in the TARDIS, Ace's guns, the Doctor's games. She could just get in the boat and go. It wasn't the late twentieth century, but it was the twentieth, she'd know enough about it to survive. If she stayed on board, continued her search, she might end up drowning, an anonymous body bobbing in the Atlantic. Even if she stayed with the Doctor, with Ace, how safe would she be?

She glanced around at the huddling crowd, some of them still refusing to get into the boats. Bodies. They were all just bodies, floating in the frozen sea.

Somewhere the Doctor was dying, and he needed her, he needed her to save his life.

She kicked the sailor in the shins and ran for it.

12.44 am

Captain Smith was in the wireless room, adding up the chances. The *Carpathia* was coming at top speed; the *Titanic*'s sister ship *Olympic* was *en route*, but she was five hundred miles away or more.

'What call are you sending?' he asked Phillips, who did not stop his rapid tapping.

'CQD,' said the radio operator.

'I've an idea,' said Bride. 'Use that new call. It might be your last chance to send it.'

Phillips laughed dryly, and the pattern of his rapping changed as he sent out the world's first SOS.

12.52 am

The sailors worked in small swarms, tugging the canvas loose to reveal the lifeboats underneath. The crowd muttered to itself. Some people stayed to watch the seamen putting supplies in the boats, winding pulleys until they were suspended over the freezing ocean. Others went back inside, out of the chill night air.

Ace pushed her way through the crowd. She had thrown one of Bernice's jackets over her combat suit in a half-hearted effort to disguise it, figuring the multicoloured jacket would attract fewer stares than the skin-tight black outfit. She hoped they took the thing for a new kind of life-jacket.

She looked down at the well deck. Tons of ice had fallen onto the ship; she had kicked her way through some of it to get here, and now those idiots, they were playing football with it, kicking it around and showing bits of iceberg to one another like cheap souvenirs. They didn't know they were in trouble. Somewhere a band was playing ragtime tunes, as though this were a colossal party.

They'd obviously already struck the berg. How long before the boat went down? She was already noticing a tilt to the deck, as subtle as the pitch and yaw of a turning ship in space. How long? Damn it, how long?

There was a first class cabin that had no window. Sparkling slices of glass had rained on the deck, impeding the progress of the ladies as they hurried in no particular direction. Something had exploded inside the room, hurling the glass outwards.

It was worth a look. Benny made a mental measurement

of the cabin's position, and scooted back inside, counting doors as she ran along the corridor.

The door was locked. Bernice yelled something obscene and kicked the door in.

The cabin was in disarray, stuff lying everywhere. Cristián was sitting on the floor; she nearly tripped over him, stumbling into the room. He held a gun in one hand, loosely, his face dazed. He was crying, but he didn't seem to notice. The air stank of burnt hair.

The Doctor lay on the floor.

Christ Jesus, she could see the carpet through him.

She took a hesitant step towards him, and then stopped. Should she touch him? How did you administer first aid to a ghost? What should she do?

As she watched, the tenuous outlines of his body began to fill in. It began with his hands, the colour thickening until they were properly visible. Then his face, first white, then pale, tinged with blue, but he was there, trembling and gasping, his fingers twitching in the shag pile.

Bernice knelt down and picked him up by the shoulders. He gasped and gasped, as though he had forgotten how to breathe. His hands were cold, unpleasantly blue, and he was shaking all over. His eyes were all blue, the pupils shrunk away to nothing, staring over her shoulder into nothing.

'I shot him,' said Cristián. 'I shot Huitzilin. He's dead. We've won.'

'What have we won?' said Bernice, her voice catching painfully in her throat.

The Doctor's hands came up suddenly and he wrapped his arms around her, leaning on her heavily. They held onto one another for a few moments, tightly. Just being together, being alive, being real.

Benny pulled herself out of his grip, looking at Huitzilin's corpse. White-haired, almost naked, with feathers sprouting from a distorted foot ... already fading into shadows, back into the ocean of the unreal. Gone forever.

'Don't talk about it now,' she told the Doctor. He

251

continued to lean on her, his breathing becoming more even. 'Can you walk?'

'I think so,' he said thickly.

'Hey,' said Cristián from the floor, 'I shot him.'

'Cristián,' said Bernice, 'we are leaving.'

1.32 am

'If anyone else tries that, this is what they'll get!'

Three shots sounded, startlingly loud, silencing the crowd for just a moment. The men who had been trying to force their way into a lifeboat stepped back, cowed.

Cristián found himself being pushed back with the little group. At last he had to give up and go back the way he'd come.

He glanced at his wrist-watch. The Doctor would be furious if he found out Cristián had brought such an anachronism on board, but the Mexican hadn't dared to venture onto the ship without some sort of clock. He'd been trying so hard not to say anything, not to do anything wrong for the time – Mother of God, it had been twenty minutes since he and Bernice had split up. He'd last seen her fighting her way through a crowd of confused second class passengers, supporting the stumbling Doctor.

He turned and wandered past a small group of women being stuffed, half-hysterical, into another lifeboat. No sign of Ace. He wondered if she had taken a seat in one of the little boats, not wanting to risk being aboard when the ship went down. There was perhaps forty minutes left before that happened.

Just for a moment, he caught a flash of her multi-coloured jacket in the thick of the crowd. 'Ace!' he shouted, but the crowd jostled him away from her. If she answered back, he couldn't hear her over the cries of panic and the shouting of the sailors. He snarled in frustration, trying to fight his way back up the tilting deck.

Somewhere below decks, Benny leaned against the wall, trying to get her breath back. The Doctor was surprisingly light, but he had to keep stopping to rest. He didn't seem aware of his surroundings.

At least, not until they passed through a hallway where the band could be heard distantly, playing a sweet tune. '*Song d'Automne*,' he muttered, incomprehensibly. 'I knew it.' Benny threw his arm back over her shoulders and staggered on.

'Hey,' said an English voice, 'do you need a hand with him?'

A sailor had come out of a connecting corridor. His face was smeared with soot and sweat.

God yes. Help me. I don't know whether I'm going the right way, I don't know if I can carry him much further, and we could save you. Take you off the ship.

'No,' she said. 'Tell me your name.'

He told her. She remembered it. She kept going.

Cristián fought his way below decks, pushing through little groups of women being led to the boats. At the bottom of the stairs, he stopped in horror. A huge crowd of third class passengers were milling about anxiously. While the boats were leaving, these people didn't even know the ship was being evacuated.

They shouted questions at him, questions he couldn't answer, and he raised his hands as if to fend off their frightened voices. But a hand caught at his sleeve, and he found himself facing an elderly woman, sobbing, holding something out to him.

'Please,' she said brokenly, 'please.'

He asked her what the matter was in Spanish, but she just shook her head, pressing the little bundle into his grasp. 'Please,' she said again.

He hadn't been able to find Ace. There was no time left, no time, no time to make decisions. Dear God, this was wrong, he mustn't do it, he mustn't!

Cristián cursed the saints and nodded, clutching the object to his chest. He turned away from the crying woman and ran for the TARDIS.

* * *

253

Benny found herself in the coolness of the storage room, at last. She took the Doctor's torch out of his pocket and flashed it about the cabin.

Oh God! Where was the TARDIS?

It was right where they'd left it, disguised as a crate. She bit her lip, letting her hammering heart slow down.

They'd left the door ajar. Her searching fingers found its edge, pushed it open. She carried him the last few feet into the sudden brilliance of the console room, squinting in the alien light. Home. Safe.

They were alone in the room. She put him gently into the big wicker chair in the corner. He sagged into it gratefully, his eyelids flickering slowly. His face was worryingly pale.

Huitzilin was dead. It ought to be over.

Benny peered back out into the dimness of the cargo room, anxiously. Should she go and look for them? No, it made more sense to wait. She shouldn't even have let Cristián go off by himself.

Cristián! He was battling through the darkness, in tears, shouting her name. She grabbed him as he stumbled into the TARDIS, exhausted and terrified, clutching something to his chest in a death-grip. His teeth were chattering.

'It's sinking!' he said. 'The boat is sinking!'

'Help me get him to the sick-bay,' said Benny. She realized what it was that Cristián was holding, and gaped at it.

Behind her, the Doctor muttered something. She tore herself away from Cristián and knelt beside the chair, lifting a damp lock of hair from the Doctor's forehead.

'Ace,' he said.

2.11 am

Captain Smith had released the wireless operators from their duty, but Phillips clung to his set as though it were a life preserver. He tapped at it, twiddling with dials, trying to adjust the set. Bride was feeding a glass of water to a half-conscious woman who perched on his chair. She sputtered and clutched at her husband.

'Why don't you get her to a boat?' said Bride.

'They're all gone now,' said the man. His eyes were unnaturally huge and dark, seeing into places he normally would never have looked. 'All gone.'

Phillips did not look up. Experimentally, he clicked out two letter Vs, dot dot dot dash, dot dot dot dash. It was the *Titanic*'s final, meaningless message. Outside, the water was already sloshing up the deck.

Ace moved through an inch of water. The boat was tipping down towards the front, and she slipped and skidded as she tried to run. All the boats were gone. All gone. A sudden hush had fallen over the hundreds on deck, almost a reverent hush. She'd heard that non-sound in the seconds before battle, the sound of human beings looking the universe in the eye.

The wave seemed to come out of nowhere. She caught a rushed glimpse of people leaping off the side of the ship, launching themselves out into the darkness, a woman's skirts billowing ludicrously around her as the water lifted them. Then the wave picked her up and threw her overboard.

She tasted Atlantic, and restrained the urge to thrash, disoriented in the darkness, tumbling over and over. She struck other objects repeatedly – other people, parts of the ship? – and then she was spinning, seeing the *Titanic*'s lights flash past her.

Suddenly she was aware of the cold. She was instantly chilled, her hair full of salt. She felt the combat suit's temperature regulators kick in on full power to compensate. She steadied herself, treading water slowly. The ocean was full of garbage. Something floated past that looked horribly like a baby . . . no, it was a child's doll. She grabbed hold of something, a plank or a piece of someone's luggage, and clung to it.

The *Titanic*'s lights flickered maniacally and went out. The ship tilted back, faster and faster, and Ace saw the vague shapes of people leaping into the water. The ship

roared as its insides fell sideways, engines and people and
cargo all falling to the stern in a single cacophony.

There was an almighty splash as one of the funnels top-
pled over, smashing into the water like a missile. The wave
from it lifted her and pushed her away from the ship. And
now the *Titanic* was standing as upright as an office block,
blotting out the stars.

What a sight! Ace was laughing. What a sight!

Majestically, with perfect finality, the *Titanic* slid
beneath the waves.

Then the screaming started.

Benny had been looking out into the cargo hold, listening
desperately for any sign of Ace, when the TARDIS's doors
had suddenly closed. She'd had to step back quickly to
avoid them.

'What is it?' cried Cristián, almost hysterical.

The time rotor started its shaky movement. 'No!'
screamed Bernice, aiming a blow at the console. 'No! Give
her time! Give her more time!'

Suddenly, the console room was half-full of water.

Cristián shouted as a salty wave washed around his hips.
Ace appeared in the middle of the freezing fluid, coughing
and spluttering. It ran out through the open internal door,
washing down the corridor, beaching her like an exhausted
whale.

Benny and Cristián knelt beside her while she vomited
Atlantic. At last she took a great breath and said, with the
deep profundity of the foxhole, 'Shit.'

'We thought we'd lost you.' Bernice was almost crying in
relief.

'I thought I'd lost me,' Ace said weakly. 'Thanks for the
rescue.'

'Thank the TARDIS.'

2.20 am

Then the screaming started.

It was the people in the water, shouting for help in a

256

dozen languages. There were children's voices in that Babel, and the high-pitched screams of men.

In the row-boats, the women shivered and clung together. Some of them wanted to go back, imagining husbands and friends amongst the howling hundreds. But they were cold and frightened, and the ship might drag them down with it, and the swimmers might crowd on board and sink their little boats.

So they waited, bobbing up and down, listening to the screaming until each of the screams went out, one by one, like little candles going out, each snuffed flame dampening the bonfire of the screaming, until they were left in the darkness, alone, alone under the stars.

Chapter 16

Tomorrow Never Knows

New York City, December 15, 1980

There was something deeply comforting about the crowd. Perhaps it was the silence, tens of thousands of people all sharing the same space, speaking in whispers, holding flowers or holding hands. Many of them were crying, and lips moved in silent prayers.

Perhaps it was the chance to be off centre stage. In a crowd, you can't be the main players, you can be quiet, keep still, be anonymous. The universe isn't depending on you.

The vigil ended but the crowd stayed on, singing *Imagine* in hoarse voices and milling in tiny circles. The time travellers found themselves separated for a time.

Bernice and Cristián walked slowly through the crowd, not going anywhere. From time to time Cris would check the little bundle he was carrying, in one of those reverse harnesses that let you haul the baby around on your chest, as though he couldn't quite believe it was there.

'Have you decided what to call him?' Benny asked. She waved a finger in front of the baby's eyes, curiously, watching as it followed the movement.

'I thought I would name him after the Doctor,' said Cristián, 'and then I realized that I don't know his name.'

'No,' said Bernice. 'I wonder if anyone does.'

'I don't think I'm ever going to understand all of this,'

sighed the Mexican. 'Like John Lennon dying. It doesn't make any sense, it's, what's the word, gratuitous. We don't need it. We don't need it.' He looked at her hopefully. 'Will anything change?'

'Reagan won't budge. Even after he gets shot next year,' said Bernice. Cris raised both his eyebrows, and she put a finger to her lips, conspiratorially.

Cris rearranged the nameless baby's woollen cap. 'But I'll never have to face the Blue again. Never, never again. Have you ever seen a bit of grass that a box or a table has been sitting on, and when you take the weight of the box away, the grass is all brown and dead? But it grows back once it's back in the light. I have a chance to grow back.'

'That's very poetic, Señor Alvarez.'

'Thank you, Professor Summerfield.'

Benny kicked a puff of snow into the air. 'What are you planning to do?'

'I'll decide sometime.' Cris shrugged. '*Mañana*.'

There were hot dog carts working the edge of the crowd. Benny thought she ought to be annoyed with the little vendors, but she decided to take it as a good omen instead. Life went on, and that was its big secret, like Cristián's patch of withered grass. You couldn't ever crush it completely.

They bought hot dogs with sauerkraut and mustard, and stood at the fringe, watching the crowd slowly disperse. 'I wish,' Cris said, 'you would tell me what is going to happen to me.'

Benny smiled at him. 'The time streams are so muddled up I don't want to tell you something that's probably going to be wrong. I don't even know what I'm going to do next.'

'Are you going to leave the Doctor?'

She swallowed a mouthful of lukewarm sauerkraut. 'I missed Tenochtitlan, and the *Titanic* – I'm not getting to do any archaeology, I'm just getting dragged from one muddle to the next.' She shrugged, 'I might stay. I might not. But whatever I do, it'll be what I've chosen to do.'

'Like the man says,' Cristián said, 'life is what happens to you when you're busy making other plans.'

* * *

The crowd were praying for peace. Ace wasn't ready for peace. There were so many battles to be fought, so many . . . she had been born fighting, punching and kicking in the playground, screaming at her mother, wrestling with the world. Fighting was like breathing now.

She tried to imagine peace, closing her eyes. She couldn't feel the cold of the snow. Her combat suit was hidden under boots and jeans and wind-cheater, insulating her from the world.

There was an old joke about a church bell that was rung every morning at seven for a hundred years. Then one night the bell was sent away for repairs, and the whole village woke up at seven, shouting 'What was that?' That was peace.

She looked at the Doctor, who was eating an ice-cream cone with intense concentration.

He'd slept for a week in the sick-bay; they'd taken turns watching over him, sitting next to the little bed and reading books in the dim light. From time to time his hands had clutched the covers, the way that she had clutched her plank in the ocean, and he had mumbled alien words that the TARDIS declined to translate. Sometimes she wondered about his nightmares. But not too often.

'Where'd you pick up that wound?' she murmured.

He was looking out over the crowd, his face part way between concentration and dreaming. He didn't turn to her when she spoke. 'What was that?'

'A cut or a deep bruise on your left side. Over the lung. I can tell by the way you're breathing.'

He didn't answer, and Ace wrinkled her forehead. At last he said, 'I see you have the suit back on.'

'I'm ending our agreement,' she said. 'We tried it and it didn't work.'

'Mmmm.'

Ace watched a couple who must once have been hippies embrace, probably feeling their childhood slide away from them. John Lennon was dead, and they had mourned him, and now the whole world was different.

'It's not the suit,' she said. 'It's me. I can't pretend I'm

260

something I'm not. Even when I take off the armour and weapons, I'm still wearing them.'

He didn't answer, but his old face seemed terribly sad, and she could guess what he was thinking: he'd destroyed one killer, only to find another waiting by his side.

I don't see what the problem is, she thought. *You used to work with UNIT, happily work with soldiers and weapons.* And she had found Benny sobbing by the side of the pool, clutching that little typewritten list of the survivors. When Ace had asked her what was up she'd just handed her the list, muttering a name. The name wasn't on the list, but it was luck, just luck, like one of the radio operators drowning and one surviving to tell the tale. The world still had to be saved. It was just luck whether you got saved too.

The Doctor's meddling was like her suit: dangerous, but ultimately useful.

Or maybe that was it. He was still trying to walk the fine line between being the healer and the warrior. It frightened him that he might be both. He couldn't accept it.

'I am who I am,' she said, 'and you can't change it. You can't tell me what to do. So we're just going to have to make room for one another, aren't we?'

He didn't answer, and after a moment she turned away. Something between them was falling apart. Not broken yet, but slowly disintegrating. She could feel it.

She really wished she knew how he'd got that wound.

July 1986

'What about bodies? Did you find any bodies?'

'Did you really find an intact chandelier?'

'Did you find the Renault?'

'Are you planning another expedition?'

'What about other valuables?'

'What things did you bring back to the surface?'

'We didn't bring anything back to the surface. There just wouldn't be anything on the *Titanic* that would be worth salvaging.'

'But you could make a mint – '

'What about the mummy?'

'Private collectors – '

'Treasure – '

'Artefacts – '

'Let me tell you what we did when the video cameras picked up that shape in the sand. We all shouted and cheered for joy. And then we realized we'd found the unmarked grave of a thousand and a half souls. When we saw that little girl's doll . . . Well, everybody just stopped work for a quarter of an hour.

'We're not planning to bring any mementoes to the surface. No, no, we're not. Let them rest. Let them rest in peace.'

Somewhere, sometime

Swoomsh.

Swiiiiiish.

Over the magical scrawls on the floor. Back and forth in time to a silent, chaotic rhythm, never tracing the same pattern twice. *Swooomsh. Swiiiiiish.*

A bright dance of sparks across the surface of the jet-black glass. A single claw of electricity jumping down to scar the pentagrams and the sacred names. *Shcrakakak. Swiiiiiish.*

Dark liquid drips from the globe as it swings, and the air is as cold as a butcher's freezer. A spatter of condensation strikes the floor and walls as the globe swings, its equilibrium upset by some internal event.

Imagine there's a bee on the palm of your hand. Now make a fist.

Swooomsh. Swiiiiiish.

The globe buzzes angrily to itself as it moves, its violent arcs beginning to quieten even as a final shower of sparks erupts across the surface. It traces dizzy circles over the central pentagram, all the while buzzing, a ball of anger.

Someone watches the ball, and the ball watches him, buzzing. It spits out a handful of sparkles and is still.

262

'Well, that didn't work, did it?' says the man who is watching.

The song of the sphere changes, the angry buzz echoing his words. *Zwell, thdiiiidn't zwaaaark, dyd yt?*

'Time to try something else, then.'

Diiiidn't zwaaark, diiiidn't zwaaaark, teases the black globe, or whatever is inside it. For a moment an eye appears at its surface, stretched into a convex smear, and the eye is laughing. *Thyall liiivd happileeeeverafter.*

The watching man spits a curse at the globe, and it shimmers with electric laughter.

October 31, 1993

Cristián went shopping in the *tiangui*.

He should have gone to the *cine*. He should have gone to Chapultepec Park. He should have visited his sister. He should have stayed home.

But he went shopping in the market on Guatemala Street, and bought three courgettes and a bag of tomatoes. He carried them in a string bag that bumped against his leg. He put down the bag as he stopped at a refreshment stall to buy himself a slice of watermelon. He never did pick it up again.

At 4:33, the Hallowe'en Man pushed aside his coat to reveal a Chinese SKK semi-automatic rifle.

Cristián had been buying a slice of watermelon from a fruit stand. He shouted, 'Look out! There's a man with a gun!' and dived behind the fruit-seller's cart, dragging his son down with him. They quivered in the road for thirty-seven seconds while the Hallowe'en Man sprayed the air with bullets.

He heard the snickering of the gun, the high-pitched voice of ricochets, the cries of people being shot or being terrified. He pressed his face to the road and held Ben down each time he tried to get up and run away. A

263

cucumber in the cart above them exploded, showering them with wet chunks.

There was a final shot.

Then there was silence.

Enough of this.

WHO ARE YOU?
Help us to find out what you want.
No stamp needed – free postage!

Name _____

Address _____

Town/County _____

Postcode _____

Home Tel No. _____

About Doctor Who Books

How did you acquire this book?
Buy ☐ Borrow ☐
Swap ☐

How often do you buy Doctor Who books?
1 or more every month ☐ 3 months ☐
6 months ☐ 12 months ☐

Roughly how many Doctor Who books have you read in total?

_____

Would you like to receive a list of all past and forthcoming Doctor Who titles?
Yes ☐ No ☐

Would you like to be able to order the Doctor Who books you want by post?
Yes ☐ No ☐

Doctor Who Exclusives
We are intending to publish exclusive Doctor Who editions which may not be available from booksellers and available only by post.

Would you like to be mailed information about exclusive books?
Yes ☐ No ☐

About You

What other books do you read?

Other character-led books (which characters?) _____

_____

Science Fiction	☐	Thriller/Adventure	☐
Horror	☐		

Non-fiction subject areas (please specify) _____

Male	☐	Female	☐

Age:

Under 18	☐	18–24	☐
25–34	☐	35+	☐

Married	☐	Single	☐
Divorced/Separated	☐		

Occupation _____

Household income:

Under £12,000	☐	£13,000–£20,000	☐
£20,000+	☐		

Credit Cards held:

Yes	☐	No	☐

Bank Cheque guarantee card:

Yes	☐	No	☐

Is your home:

Owned	☐	Rented	☐

What are your leisure interests? _____

_____

Thank you for completing this questionnaire. Please tear it out carefully and return to: **Doctor Who Books, FREEPOST, London, W10 5BR** (no stamp required)